Jonah stays seated, and while I anxiously race around the room, he presses on. "Where do you think mythology came from? Why do you think there are so many fairy tales? So many versions of the same stories? Sit, Agatha. Let me continue. It will make sense. Just give it some time."

I throw my hands up in frustration. "Here I am, in a cottage deep in the heart of a subway line. Yeah, that could happen. You know, when they find me, if they ever do, I'll be sitting in a pile of filth somewhere in the subway tunnels eating dirt and talking to myself. Or I may not even be in the tunnels. I could be wandering the streets of New Jersey somewhere."

"Agatha, you're not insane," Jonah says calmly as he walks over to me. "First off, crazy people don't believe they're crazy. They believe they're thinking more clearly than ever."

"Oh, okay. Good. The Grim Reaper thinks I'm sane."

THE LOST KNIGHT SERIES

First Published in the
United States of America in April 2016
By Monster Publishing
ISBN: 978-0-9889012-2-3

For information about permission to reproduce selections
from this book, write to Info@CandyAtkins.com
For information on bulk purchase please contact Premium
Sales Department at Sales@CandyAtkins.com

Cover art by Sebastian Sánchez Carballo
Illustrations by Lajon Tanganco

Visit us at:
www.CandyAtkins.com
twitter.com/Candy_Atkins
facebook.com/CandyAtkinsAuthor
Instagram.com/Candy_Atkins

For my family
Michael, Liv, Harrison, Cortney and Scott.
I wouldn't be who I truly am and be able to do what I truly love without your love and support.

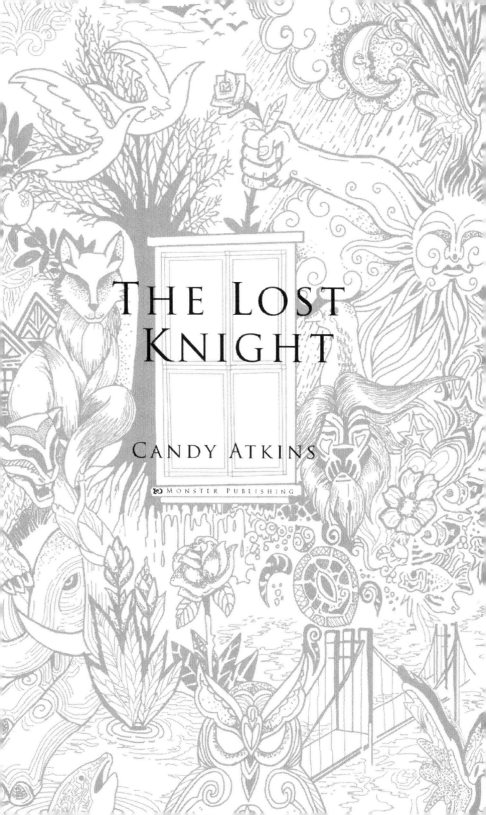

THE LOST KNIGHT

CANDY ATKINS

MONSTER PUBLISHING

CHAPTER 1

I grab the box of midnight-purple hair dye from my book bag and squeeze my way down the narrow, overstuffed hall into the only bathroom in our apartment. The shower hasn't worked since it was turned into a storage closet, so I clear the sink of the old cat food cans Auntie has stockpiled, turn on the cold water, and dream about the day when I'll have my own apartment with a shower, hot water, and food.

"Agatha, are you still pouting?" Auntie yells from her recliner. "I told you, Uncle will pick something up when he's done with work."

My foster parents, I call them Auntie and Uncle, are not what I would describe as parents, or even aunt and uncle, they're more like babysitters. Uncle hasn't been home for three days, and I doubt she believes he'll be here tonight. She just wants me to tell her that I'm okay with her not picking up dinner. I'm not.

Today is my thirteenth birthday. It's not like I was expecting a cake, but something to eat would've been nice.

After I dye my hair, I take a shirt from the pile of laundry I'm standing on, wrap it around my head, and carry the remaining hair dye back to my bedroom. I love my tiny room, mostly because I've been sketching and painting jumbled and disjointed art on these walls since I was old enough to grip a pencil. Part of the reason I chose what the

1

box calls *boysenberry* for my hair is because the extra dye is the perfect hue for the raven I'm painting on my ceiling.

Dipping the number-three flat brush into my dye calms me and all is forgiven. Auntie's not a mean person, she's just a bit *off.* Being angry with her is like being mad at one of the cats—pointless.

I wrap a blanket around my shoulders and open the window. Queens is especially chatty tonight with the noise of cars, people fighting, dogs barking, and the laughter that only I can hear. I stand on the bed and fill in the gentle face of my birdie while humming along with the chorus of voices outside.

Tonight, the singing is boldly wafting through my window. I can't understand the words and don't know the tune, but the music is sweet and peaceful. It's sad that I can only hear my songs some of the time, when I'm tired and relaxed, and sadder still that no one else can listen with me.

My dye runs out long before I'm satisfied with my raven so I give up and climb into bed. The song I'm listening to now is particularly soothing, a hymn or possibly an opera. Maybe one day I'll be a great songwriter or something.

A muffled thud near my window startles me from a sound sleep. There's an eerie red glow casting moving shadows across my room. I blink a few times to make sure I'm not still dreaming and follow the source of the light. Just to the side of the foot of my bed kneels a tall, hooded figure with luminescent red eyes. It's stroking the long ears of a much smaller creature that looks withered and dying.

I'm not scared, which is weird, but it might be because I'm not sure I'm awake. I turn on the lamp to make the dream disappear and end up blinding myself. When my eyes adjust, I see the sickly green skin of a long-eared frog-boy lying on the floor and the tall cloaked being that's

2

cradling it. The tall black monster who closely resembles the Grim Reaper appears to be even more stunned than I am. We stare at each other while my brain struggles to figure out what I'm looking at. These things don't exist, so how can I be seeing them so clearly?

The black-hooded creature never takes its red eyes off me while it stands and lifts the small sickly frog-boy off the floor.

"Agatha?" it whispers.

This monster is actually in my room! My insides seize, trapping my scream. What is this thing and how does it know my name? I want to run, but I can't move or look away. My fluttering heart stops when my door flies open with a crash. A scream unseals my lips, amplifying my terror.

Auntie charges in, wielding a large kitchen knife. She's yelling in her nutty made-up language, but it works. The creature jumps out my fifth-floor window, taking the frog-boy with him.

She whips around toward me, still holding the knife, and looking like she means to use it. "What did you see! What was that? What were you doing!"

Auntie has her kind moments, but she's crazy. I mean, truly mental. Whatever just happened, she mustn't know that I saw it too. She probably suspects I did, but if I confirm it, she'll nail my window shut and my songs will disappear forever. "I had a nightmare. Was I yelling in my sleep? Did I wake you?" I'm trying to sound calm, but I'm failing.

She takes a few deep breaths while she sizes me up. She pauses and tilts her head to the side. "There was something here. I saw it. Did you see it?"

"What was here? What did you see? And what's with the knife?" I want her to tell me if she saw the Grim Reaper and a dead rabbit-frog-boy at the foot of my bed. If she saw them too, then I'm not crazy. But then again, if I see the same thing as a crazy person, we're probably both insane.

Auntie attempts a comforting smile and mellows her tone. "I thought someone broke in. I thought you were in danger. It's not safe for you to sleep in here. Come to my room."

I've never been invited to sleep in her room before, not even when the heat went out last February and I thought I'd freeze to death.

I follow her round body out my door and into the maze that was once our kitchen. I cautiously climb over the avalanche of junk that Auntie caused in her haste to get to my room. How did she know I was in danger? The creature whispered and I did nothing.

"We should clean this up," I say right before I take a nasty tumble over hundreds of old magazines.

"Leave it. I'll take care of it in the morning."

Translation: I'll be stacking them up again when I get home from school. Hopefully she won't add to the pile while I'm gone.

Auntie's room smells of cat, body odor, and rotting garbage, but I'm happy for the company. I'm still shaking from what I hope was a nightmare. She doesn't say a word to me as I climb onto the pile of dirty clothes next to her bed. I try to watch the old movie on the television, but my mind keeps going back to the strange creatures and Auntie's reaction to them.

Finally, in the wee hours of the morning and well past the time Auntie started snoring, I chalk it up to an overactive imagination. I was probably still dreaming when I thought I saw something. Auntie is skittish by nature, so her response wasn't that strange. At least, this is what I tell myself so I can get some sleep.

"Get up, my dear. It's your birthday," Auntie says with false cheeriness.

I wake up groggy and sore from my terrible night's sleep. I slept on a mound of what I thought were clothes, but something under the pile is hard and lumpy. What sleep I got was far from restful, and I desperately need to go back to my bed.

Auntie is standing over me with a bowl of cereal, which she thrusts at me as soon as I sit up. I sleepily grab it and shovel the soggy flakes into my mouth. I can't remember the last time I ate breakfast at home. She must have gone out early this morning to buy the milk and cereal.

"Stop looking at me like that." Her smile doesn't reach her eyes. "It's your birthday. I wanted to do something nice."

My birthday was yesterday. Auntie never cares if I eat, and certainly never does anything for me on my birthday. Maybe she's getting thoughtful in her old age. However, I change my mind when, before I can finish my cereal, she yanks the bowl out of my hands.

"Okay, that's enough. Time for the birthday tradition," Auntie sings with genuine enthusiasm.

From the bed, she lifts a small wooden chest that's crafted out of many different colored woods. It's intricately carved with depictions of strange beings standing guard over a door with an eye in it. The case is truly beautiful, but what's inside confirms that Auntie has truly lost her mind.

I do this ridiculous tradition every year somewhere around my birthday. I used to ask questions about the box and the ceremony, but she never answered me. She just tells me to enjoy it. However, there's nothing to enjoy. I'd rather have a cake.

Auntie lifts the chest in the air and mutters her strange guttural words. Then she puts the case back on the bed, kneels beside it and opens the lid. Inside is a small crystal sphere nestled in red velvet. She brings the ball close to my face, waves it above my head and utters more strange things.

Not only does Auntie dance around like this on my birthday, but she also talks to herself nonstop in a made-up language, and barricades us with garbage in this tiny apartment. Nevertheless, she's all I've ever had for a caretaker and I want to make her happy. I usually fail, which is why I always dread this ceremony.

She lowers her arm and I reach into the chest to grab the ordinary glass marble. It's about the size of a golf ball and rather plain compared to the box it comes in.

She crouches down near me and whispers the words I loathe. "Now, what do you see?"

I see a crazy lady with a glass ball is what I want to say, but this ritual makes her happy and it's the only thing she ever asks of me. I would play along if I knew what it is that I'm meant to see. One year I made up a story about seeing the future and that made Auntie livid, so I never lied again, and this year is no different.

"I see a crystal ball."

"You're getting older. You should be seeing something. Concentrate. Relax. Look at the orb."

I gaze at the marble with what I hope is an expression of concentration and relaxation, but it's just a ball. I stare at it for what I deem is an appropriate amount of time and repeat, "I see a crystal ball."

Auntie scowls and follows it with a sigh. "Well, next year."

As she puts the marble away, the light catches it for a second and it takes on an orange glow, but by the time my lips part to say something, it disappears.

When she hears my intake of breath, she jumps. "What! What is it? What do you see?"

"Nothing, the light just hit it funny. I thought it was something, but it was nothing." I tell myself that sane people don't see things in glass marbles, but her disappointment makes me feel like I should.

Auntie snaps the case closed. "Go get dressed before you're late for school. And fix your hair. You look ridiculous."

CHAPTER 2

I get ready for school and ignore Auntie's request that I change my hair. I grab the black jeans I wore yesterday and pick up the black sweater that's lying next to them, but a quick smell check informs me that I need to wash it before I wear it again.

As soon as I hit the sidewalk, I slow my pace. Goosebumps race up my arms and my feet stop moving. I scan the street for anything out of the ordinary but everything seems to be as it should. I shake off my willies and head off to school.

The feeling won't leave. Something isn't right. Then I hear it. I never hear the laughter or singing during the day, but today I hear both. In fact, the singing is louder and clearer than it's ever been. It's in a language I've never heard, so that's probably why I couldn't understand it before. Last night I saw creatures at the foot of my bed, and today the singing. Did Auntie see them too, or am I going crazy?

"Shhhh. Shhhh. That's her," whispers through the air, but there's no one around.

Mrs. Belmonte is taking her garbage to the curb. She's the only one on the street and I can see she's not talking.

"That's the Agatha."

I stop and thoroughly scan the area. Someone must be playing a prank, but I don't understand how they could do it without an elaborate setup. Plus, I'm not important enough for anyone to go to that much trouble.

"Yep. Her."

The sound seems to be coming from the maple I'm standing next to, almost as if one tree is talking to another, but there are too many voices. They're exceedingly high-pitched and talking in unison. Can bugs talk? Can I hear bugs? No, bugs don't talk, so obviously that's not what I'm hearing.

My gaze darts down the street. I don't want anyone to see me listening to the tree. I used to believe that the singing was something everyone heard. People always talk about a song they can't get out of their head, or maybe an argument they had with themselves, but when I told Auntie about my songs, she told me that only I can hear them. She said I must never tell anyone or they'll take me away. I never asked where they would take me or who *they* were, but I've never told anyone anything ever again, not even Auntie.

The voices used to be just songs, but now they're talking to me, or more accurately, about me. *Delusional,* that's what this is called. I'm imagining things in my room and hearing voices.

I can't get enough air into my lungs. My fingers are tingling and my arm is going numb. I need to get away from the bugs, or whatever they are. I don't want to run and draw attention to myself, so I walk as fast as I can while trying to look relaxed.

"Which one?" the voices continue.

"That one."

"That's the Agatha."

"Goes to school down the street."

"Why did she do that to her hair?"

The bugs in each tree speak as one voice and discuss me with their neighbors in the next tree. I don't care who sees me, I'm running.

The wind in my ears and the blood thumping through my veins make it impossible to hear the voices, so I sprint faster. I cross the street against the light and weave around the honking cars. Even though I don't go far, my lungs almost implode from the effort. My right thigh is cramping so intensely I'm afraid I might fall.

As I reach the school, I have to slow down because the other students are clogging the sidewalk. I shove anyone who is in my path out of the way. Some of the kids complain and a few push back, but I keep running.

Once I'm safely inside, the noise of the other students drowns out everything else. I bend over and rub my thigh as I try to fill my burning lungs. I'll never run again for as long as I live. When my air returns and I can keep my breakfast down, I stand. There, on the locker right beside my face, is a fly. Without thinking, I smash it with my bare hand. There's no way I'm letting them follow me in here.

"Gross," a girl across the hall says to another.

The burning in my face replaces the fire in my lungs. I can't believe I just did that, and in front of Trishel Gomez, of all people. My hand is covered in fly guts and Trishel is witnessing the whole disgusting episode.

"So Aggi," she says, leaning against the lockers. I wipe the fly guts on my jeans and see her flash of revulsion. This day couldn't get any worse.

"What made you decide to dye your hair?" Trishel asks so sweetly it's easy to tell she's faking. "I'm thinking of dying mine, too. Where'd you get yours done?"

I don't answer. I just put my head down and walk away, hoping she doesn't follow. She's making fun of me the way mean girls do. I don't know how to fight back when they pretend to be nice but really aren't. Her friends laugh at me as I walk down the hall, and I'm relieved they let me go.

First period is science. I share a lab desk with Joe Thompson, one of the most popular boys in school. I'm not up to facing him, so of course, he's waiting for me when I arrive. I keep my head down and hope Joe loses interest in whatever he has planned for me today, but no such luck.

When I reach the desk, I notice he's left a white carnation on my side of the table. I ignore it as I sit down and chide myself for getting to class so early. Joe is unfazed by my lack of reaction as he waits for more of his followers to arrive.

When the class is full, except for Ms. Quraishi of course, Joe picks up the flower and drops to one knee. "Agatha Stone, you are the prettiest thing I've ever seen. I must have you. Will you marry me?" The last part is hard to understand through his laughter.

My blood stops circulating and I freeze solid, praying he'll tire of this game, and willing the teacher to hurry up.

"You just got rejected by Agatha Stone!" a girl in the back of the room shouts. The entire class erupts into laughter.

I don't understand why this is funny, especially since he does stuff like this all the time. He asks me to every dance, recites obscene poetry, and tries to hold my hand on a regular basis. It wasn't funny to begin with, but the repetitiveness of his torture should be boring his audience by now. It's been going on for years, though, so I guess I'm wrong.

I make it through the rest of my morning classes without incident and, as is my ritual, I hide in the library during lunch. I get some chips and a soda out of the vending machine and peruse the aisles.

My nightmare rattled my nerves. Only now I can't remember what I was dreaming about, just the events that happened after I woke up. I try to find a book in the psychology section that can explain what's going on with me.

I've always been different. I don't know how to talk to people, and I don't know why people do the things they do. I also don't like the stuff others seem to like, and they certainly don't like what I like. *Different* had been hard, but this new delusional twist is terrifying.

I open a book at random and then slam it back into place. I'm not insane. I'm in the wrong section. Where I should be is in mythology. That thing last night looked a lot like the Grim Reaper. Maybe I read something that stuck in my head and came out in the nightmare.

Death is dark and cloaked like that. Every cartoon wanting to depict something scary has the red eyes in the dark. The devil sometimes appears like that, too. But what I saw wasn't scary. Maybe that's the trick: like a Venus flytrap, it makes you comfortable, then eats you.

Frustrated, I leave the library to get an early start to my next class. I don't pay any attention to my teacher and try, without success, not to think about the weird events of the last few hours.

"Ohhh! Ohhhh! Ohhhh! I know this one! I know it!" say the high-pitched bug voices.

I snap my head around and scan the room. No one is talking, and no one hears the bugs. The teacher continues his lecture as I search for the source of the voice or voices—many voices saying the same thing.

"Agatha," the teacher says.

Mr. Hallman has asked something, but I have no idea what the question was. Why do teachers get such a thrill from picking on the weak? Mr. Hallman knows I don't know the answer but called on me anyway just to humiliate me.

"Cape of Good Hope! I know! I know! Ohhhh! Ohhhh! Cape of Good Hope!" the bugs chant.

I don't know the question Mr. Hallman asked, and I've never heard of the Cape of Good Hope, but the bugs seem to know. "Cape of Good Hope?" I mumble.

"Very good," Mr. Hallman affirms, sounding surprised.

I'm surprised, too! How do I know that? Maybe I heard the question and somehow knew the answer, but I don't know what the Cape of Good Hope is.

The bugs are singing again. This time it's in English and about famous explorers. I'm definitely not writing these songs. It's one thing to make up a language, but I don't know these explorers. It's coming from a large Yucca tree in the corner that's swaying in the breeze from the open window. However, there's no breeze on this side of the building. The tree is dancing. It's singing a song and dancing to its music.

I'm as nutty as Auntie. The thought makes me jump out of my chair and gaze helplessly at the startled faces staring back at me. I need to get out of here. I grab my book bag and walk out the door. Mr. Hallman says something about my leaving and the Yucca bugs say goodbye, but I ignore them.

I run as fast as I can toward home, but even though it's just a block and a half, I'm not going to make it this time. I'm almost there when my lungs won't take any more. This is the most exercise I've ever had in my life and it might kill me. I'm nauseous, but once some air gets into my lungs and I walk off the leg pain, I notice that the bugs have stopped talking. Relieved, I walk the rest of the way home.

Just as I reach my stoop, the bugs mock me. "You're in trouble. You're in trouble," the high-pitched voices chant in unison.

I try to jump up the first three steps at once, but miss and crash painfully into the concrete.

"You don't want to go in there," the bugs tease, shaking the trees branches.

I ignore them and limp inside. Is it rude to not speak to one's delusion? Walking up the stairs clears my head and I relax for the first time today. Auntie won't be mad that I'm skipping school because she doesn't care if I go or not.

When I walk into the apartment, the air leaves my lungs with an audible whoosh. My body refuses to draw in another breath as my eyes travel around the empty room. Before I can form an explanation, I leap backward out the door. I bend over to make the oxygen rush to my brain faster. I can't believe I was so distracted I accidentally walked into the wrong apartment. I turn in a slow circle and press my hand to the bridge of my nose. I'm in the right place, but I check the number to be sure.

I cautiously step back in. Everything is gone, including the carpets. Moldy stains cover the floor and walls, and the entire place has been swept clean and wiped down. The smell of garbage-cats has been replaced with the scent of rotting lemon-pine trees. Funny how our apartment looks smaller with the stuff out of it. My vision spins but straightens out before I can faint. How is this possible?

CHAPTER 3

There's no furniture except for a naked table and chairs standing alone in the family room. I remember the table being a lot bigger, so I must have been about five the last time I saw it. We have a fireplace? A sad sigh escapes my lips. It would've been so nice to sit by a fire on cold nights.

I numbly inspect the apartment and try to fathom how this happened. It's impossible to remove everything from this place in the few hours I've been gone. Even with a crew of twenty and heavy equipment, it should've taken at least a week.

Auntie steps out of the kitchen and greets me with a ridiculously wide grin. "Oh, there you are, dear."

The *dear* at the end of Auntie's statement must mean she wants to impress the tall man standing next to her. Just looking at the guy, it's obvious he's important. His perfectly tailored wool suit is an expensive shade of charcoal, and his black shoes are very shiny. *Lawyer*, obviously.

Auntie's treasures are the most important things in the world to her. They're gone, and she's delighted. She should be bawling her eyes out or, more accurately, screaming her head off. She's definitely enthralled with the stranger beside her. Maybe she's just happy she was able to keep her cats, which are sitting in a row against the wall, staring at her. I've never seen cats line up like that: twenty cats, each sitting an equal distance apart.

I'm still dreaming. I bet I never woke up. This is part of my nightmare. At least, I hope it is.

"Well, say hello!" Auntie demands.

I drop my gaze to the floor. "Hello."

Auntie's visitor nods as he walks past me, closes the door and ushers me in to sit at the table. His long braid falls over his shoulder when he sits in the other chair. He gives me a self-conscious smile when he flings it back over his shoulder.

I shiver when he slides Auntie's beautiful carved chest with the crystal ball in it over to me. Maybe it is valuable if a lawyer is involved. "Do you know who I am, Agatha?"

"No, sir," I whisper.

"This is Grand Wiz—" Auntie begins, but he silences her with a wave.

"My name is Duradin. I'm a friend of your foster mother, and I knew your parents."

This information is supposed to give us a connection, but I don't want to talk about my parents. I want to know why he's here. He's expecting a reaction, but I just sit there and wait for him to tell me whatever it is he wants me to know. We stare at each other for an uncomfortable amount of time until he gives up and nudges the chest. "Do you know what this is?"

"It's Auntie's box."

Duradin smiles. "No. It's your box. More precisely, it's your Orb."

By the way he says it, he's trying to impress me, but it's just the crystal ball that Auntie always makes me look at. This man is crazy. Auntie is crazy, and it's becoming quite clear that I'm crazy, too.

16

Duradin lifts the box, opens it carefully, and formally presents it to me. I grab the marble and he places his hands over mine, closing my fingers around the orb. The contact causes waves of revulsion to travel up my arms, but I don't know how to yank my hands back without making Auntie mad.

He leans in and puts his face close to mine. I can smell the mint on his breath as he stares into my eyes. "This Orb has special powers, and I'm here to help you use them."

The marble slides around my sweaty palm as I fight the urge to stand. I put my head down to break his stare, and glare at the hands holding mine captive. I just want to get this over with so this man will leave and I can ask Auntie what happened to her stuff.

"I need you to relax," he instructs as he shakes my arms. "Take a few deep breaths. Close your eyes."

I do as he orders, but I'm not relaxed. My heartbeat is matching pace with my anxiety. Mr. Duradin starts chanting in the weird language Auntie always uses when she makes me do the birthday ritual. His chant is longer than Auntie's and more powerful, if that's possible.

"Now, open your eyes and peer into the Orb," he whispers.

I do what he wants, but as always, it's just a ball. I want to lie to him and tell him I see something, but then he'll ask questions, and I won't answer them correctly, and then everyone will be mad at me. So I look at the ball and wait for the question I dread.

"This isn't an ordinary orb, Agatha. Look at it. See through it. How deep does it go?"

I figure it goes about an inch, maybe an inch and a half. I've never measured Auntie's ball—I mean, Orb. However, I can't answer because he's chanting again. If everyone around you loses their mind, does that mean you're really the one who's insane?

"Look into the eyes of the Orb," he whispers. "Look into it."

I do my best to appear as if I'm trying. I would laugh at this man if he weren't so scary. I want to throw the ball in his face and inform him it's just a glass marble—so no eyes. I gaze down at the distorted reflection of my hand while Duradin chants louder and Auntie joins in. I focus on keeping my trembling hands still and my breathing even. I don't want them to know how badly they're scaring me.

I'm fixated on keeping an appearance of concentration on my face when a dim orange pin-light appears in the center of the Orb. I glance around the room, trying to find what the ball is reflecting.

"You saw something! What do you see?" Duradin grabs me by the hair and forces me to look down at the ball.

Tears spring to my eyes, blurring my vision. Why does he need to hurt me if I'm doing what he wants? I try to lift my head, but he pulls my hair again. The ball is glowing brighter, but I won't say anything. After he's gone, I'll tell Auntie what I saw, and maybe she can explain what's happening. Until then, I open my hands and let the ball drop to the floor.

Auntie yelps and dives for the ball. Her bulky body bounces me out of my chair. A shriek bursts from my lungs, more from surprise than from the actual fall. I land with a thud and hit my head on the now uncushioned floor.

Duradin's fingers bruise my skin when he grabs me and drags me to the Orb. "Pick it up." His tone is quiet and more terrifying than Auntie's ranting. I do, and he forcibly sits me back down in the chair. He grips the back of my head and demands, "Look at the Orb. What do you see?"

My head hurts, my stuff is gone, and this vile man is forcing me to stare at a marble. I refuse to tell him anything until Auntie explains what's happening.

"Tell me what you see!"

There's a hiss, and the man hollers. I snap my head up. Oberon, one of Auntie's cats, is wrapped around Duradin's head, sending him to the floor. I launch myself out of the chair toward the door, but Auntie tackles me. I crash to the bare subfloor and slam the air from my body.

"You're not going anywhere!" she screams, trying to pin me to the ground.

"Let me go!" I try to wiggle out of her grasp. I've never been in a fight in my life, and I never in a million years thought Auntie would attack me. She's never been a violent person. Who is this man, and why do they care so much about a stupid marble?

The other cats join the fray, and the scary guy gets caught in the middle. Auntie's tiring, so I'm able to squirm free. I only take one step when the man seizes me by the ankle and knocks me down, smashing my face against the floor, and jarring the ball loose. The cats rush after it.

"What did you see?" Duradin demands as he picks me up and shakes me.

My body shuts down and my brain follows. I go limp and close my eyes tightly. They fly open when he drops me. My elbow connects with the wood floor and sends an electrical shock up my body. I flip onto my stomach, ready to run, but freeze when I see what made him let me go.

The large black monster that came through my window last night is in my family room, brutally striking Duradin in the stomach with a long white staff. It follows that hit with a blow to his face that sends him tumbling backward. Then the hooded creature turns toward me.

Auntie leaps onto its back. She's only there for a second before the monster shrinks into nothingness. She hits the floor with a loud smack and a groan. It's only gone for a second before it's back and lunging at the man.

Duradin shouts, and ten soldiers appear from thin air. They're in red armor with raised gold swords, crowding our tiny apartment, and charging the monster. They end up crashing into each other when the hooded creature vanishes and reappears again a few feet away. It swings its staff and bashes the soldier in front of it. Then it thrusts the staff back, taking out two behind him.

That buys it some time. The glowing eyes search the room and find me.

Maybe if I play dead, the monster won't come after me. I lie still so it can tell I'm not a threat to it.

"Run!" it screams.

I spring to my feet, but only make it a few steps when I trip over one of the cats and hit the floor again. It's Oberon, the small black and white tabby that attacked Duradin. The cat trots to the side of the room where the glass ball rolled and bats it to me. I capture the marble without thinking and sprint out of the apartment.

CHAPTER 4

I run outside, jump from the top of my stoop to the sidewalk, and fall to my knees. Blind panic brings me to my feet and starts them moving. I have nowhere to go.

Oberon bolts in front of me and I follow. He's fast, but I manage to keep pace while we weave our way down multiple side streets until I'm completely lost. I run until my legs fail, sending my body tumbling through a narrow, garbage-filled alley. The fire in my lungs distracts me from the filth I'm lying in as I gasp for air.

The need to vomit jolts me back to my feet. I barely make it to the side of the dumpster when my stomach violently empties. Never in my life have I exercised like this. My heart might explode. I sit back down on the grungy alley pavement, and Oberon rubs himself against my shins, purring loudly. He probably thinks I'm dying. He's probably right.

When my breathing returns to normal and I'm relatively confident that I'll live, my brain flashes back to my real problem. "What am I going to do, Oberon? Why am I following a cat? I don't know where to go. I can't report this to anybody. I have no friends and nowhere to run. Tell me what to do."

Oberon stares at me for a moment, then holds his head up and opens his mouth to speak. "Murr, murr, mow," he says with confidence.

I roll my eyes. "Great. Bugs can talk, but cats can't."

Tears fall in abundance down my cheeks. I can't remember the last time I cried. "I'm scared, and alone, and have no idea what to do next."

Oberon continues to rub his body against mine, almost as if he's petting me, but in spite of his solace, I sob for a long time.

The little tabby offers quite a bit of comfort, and my crying fit abruptly ends. It's getting dark, and I'm afraid I may have to spend the night in the alley.

"Maybe we should head back, Oberon. I'll tell them what I saw," I say, not liking that idea but not having many options. I can't even think about what happened in the apartment without my chest seizing. I should do nothing and just sit here with my cat. "I don't like that plan either."

The sun sets, and I'm glad that it never gets too dark in the city. I almost convince myself to relax when a long shadow creeps down the alley. I look for the source but there isn't one. No one is coming. When it reaches my feet, the black monster from the apartment oozes up from the ground.

"Agatha Stone," it says in a deep gravelly voice.

That's the second time this thing has said my name, only now I'm not scared. And because I'm not scared, I'm worried. I'm not a brave person. This monster should be terrifying me out of my mind, but instead, I'm overcome with relief. I'm less afraid of this monster than of being alone in the alley.

"You must come with me, quickly."

"Why?" I ask with astonishing composure. I'm grateful to have a place to go and thankful someone else is making the plans. I've never been in charge before, and I don't want to start with life-changing decisions.

"You are not safe here. It's essential that we leave."

"Leave? Where?"

"Come, and I'll show you."

Oberon leaps from my lap and runs to the monster, rubbing against the bottom of his robe. He reaches down, strokes the little cat's head and makes meowing noises. Oberon meows back.

His suggestion doesn't alarm me, which is odd because I know that I shouldn't go anywhere with strangers, especially if they're real live monsters.

"I'm not going anywhere with you. What are you?"

"I'll explain everything. We'll not go far, just out of the alley and away from—*them*."

"Who's *them*? You came into my room last night, and today my whole world falls apart!" I shout, trying to sound brave, but the tears have already started.

"Agatha, I can explain everything, but your hiding place is not a good one." He sounds worried. "Come with me. I'll get you some food and expound on what transpired this evening."

I can't go home; just the thought of facing Auntie and her weird friend makes my fingers cold. This creature is my only solution. He did defend me against Duradin, and if he found me, the others will too.

"Okay, I'll go. But not far."

Once he has my consent, he leads Oberon and me down into the subway. While we're waiting on the platform, I have time to think. I agreed to go because I couldn't come up with a better plan. However, leaving with my new friend might've been a bad idea.

"You could at least tell me your name," I say to stop my brain from continuing down this line of thought.

"Jonah. Don't talk to me here. Humans can't see me. You'll draw attention to yourself."

"I'm human." The way he said humans makes it sound as if I'm not one, which is just rude. But if humans can't see him and I can, then that means—"Right?"

"You're human. Now stop talking."

"But I see you."

"Stop talking."

We stand by the yellow line waiting for the subway. The station is busy, but no one notices the seven-foot Jonah next to me. I'm beginning to wonder if he's real.

It's crowded inside the train and although people can't see Jonah, they've made room for him. In fact, I'm jammed against two women, yet there's space all around him as if the passengers know something is there and don't want to touch it. Even when the movement of the car jostles them in his direction, they maneuver to avoid him.

"This is our stop," he says loudly.

I look around to see if anyone heard, but no one cares. He grabs my arm and shuffles me toward the door. It's amazing watching New Yorkers wordlessly shift aside for him as we make it to the door in record time.

"Get ready to jump."

"Jump?" I yell and although their heads never turn, many an angry eye shifts my way. Not only are the doors shut, but the train is racing down the track. How does he expect me to jump?

"Shhh! Now go." He places a hand on my back.

I try to brace myself for the impact with the door when he pushes me, but it's gone. I fall through the air for less than a second and hit the dirt with a grunt. Lying in the muck as subway wheels pass close to my face, I'm amazed I'm uninjured. It wasn't a bad fall. Had I known what to expect, it wouldn't have been an issue to stay on my feet. It was like jumping down from a high step.

"Where'd the doors go?" I ask, brushing myself off.

"The portal makes the physics weak here. The humans built the track just on the edge of the bubble. When the trains pass, the entire wall of the car is compromised, but I thought the doorway would be easier for you."

I have no idea what he just said, so I ask another question hoping for a better answer. "I can't talk to you, but I can jump from a moving train?"

"The humans will believe they imagined you, or that you moved to another part of the train. If they can't explain what they see, then to them, it didn't happen."

"I am human, right? I can see you, jump from moving trains and go through walls..." It sounds crazier when I say it out loud.

He starts down the track, and I have to jog to keep up with him. "Yes, you're human. I'll explain everything in a moment. Just a little further."

We're deep in the subway tunnel. It's dark, dirty and smelly, and everything has a damp yuckiness to it. We go only a short distance when Jonah stops at an old wooden door barely visible under the grime. He knocks and an eye peers at us through the peephole. The hole closes, but the door opens with an unnerving creak.

"Come in. Come in," a gnarled old man prattles as he shuffles to the side, making room for us to pass.

"Finnegan's my name. Haven't had a Knight Crawler here in some time. What brings you to this side? And who's this?" He seems thrilled by our company.

My confused gaze scans the area as I cautiously enter the small kitchen. It's a cottage, with wood floors and petite furniture. It's dim because there are no windows, but it's clean and, oddly enough, it has a certain charm about it that's warm and welcoming.

I stare at the herbs hanging from the ceiling. "Is he human?" I whisper to Jonah.

"Yes," he whispers back.

"Let me get you some tea," the old man chatters, opening the icebox to pull out a tray. "I just made some cookies. Are you hungry? I might have a few bananas."

"Yes, please," Jonah says. "This is Oberon Thunderclaws and Agatha."

Finnegan stops so abruptly I'm afraid he might fall over. He whips his head around and in one rather agile hop, we're nose to nose. He's staring at me as if his mouth and eyes are competing to see which can get wider. "Agatha Stone?" he whispers.

A shiver runs up my body. The kids I've gone to school with my entire life don't know my name, but now people and *things* I've never met know it. Jonah's not giving any indication of what I should do, so I nod.

The feeble old man's face lights up as he loudly claps his hands together. "Agatha Stone!" He grabs my hand and shakes it vigorously. "Agatha Stone, you're alive! Well, that explains everything. Come in, come in. This is cause for celebration!"

"No!" Jonah shouts, startling both Finnegan and me. "No celebration. She's had a difficult time. I need a place to speak with her, and she needs to eat."

"Oh, of course. How rude of me. This is so exciting. Agatha Stone in my humble home," he whispers, and then claps again and exclaims, "Agatha Stone!"

He attempts a few weak coughs to cover his excitement, but fools no one. Then he gently grabs my elbow in order to steer me across the kitchen and through the door to another room.

"Here, come here. In here. You can sit and talk for as long as you need. I'll get you some food." He tries to keep his tone serious, but by the third *here*, the big grin is back as his voice rises with each syllable.

The three of us are ushered into a modest room that appears to be Finnegan's office. There's a table and chairs piled high with papers and books, and a small sofa in front of the fire. The place should be damp and eerie, but it's not, especially with the bookshelves and glowing coals in the fireplace. Oberon makes himself comfortable near the hearth while I flop down in the closest chair and watch Jonah clear the table in front of me.

"Are you the Grim Reaper?" As soon as the words leave my mouth, my face burns because I didn't mean to ask that out loud.

Jonah's eyes widen for a moment and then he chuckles. He sits in the chair across from me and rests his elbows on the table. "Humans ask me that a lot."

"I thought humans couldn't see you."

"Sometimes some can." He's got that look adults get when they figure you're too stupid to understand what they're about to say. "Let me explain in a way that might make more sense rather than you asking me random questions."

He's looking at me as if he's expecting me to do something. We gawk at each other for an uncomfortable moment, and then he shrugs. "I'm a Knight Crawler. We are guardians. I'm your guardian. I'm not Death or the Reaper. However, most humans use my image to depict death. Does that scare you?"

My first reaction is *no*. His presence is just too soothing for him to be the eerie specter of death. It's odd because when I look at him, my brain says *monster,* but my impression of him is all warmth and caring.

"No. I didn't think you were. But if humans can't see you, how can they use your image?"

"Well," he sighs. "There was a time when humans and my kind peacefully coexisted. People like you can see me all the time, but most are blind to me now. Some can feel my presence, especially children, but it usually frightens them. However, many times when an individual is near death, their vision clears and they can see us. Often when a person is alone and dying, a Knight Crawler will sense that and sit with them. It goes against our breeding to let a being die alone. Mine used to be a comforting image, but people have changed it over the years."

I'm so riveted by what he's telling me that when Finnegan knocks on the door I jump and slam my fist on the table.

"Here you go," the old man jabbers as he sets a bowl in front of me. "I heated up some stew and bread. That should warm you up nicely."

He places a sad-looking plate in front of Jonah. "I have some tomatoes and a banana for you. Sorry. I wasn't expecting company. I don't have much…unless you want a salad or a potato?"

"Thank you, Finnegan. This will be fine."

"For Master Thunderclaws—tuna," Finnegan announces with a flourish, and Oberon jumps up, mewing his appreciation.

"If you need anything else, just holler," he says before closing the door behind him.

I dig into the stew with gusto, and don't stop until I can't scrape any more off the sides of the bowl. As I stuff the bread into my mouth, I watch Jonah eat the entire banana in three bites, skin and all. When he talks, his mouth is hard to see, but when he eats he looks like one of Auntie's yawning cats.

"You're a vegetarian?" I ask it as a question, but it's more of a statement. I'm proud of myself for figuring it out.

"Not quite. My kind only eats fruit, but we'll eat a vegetable if we're desperate."

With his answer, I'm out of conversation, so I sit and wait for him to speak. When he finishes his paltry meal he pushes his hood back, exposing more of his face. I lose all pretense of manners as I gawk openly, studying everything about him.

His skin is as black as his robe. Most of his face is comprised of two enormous red eyes that are surprisingly expressive. There's no white to them, but they're kind eyes, like those of a horse, only larger and much more angular. They take up a sizable portion of his face, and are changing shape as he thinks of something to say, discards the thought, and considers something else.

"What's with the marble and the weird guy who attacked me?" I ask, giving up hope that he'll just explain what's going on.

"You have the Orb, yes?"

"Yeah, in my pocket. Why's it such a big deal? Who was that lawyer guy?"

"Grand Wizard Duradin."

"Wizard? Like, a wizard? Like a magic and potions wizard? Or like the *Hey, this is a fun title. I'll call myself a wizard* kind of wizard?"

Jonah's eyes slant as he processes my question, "The first kind. Although magic in the way you understand it doesn't work on Earth."

"Umm, he made an army appear."

Jonah laughs. I'm not being funny. "Not an army. A few soldiers. They didn't materialize from thin air. It's a cloak. I could show you how to do that."

"Why did he attack me?"

"Because he doesn't know any other way."

That's not helpful. I expected a better answer.

"Grand Wizard Duradin works for another man. I'll tell you about him in a minute. That marble is an Orb."

29

He stops and his eyes get slanty again. "It's like the subway doors. I can explain things to you, but until you have the whole story, you won't understand. It would make more sense if I just start at the beginning."

How is any of this going to make sense? I think back to yesterday when I was just a girl from Queens, hating school and painting my bedroom. How did I end up talking to the Grim Reaper about wizards?

"You should tell me what you need to tell me in the way you want to tell it to me," I say.

He takes a deep breath. "Honestly, I don't know where to start. You should've been raised with this information, so it's difficult to give it to you all at once." He stops and lowers his eyes. After a brief moment, he looks up again, somewhat less defeated. "Okay, well...there are two populated worlds. One you know about. You call it Earth, and the other is Ashra."

I take it back. Maybe I shouldn't know.

CHAPTER 5

I'm not ready to hear this. I'm having trouble believing everything that's happened already, and it's getting more ridiculous the more he explains.

"Earth has one type of sentient being; they're called humans," Jonah continues. "Ashra has many types, but together they're called *curramonstrusos*. We call ourselves *curra*, but humans call us monsters."

"Monsters? Monsters are real! You're a monster?"

He grimaces. "I prefer 'curra.' And yes. You even said yourself, you've seen my image portrayed as a monster. I'm sure you've heard about some of us in myths and fairy tales."

A groan gurgles from deep inside my throat. I'm looking at the Grim Reaper while he tells me about other worlds and monsters. I can see and hear him, so he has to be real. I also touched him, and he moved the papers and stuff. Finnegan can see him, too. Finnegan, the guy who lives in a quaint cottage in a subway tunnel.

"All of us, humans and curra, lived together for centuries connected by portals. Then several hundred years ago, the humans sealed the portals without warning."

"What portals? And if they're sealed, how are you here?"

"They are doorways connecting my world to yours, but they were locked. Someone tried to open them, but they failed. However, because of his actions, now some of the portals let certain humans and curra get through, like you and me."

"Okay. Yeah. I've lost it." I jump out of my chair so fast I knock my empty bowl to the floor and spill my tea. "I had my doubts. I mean, I could almost accept the Grim Reaper and soldiers materializing out of thin air, even a wizard, but a whole other planet filled with monsters, connected to Earth? That can't be right. Someone somewhere would know about it. An entire planet is a tough thing to keep secret."

Pacing around the room isn't helping to make sense of all the stuff that happened today. My fear is making me mad, which confuses me because as a rule, I'm not an angry person. My brain is making a buzzing noise and flashing images as it rearranges the events in my life. How did I get in this situation, and more importantly, how do I get out of it?

Jonah stays seated, and while I anxiously race around the room, he presses on. "Where do you think mythology came from? Why do you think there are so many fairy tales? So many versions of the same stories? Sit, Agatha. Let me continue. It will make sense. Just give it some time."

"Here I am, in a cottage deep in the heart of a subway line. Yeah, that could happen. You know, when they find me, if they ever do, I'll be sitting in a pile of filth somewhere in the subway tunnels eating dirt and talking to myself. Or I may not even be in the tunnels. I could be wandering the streets of New Jersey somewhere."

"Agatha, you're not insane," Jonah says calmly as he walks over to me. "First off, crazy people don't believe they're crazy. They believe they're thinking more clearly than ever."

"Oh, okay. Good. The Grim Reaper thinks I'm sane."

"Secondly, you saw your Auntie tonight. I'm sure you thought her behavior strange. I can help you understand. If you let me continue, I'll do my best to explain."

I don't believe him, or myself, or my delusion. However, after much more pacing and a lot of deep breathing, I question if I'm creative enough to think this stuff up. I'm not this clever. Maybe I should just let whatever is happening happen, and trust that it will all work itself out.

I pace for a few minutes, and once I'm more in control, I flop back into the chair across the table from Jonah. I take a cleansing breath. "Why humans like me?"

"There used to be Knights posted on both sides of the portals. Human Knights guarded the Earth side and curra Knights guarded the Ashra side. You're a descendent of a human Knight. Human Knights can get through."

If what he's saying is true and I'm one of these Knights, why didn't Auntie know? Why aren't there others? He said portals with an *s,* so that means there's more than one. How many are there? Where are the other Knights? I want to ask all of these questions but I'm only brave enough to ask one. "How many are there like me?"

"One. You're the last."

Jonah states this so flatly there's no way I could've heard him right. I'm not special. This doesn't make sense. My mind is racing with questions, but then I remember that I'm hallucinating. Of course I'd be vital in my own fantasy. But this feels so *real.*

"Is that why you knew who I was? Why Finnegan acted the way he did when you said my name?"

"Agatha…you're a legend on Ashra."

I stand again and my head swims with the movement or maybe with the shock of being a legend. What are these people expecting of me? "I'm not a Knight! I mean, I don't know any Knight things. I don't know anything about being a Knight. Or anything about what you're talking about." I stop speaking because I'm hyperventilating.

"Relax. You're a thirteen-year-old girl," Jonah says calmly. "You know what a kid your age should know. You just missed out on some of your heritage, and that's easy enough to get back." He makes it sound like it's less of a big deal than it actually is.

"Nothing about this sounds easy. Finding out about one's heritage should be finding out your great uncle was a drinker or fought in a war. Not that there are two worlds and monsters are real, that you're a Knight and apparently a legend."

I can't breathe. The cottage is growing dim. "I'm going to faint. I've never done that before."

My body tenses when Jonah grabs me. Is he hugging me? "I'm not used to people touching me," I say to his upper arm. "But this is nice."

He holds me for a long time and when I become uneasy with the contact, he guides me back to my chair. My wide eyes meet his sad ones when he sits across the table. He needs to tell me that I'm okay. And that soon I'll wake up in my own bed with this nightmare behind me. However, if he insists on continuing this story, he has to make it make sense and convince me that this is normal. Convince me that I'm normal.

But he's waiting for me to begin the conversation again. "Why am I the only one?"

"Humans sealed the portals and then they killed all the Knights. Have you ever heard about the Knights Templar?"

I shake my head. "No. History's boring. I'm not good at it."

"Well, they were famous Knights. Humans don't know much about them except that they escorted people through the Holy Lands and held secret ceremonies. They're most famous for being slaughtered all at once for what most humans believe to be unknown reasons."

"If they killed everyone, how am I here?"

"Well, it was the thirteen-hundreds," Jonah says carefully. "They killed the men. Women of that time were not considered worth bothering with. However, it didn't take long before they realized their mistake and murdered the women for being witches. That was a brutal time. They killed off most of the remaining Knights and many innocent women."

"The Stones were one of the few surviving legacies. When your parents died, it was never clear what happened to you."

"How did my parents die?"

"They were murdered," Jonah mutters after a pause. I think he might have been debating if he should tell me, but I'm glad he did.

I should gasp in shock or feel some kind of remorse, but news of my parents is a relief. I want to ask him more, but I'm afraid of the answers. Plus, my brain is no longer forming coherent thoughts so I stare blankly at him, waiting for him to say more.

"I'll tell you everything, but for now, I don't think you'll understand. I can see that you're overwhelmed by the events of today and everything I've told you. Give yourself some time. It's late. Rest. I promise, I'll help you understand, but you can't learn it all in one night."

I sit back in my chair and try without success to comprehend everything he told me. I'm not smart enough to make something like this up. He might be telling me the truth. If he is, what's going to happen to me?

His wide red eyes seem so sad. "I'm sorry I'm the one who has to tell you these things," he says. "And I'm sorry it's being told to you in this way."

"I don't want you to feel bad." I wish I were able to reassure him as well as he's able to reassure me, but I'm new to comfort so I don't even try. I stare off into space and let my mind race. It doesn't run for long before my eyes close. I snap them open, but it's no use. My brain is shutting down and my body is following.

"We will spend the night here," Jonah says as if he just decided that.

Finnegan is thrilled to learn he'll have company for the night. He joyfully makes a cot up for me by the fireplace. Oberon, equally happy with the bed, stands on my chest, exuberantly head-butting me in the face. When I stop petting him, he licks my eyebrows a few times then plops down on top of me purring loudly.

Wrapped in my comfortable bed with the sleeping cat, I listen to Jonah and Finnegan speaking softly in the other room. I can't understand what they're saying until Finnegan whispers, "Poor girl. She has no idea what lies ahead for her."

The rough tongue of one of Auntie's cats scrapes across my nose, stirring me from a deep sleep. I grunt and shoo the little beast away. Why is my room so warm? Because I'm not in my own bed! I jerk upright, sending poor Oberon scurrying to the floor. The Cuckoo clock on the wall says ten fifteen, but I can't tell if that's a.m. or p.m.

I glance around the strange dim room with the images from yesterday flooding my brain, and my heart sinks. How long can a delusion last? I don't think I could go to sleep and wake up with everything being and feeling exactly the same if I'm making this up. Jonah is chatting with Finnegan in the other room. This has to be real.

My sore muscles complain when I reach down to give Oberon a few apology pets. I hate exercise, and I certainly got a lot of it yesterday. I stretch to relieve some of the aches, but I'm making it worse so I give up and hobble out to join them.

"There you are! Good morning, good morning! Let me get you some breakfast," Finnegan exclaims. Is he always this happy?

"I want to take you to Ashra. You'll be safer there," Jonah informs me as soon as I take a seat at the kitchen table. I shrug my shoulders. He's in charge, so if he thinks I'm safer there, then we'll go. Although I highly doubt Auntie would ever find me in a cottage in a subway tunnel.

The little tabby jumps up on the chair next to me, and Finnegan rubs its head. "You're welcome to stay with me for a few days, Oberon. I know cats don't like the underground, but just until you can find a new home."

He sets down a wonderful-smelling plate of eggs and bacon in front of me. "Are cats curra?" I ask.

"Oh, yes. You couldn't tell? Why, the air of superiority should've been your first clue," Finnegan says with a wink to Oberon.

"Are all animals curra?"

"No, no, just felines and serpents," Finnegan says.

"All cats are monsters?" Oberon meows at my use of that slur.

"Cats are curra. They liked their human servants and chose this side a long time ago," Jonah explains.

"Is that why a black cat shouldn't cross your path? And that weird Egyptian thing with the cats?" I ask, placing some facts with his story.

"The Egyptians knew the cats were curra and used them to help manage their civilization," Jonah answers. "Black cats were spies working for the Circe Mystics. They're not anymore, although they're still sneaky."

Sometimes Jonah's answers leave me with more questions. How can cats be spies or run governments? And that group he named sounds like a circus act, but they're probably something awful that I don't want to know about. I want to tell him I'm scared, but I don't know how. "If I go with you, can I come back?"

"Yes, you're able to go through the portals anytime you wish."

"Can Oberon come with us?"

Jonah shakes his head. "No, just human Knights and Wizards. And a few choice curra. No cats."

I stop asking questions because the less I know the better. I wish I didn't know what I already do.

After we finish eating, I thank Finnegan for his hospitality and say my goodbyes to Oberon. When we step out of Finnegan's cottage, a pang of regret touches my heart because I wasn't closer to Oberon when we lived together.

We all walk a few steps to a beat-up old archway that's been boarded up. Jonah places a comforting hand on my back while Finnegan wipes the decaying planks down with his dishtowel.

"This will feel strange," Jonah says before he pushes me straight into the boards.

CHAPTER 6

My face connects with the wood slats but the beams easily fall away. And then I sneeze. A moment later, Jonah appears beside me.

The light is dim like the sky before sunrise. It's a deep purplish blue with pink and red streaks. I can see stars and a muted sun. Two moons, right next to each other, are directly overhead. One is brighter than the other, almost like a reflection. There are also several large dim circles in the sky that I assume are other planets.

"We're outside," I say.

We're in an expansive field with trees dotted throughout. They appear to be ordinary trees in fall colors with fiery reds and oranges, but they also have deep blues and indigos. Everything seems so much more luminous than the gray and green I'm used to.

The field is crowded with people who appear to be having a party.

"They're flying," I whisper. They're ordinary people but they're flitting from tree to tree, chatting, laughing, and dancing with each other. Dizziness flips my stomach. I turn to leave, but Jonah puts an arm out to stop me. "I want to go back. This is too much."

"You know where the door is and you can leave at any time, but I'd like you to stay and meet some of the faeries who live here."

Winged people are beautifully engraved into the heavy wooden door in front of me. An intricate stone archway surrounds it, and at the top are statues of larger winged people brandishing swords. The door is housed in a small but ornately decorated building that looks like the tomb of a very important person. The subway arch might have been as pretty as this one before time, trains, and people wrecked it.

Faeries are just too tempting to pass up. I'll take a few minutes, have a look around, and then head home. I look up at Jonah's smiling face. "I can leave when I want?"

He nods. "I'll escort you back myself."

Now I'm nodding. He takes my hand. And my body locks in place. He doesn't pull me or drop my hand. Instead, he waits while I study his face. This is like hugging. Hand holding. I like it.

We only take a few steps when the high-pitched chorus of bugs starts talking. "That's her! That's the Agatha!"

The bugs give me such a fright, I nearly jump into Jonah's arms. He puts a reassuring hand on my shoulder. "Trees are an excitable bunch. They're happy to see you."

"That's a tree?"

"Yes," he says. Then he chides the tree for scaring me.

"Booooo!" the large oak says while rustling its leaves. Then it breaks out in laughter at its joke.

Jonah grunts and ushers me away from the trees. I'm not watching where he's taking me because I can't keep my eyes off the flying people. They look like regular New Yorkers, only taller, prettier and better dressed.

Jonah guides me down a stone path. When we come to a clearing, my heart leaps when I see the Manhattan skyline. It's shaded and purple, like mountains in the distance. The lights from many windows are shining in irregular patterns that blend with the starry sky, but the buildings themselves look to be just a mirage and not like they're part of this world. I've always thought the buildings of Manhattan were beautiful, but seeing them like this adds to their splendor.

"We're in Central Park," I announce.

"Sort of. The veil is thin here, so it's easy to orient yourself."

"So we're still on Earth. We haven't flown through space to some distant land." I'm so relieved, I'm giddy. "I'm much more at ease now that I know where I am. I've grown up with these buildings. I never realized how much a part of me they were until I saw them in this unexpected place." Jonah shakes his head, but says nothing. "I've lived in Queens my entire life. I've never been anywhere. Not even Philadelphia."

He gives me a look. I can't tell if it means he's worried about me or he pities me. I guess that is rather pathetic. He silently guides me up a pathway that's lined with numerous glass streetlamps with actual flames in them. I've seen all forms of streetlights in my lifetime but never anything as exquisite and detailed as these. Intrigued, I ask Jonah if we can stop so I can inspect one.

The post is made of water, solid water if that's possible. It even has tiny iridescent fish swimming in it. The water forms a globe at the top and inside is a fluorescent pink flame, which attracts the tiny fish like moths. The globe is casting off large plumes of pinkish-orange steam that lights up a considerable portion of the park around us. I reach out and touch the post and it ripples like a puddle in the rain.

Mesmerized, I study the lamp for a long time until Jonah gently pulls me away. He's leading me to a tall, ornate platform that's weaving through the tree canopy. It's made of thick interwoven vines in varying shades of blue

41

and purple. Jonah hasn't taken his eyes off it, as if he's trying to figure out who or what might be up there.

The trees are singing a lovely chorus and swaying to their music. We climb the many steps of a stairway that's definitely alive. It has a few leaves sticking out here and there and an overabundance of lavender flowers draped down its sides. With no evidence of a support structure, how did they get the vines to grow in this peculiar way?

When we reach the top, the platform is packed with faeries that are just as curious about me as I am about them. I want to grab Jonah's hand, but mine is sweating. I don't want to gross him out. I need to go home, or at least get away from the scrutiny and whispers. I'm not what they expected.

They're opulently dressed in fine fabrics in a multitude of deep rich colors. They're much taller than I imagined. In fact, every one of them is over six feet tall, which is weird; I thought they'd be tiny. Of course, I also thought they were imaginary. They look human, too, with the exception of two sets of translucent, shimmering black wings on each side of their backs, like a dragonflies. The wings are as long as the faeries are tall. When not in use, the papery wings have a joint in the middle that folds them neatly down their back. I've never felt pretty, but in the company of such profound beauty, I'm even more plain than usual.

Jonah leads me through the crowd to a dais, which has one large throne with two smaller thrones on either side of it. On the center throne sits an imposing man wearing a crown made of vines, flowers, and jewels that covers most of his long, black hair. He's also wearing a skirt, which is weird until I remember what a kilt is.

"Quiet!" the man orders and everything, including the trees, falls silent. The hush makes my trembling limbs weaken. Everyone is staring at me.

"Agatha, I'd like you to meet His Majesty, King Ohad," Jonah says as he bows to the King. I bow too, and then remember that I probably should've curtsied, but I don't know how.

"Agatha Stone." The King flashes an intimidating smile. "It is a pleasure to meet you. I am so pleased you are well. We have been concerned for you, and I'm overjoyed at your safe return."

"Your Majesty, if I may have a private word with you?" Jonah asks.

The King agrees, and when Jonah sits down in the throne next to him, King Ohad mutters something in a foreign language. He continues to move his mouth as if he's talking, but no sound comes out. They converse for a long time in silence. I shift my weight to different parts of my feet and concentrate on not looking at the faeries who are gawking at me.

When they finish, the King waves his hand, and Jonah returns to me. "Come sit with me, Agatha," the King commands.

I cautiously sit in the throne Jonah vacated. I've never spoken with a king before. I hope I don't say anything stupid. I wish my stomach would calm down. If I throw up on him, I'll leave Ashra and never come back.

The King mutters again, then turns to me. "No one can hear us now, so you are free to speak." I don't know what to say to a king, so I sit on my hands and rock back and forth, nervously hoping he'll do all the talking.

King Ohad sighs loudly. "Jonah has informed me that you are unaware of your heritage and that up until last night, you didn't know about Ashra or its peoples." He's watching me as if he expects me to say something, but I'm already feeling like an idiot for not knowing these things that I'm supposed to know. I don't want to open my mouth and add to my stupidity.

Ohad gives up. "Agatha, do you have the Orb with you?"

I gaze blankly at him, so he tries again. "Do you have a ball made of…glass on your person?"

My face lights up. I finally have something to contribute to the conversation. I happily reach in my pocket, pull out Auntie's crystal ball, and hold it up.

King Ohad flinches with alarm and covers my hand, forcing it down. "A simple *yes* would have sufficed." He tells me to put the ball back in my pocket and then he gazes at me with a solemn expression. "Do you know what the Orb is?"

I shake my head. I don't know what any of this is. I'm disappointing him just by being who I am.

King Ohad rubs his temples. "Someone as old as I am should not be asking this of someone as young as you." His head is down. He's talking to himself.

"Agatha, that Orb is a map," he blurts out when he looks up. "Jonah told me he explained the portals to you. The map leads to the key that will open the doorways between our two worlds. There are some that want the gates open, and others who want the gates closed. There is only one key, and it is hidden, and only one person has the map to it. That person is you."

My face reddens with a rush of pride. I'm the key holder for everyone in both worlds. I can open the gates, and everyone will know that I'm the one who did it. I'll be a hero.

King Ohad reads my face and can see where my thoughts have taken me. "Agatha, those gates must not be opened."

"Huh? Why do I need to get a key to a door that you don't want to open?"

"We need you to find the key before anyone else does."

"But I thought I'm the only one with a map."

He rubs his temples again, "There is so much you don't know." He puts his head down, studies his knees and doesn't move for an uncomfortable amount of time.

I shove my hands under my legs and rock back and forth. Should I leave? Are we done?

He raises his gaze and asks, "Do you know where you are?"

"Central Park." I'm so happy that I'm able to answer at least one of his questions.

"Are you sure? Does the park look all that familiar to you? Those buildings are a shadow. You could walk right through them. You are in the thinnest part of the veil. A place where our two worlds overlap, but you are not in Central Park. You are in Manahata, land of the faeries."

He pauses to let his words sink in. I should be pondering his statement, but all I want to do is to go over and try to walk through one of the buildings.

"Agatha," the King snaps. He caught me not thinking about the right thing. "I'll try to explain some overly complicated matters in as simple a way as I can, but you need to pay attention."

He says nothing after this and scrutinizes his knees again. I look at his knees too. When he snaps his head back up, he catches me gawking at his knees and my face gets hot.

"Is there peace in your world?" he asks.

I'm taken aback by his sudden change of topic and the odd question. I shake my head.

"What would happen if an army of humans could walk, unseen, to an enemy's doorstep? That would be a great advantage to the humans. You can see why some humans would want the gates open and why others would not. The land we are sitting on would be very valuable to the humans. You can understand why we faeries would not want humans invading our village."

I nod because I want him to think I understand, which I kind of do. Would there be two Central Parks, or would people build offices and condos here since we already have one? Either way, people would be tearing the trees down and building skyscrapers all over this place as soon as the portal opened. What if that happened in all the major cities across Earth? That would be bad for Ashra. Plus, I doubt the curra would surrender without a fight. A lot of people would get hurt.

"Agatha, look at Jonah. How would you, a human, defeat him?"

I shrug my shoulders. Why would I have to fight Jonah? Why would I have to fight anyone? "He's very big. And he can disappear and stuff. I saw some soldiers try and fail."

"I'm sorry if my question disturbed you, but the humans sealed the portals at their first opportunity for a reason. There are many things on this world that would bring chaos and destruction to yours. And there are many reasons why there were Knights posted on both sides."

"Well, if the key is hidden, why don't you leave it alone? It's been wherever it is for a long time, and I won't tell anyone."

"Because those who want the portals open will find it without you."

My specialness washes away. "So you want me to tell you where the key is so you can have it before they get it."

"Not quite. We need you to lead us to the key so you can destroy it," the King says it so matter-of-factly that the impact of his words doesn't register.

"Okay," I say meekly. I want this conversation to be over now.

King Ohad smiles grimly at me. "It's not a simple task I'm asking of you. The key is well hidden, and the journey is dangerous. You could be killed like your parents were."

A chill shoots up my spine and shimmies my shoulders. I'm not interested in dying. I'm not good at anything, especially all the stuff I'd have to do to find this key. I'm highly under-qualified. "What if I can't do it?"

"Then Stratagor Ziras will find the key, open the floodgates and dominate the human civilization."

That sounded so weird, I can't wrap my brain around it. "Who's Stratagor Ziras and why does he want to dominate humans? What will he do?"

"He's a powerful specter who would war with the humans until only one world remains."

I don't want Earth to be destroyed, or for there to be a war. A true world war, where every human civilization would have to fight or die. I don't understand any of this, but if the portals are locked now, then it's best to keep them that way.

"Okay." I agree so that our conversation will end. I'm not brave, courageous, or strong. They've got the wrong girl, and I'm telling Jonah as soon as the King lets me leave.

Ohad sighs again. "Agatha, you need to think about what I'm asking you. It won't be easy."

He studies his knees again, but this time I don't look at them. When he finally glances up, he's made a decision. "You can say no. We will not force you to search for the key. But to help you decide, I would like you to embark on a voyage of self-discovery and reflect on what lies ahead."

I nod. I don't need to go on a voyage to decide because I'm not doing it. But I'll go because I'd like to be on a boat, and I want to see more of this faerie land. I'm glad they said I can say no after I get to do that

He waves a hand and says, "Jonah, you will take Agatha on a voyage. On your way, you will ensure that she has enough information to make a decision about her willingness to search for the key."

Jonah bows, so I'm guessing our private talk is over.

The King turns back toward me. "It is understandable for you to be unsure. This is all new. Do not rush to a decision. Fully understand what is being asked of you." Then he grasps my hand and leads me to the edge of the platform. When everyone across the park stops and looks up at us, my knees weaken. I should've gone home.

"This is Agatha Stone," he announces to the crowd. Everyone gasps. "We are so pleased that she has returned to us. Tonight we feast!"

CHAPTER 7

The crowd erupts with loud cheers, and a crush of faeries surrounds me. They're speaking English, but there are so many questions at once I can't focus on one long enough to answer it. The profusion of attention overwhelms my senses, and I can't breathe. Jonah hurries to my side and extricates me from my admirers.

The party begins immediately upon the King's announcement, and Jonah is steering me away from the commotion. The trees are having a good time, singing and gyrating to the music. I never knew trees could be so much fun.

When we walk a good distance away from the festivities, the trees in our vicinity stop singing and shush each other like a class of kindergarteners. When it's quiet, one giant oak says, "Agatha, come sit under our branches."

I want to run back to Queens so I can tell everyone about the trees, and the fairies, and Jonah, but then I remember that I have no one to tell. What will happen to me if I admit that I'm not a Knight?

I sit down on a pile of leaves and lean against the oak's trunk. Jonah is looking at me with round, concerned eyes. No one has ever looked at me that way before. It makes me self-conscious.

"Why does a tree have so many voices, and how do all the voices know to say the same thing? And why can I hear them and others can't? And why is it such a high pitch? I always thought that a great big tree like this one would have a deep, wise voice," I say while imitating the deep tone.

The oak laughs.

"Humans can hear the trees. They just forgot to listen. Think of the stories where trees talk. Why do you think humans put faces on drawings of trees? The reason you hear many voices is because a tree is a multitude of parts working together for one goal. When a tree speaks, all of those parts are joining together to form words. That's why you hear all of their voices."

He stops talking like his thoughts took him away, and then he looks up. "I don't know why it's so shrill. I guess that's just the way they're made."

Thinking about something other than what King Ohad said relieves some of my stress, but now that our conversation has run its course, I don't want to talk anymore. I want to sit in the silence of the trees with Jonah on the grass next to me.

After some time passes, Jonah touches my leg. "Agatha, have you ever been to a party thrown in your honor?"

"No."

"Well, there's one right over there. Do you want to go and see what it's like?"

I was so lost in my thoughts that I forgot about the party. I've never been to a party, let alone as the guest of honor. I'm suddenly so excited that I want to run over there.

Instead, we walk quickly. The faeries look my way but none of them approach me right away. Jonah seats me at a table in the corner. I'm served an overabundance of strange food, all of which is delicious with the exception of some yellow beans. We eat and drink and I watch the faeries dancing. I've never felt so happy in my life. The party goes on for hours with all sorts of faeries clamoring for my attention. It's exhausting, and when I start to fade, a sweet faerie named Hetty informs me that I'll be staying at her home.

I nod my head. She nods back, but she's looking up. Someone grabs me under my armpits and lifts me off the ground. I try to scream, but I'm drawing air in, instead of out, so I make an odd noise and choke on my spit.

"I'm Zeal, Hetty's mate," says the deep voice of my abductor.

We're flying at high speed, and the only thing that's keeping me from plummeting to my death is the strength of his fingers. I want to get down. And I want a safety harness!

"Breathe!" he exclaims with a laugh. He says it three more times before I do. "Now, open your eyes!"

I want to shout *No!* but I'm unable to speak. I wish he'd grabbed me differently because I want to cover my eyes with my hands, as if the added protection will make this less terrifying.

"Come on. Open them. I won't let you down until you look around."

I want to yell at him for putting me through this horror and then fight my way loose from his grasp. Unfortunately, I'm not a temper tantrum kind of girl, and I certainly am not a fighter. I do what I'm told because I always do what I'm told. I open my eyes.

The brightly colored trees whirl past my feet. We're flying so fast, they're more like streaks of color than individual trees. I'm seeing the Manhattan skyline as no other human being has ever seen it: soft, shimmering indigo shadows, with gleaming points of light dotted throughout

51

and merging with the stars. The brilliant shapes erupt from a sea of radiant trees, set against the backdrop of the purplish-blue sky and highlighting the beautiful faeries flying about.

Just as I start to relax, Zeal plunges into the trees, dives down under the canopy, then swoops up. I'm in a house. A tree house.

He sets me down on the wood planks beside the door in the floor. Branches pass through the spacious multistoried home, creating screens and archways. The leaves make up the exterior walls. Hetty is walking down a spiral staircase that wraps around the thick trunk in the center of the house. Everything has the appearance of nature. There are so many flowers and candles it's like I'm in a garden.

Hetty guides me into the living room and over to a topiary with small green leaves that's shaped like a couch. "You can sleep here."

I nod, even though I'm not sure how comfortable it will be sleeping on a bush.

"We require a bed, please," she says to the sofa. The bush slowly lowers its back and sides to make a perfectly flat bed, complete with headboard. "Oh, you'll need to be a lot softer." The bush explodes into a million tiny blue flowers.

Hetty spreads out a blanket made of feathers and then says something in that language the King used, and a pillow made of clouds appears.

"Do you need anything else, dear?"

I shake my head. I wouldn't know what to ask for after witnessing that.

She looks at me with watery eyes for an uncomfortable amount of time, then grabs my hands and takes a shaky breath. What am I supposed to do if she starts crying? "Zeal and I would like you to know how terribly honored we are to have you in our home. If you desire anything, please, let us know."

She continues to stare at me as if she expects me to say something profound. I avert my eyes and notice there's no bed for Jonah. I rip my hands from hers and spin in a circle. He's not here! He wouldn't leave me without saying goodbye. But I left! I left without telling him where I was going.

"Where's Jonah?" I sound so calm, like I'm casually asking about my friend, instead of having a panic attack.

"Oh, he'll be along soon. He chose to walk," Zeal explains.

"Where will he sleep?"

Hetty smiles. "Why, under your bed, of course."

I can't tell if she's joking. It's difficult for me to figure out why some people think certain things are funny. This doesn't sound funny. Jonah can't fit under the bed. But Hetty was so genuine when she said it. It's stupid to ask her what she meant, so I ignore it. She gives me another of those weird looks and wishes me a good night.

The bed is beautiful. It's like something rich people would sleep on. I'm afraid to sit on it because the topiary might get mad that I'm crushing its flowers. It might grow thick thorny vines and strangle me to death.

I reach down and stroke the petals. "It's just a bed. It knows you're going to lie on it. Get a grip," I whisper while testing the bed with some firm pushes.

It stays quiet, so I push on it harder. Nothing moves and no thorns appear, so I take a deep breath, spin around and sit. I freeze, squeezing my eyes tight, bracing for anything, but nothing happens. I let out a breath and cautiously climb under the blanket.

This bed is amazingly plush and smells like vanilla and lilacs. I sink deeply into the velvety petals and fall asleep instantly.

I'm on a boat in a rough sea. There's a storm. The waves are enormous. We're not going to survive. I must open my eyes.

I'm in a tree. I was dreaming about a boat, but in reality I'm in a tree. How is this my reality? Why is the tree swaying?

The tree is humming and dancing to its song.

"Please stop. You're making me ill."

The tree stills without a word. I'm in Hetty's house, in the topiary bed, and Jonah isn't here. They lied to me! Hetty said he would sleep under my bed, but he couldn't be under there because that's weird. I should peek to be sure, but it's scary to look underneath a bed in the dark. He couldn't fit, either.

I muscle up some courage and work my way to the edge of the opulent bed. I dip my head down to prove to myself that he's not there. It's pitch black. I'm stupid for hoping he'd be there.

A pair of luminous red eyes appears in the dark, and my entire body seizes.

I sit up and try to catch my breath. I automatically bring my hand to my chest to check my heart, which is pounding frantically. "Jonah, you should warn a person before you do that! You scared the life out of me."

Jonah materializes from the floor up and hovers beside my bed.

"That's really creepy." It doesn't scare me that he's able to do that. I accept it as who he is, but I'm being honest when I say it's creepy.

He yawns. He has a wide mouth that I can only see when he talks or smiles. Normally, his face is a black void

54

with giant red eyes. Light doesn't reflect well off of him, so he has a shadowy form and no real shape. Although I've touched him, he's solid. He seems to know that his appearance alarms people because he often pulls the hood of his cloak over his face, which makes him scarier.

"You're very scary-looking," I say.

Jonah rubs his hand over his sleepy face and gazes down at me. He scratches his arm and says in a gravelly voice. "Really? Because you just took a few years off my life. With your big blue eyes on the front of your head, staring at me. Thought I was a goner there for a moment."

I can't tell if he's joking. "I scared you? How could someone as small as me frighten someone as huge as you?"

"I'm going back to sleep."

"Jonah?"

"Hmmm?"

"Why are you under my bed?"

"Because I'm a Knight Crawler."

"Wha—"

"Go to sleep."

CHAPTER 8

The sounds of people making breakfast wakes me from a disturbed sleep. As soon as the tree notices that I'm awake, it spreads its branches to let in the morning light. At least, I think it's morning. The sky is still the same dim purple it was the night before.

Jonah and the two fairies greet me when I stumble into the kitchen. I'm not a morning person, but I manage a polite response. I plop into the open seat across from Jonah, and Hetty promptly places breakfast in front of me.

"Thanks," I manage. This is the second day in a row that people have cooked for and served me. The attention is making me more self-conscious than usual. I don't know how to respond to their kindness. I wish everyone would stop treating me like I'm special. I want to be left alone because at least I know how to handle that.

Hetty places a bowl of cherries in front of Jonah, and a happy grin spreads across his face. He looks like one of Auntie's cats when he does that. His mouth is so large he can almost literally smile from ear to ear—if he has ears, that is. He never drops his hood far enough for me to see.

He carefully picks up a cherry, and after studying it for a moment, he eats the entire thing, including the pit and stem.

After we clear the breakfast dishes, Jonah and I walk back to the platform we were on last night. It's strange that the sky is still the same shade of dim purple and the light is exactly as it was last night, even though a significant amount of time has passed.

The fires continue to burn in the streetlamps, and everything is identical to yesterday except it's deserted. There are no faeries flying around; even the trees are quiet. When we reach the top of the platform, the thrones are gone and in their place are two guards in front of a wall of leaves. When we arrive at the wall, the guards step aside and the tree opens its branches, forming an archway.

The walls are alive, constructed completely out of living leaves in every color imaginable. The leaves attach to a multitude of equally colorful branches passing through the chamber at all angles, like Hetty's home, only much bigger and fancier.

There are doors leading off to other areas, but most of them are closed. The few that are open reveal long ornate passageways that make me want to run down the halls and see how big this place really is.

Our footfalls resonate loudly on the shiny stone floors, and my heart beats faster with every echo. I avert my eyes from the throne in the center of the room and study the few finely-crafted furnishings in the chamber.

The expansive room is practically empty with the exception of the dozens of armored guards and King Ohad, who is even bigger and more kingly today. I draw my eyes up to study the mural made of flowers. It's a faerie killing a dragon in midflight, and it seems to be moving as the plants grow.

I'm so absorbed in the painting and how it can move that I jump when Jonah grabs my sweaty hand and leads me to the dais.

"Jonah," the King says with a stern tone. This is definitely not the same friendly man as last night. "I want you to make sure that Agatha understands what is expected of her before she embarks on the voyage. I want her to know exactly what is at stake."

"Yes, your Majesty," Jonah agrees, not intimidated at all.

"Agatha," the King continues. "Learn all you can from Jonah before your voyage so you make a mindful choice. If you decide to undertake your quest to find the key, know that the odds of you succeeding are slim. You are ill-prepared and too young."

My knees weaken at his words. I was about to confess that I'm not going on any quest. I was ready to thank them for the party and good food, but inform them that they have the wrong girl. I'd anticipated them giving me some nice words before I left, but the King's tone makes me hold my tongue. Maybe he suspects that Jonah found the wrong Agatha?

"No one can properly prepare you for this task because you would not understand what you are told," he continues. "But know this, you will face horrors you did not know existed."

The King waves his hand, and an enormous dinosaur materializes twenty feet to my left. Its squat crimson body stands on four stout legs and is covered in large pink spots. Its stubby speckled head possesses two huge emerald eyes at the top and four massive fangs at the bottom.

The animal is temporarily stunned. But then it lets out a roar so loud it hurts my ears. After a deep inhale, it breathes out a plume of fire right before it charges at me. It's so heavy that the entire room shakes and the reverberations travel up my body, locking me in place.

How am I seeing what I'm seeing? My brain shuts off and makes some kind of humming noise as I stand helplessly when the monster charges.

It's so close, the musky scent of its skin wafts up my nose. Its warm breath blows past my face. A flash of black jumps in front of me. It's Jonah with his staff drawn, ready for battle.

The monster vanishes.

With the danger gone, Jonah spins around to face me. He grabs me by the shoulders and studies my ashen face. "Are you okay?"

My brain switches back on with a rush of sensory information that almost makes me faint. I can't answer because images of what just happened are flashing through my head, with each new scene increasing my terror. Jonah sounds frightened, too. That makes me even more scared, as if him being afraid validates my fear.

"That's a dragon," I manage with a shaky voice.

I want him to tell me that I imagined it, that dragons aren't real, so I couldn't possibly have seen one. When he says nothing, I point to where it was. "That's a dragon."

I shake my head. "I'm not going."

Jonah's grip tightens on my arms. It's painful, so I try to pull away, but my legs have stopped working. In fact, I can't even feel them.

"That's a dragon. I'm not going," I repeat in case he didn't hear me the first time.

Jonah wraps his arm around my waist and lifts me off the ground. He holds me close and strokes my hair with his other arm. This is the second hug in two days. "No harm will come to you," he whispers. "You're in Manahata. You are safe. His Majesty just wanted to show you something that may await you if you decide to search for the key."

He gently puts me down. "Agatha, you're being asked to make a choice. I'm going to take you to the voyage, and that will help you make a decision. No one will force you to search for the key. Do you understand? You're safe. You can leave right now if you want."

I don't believe a word he's saying. I want him to tell me that what I saw wasn't a dragon because dragons aren't real. When he says nothing, I get angry because he's not telling me what I want to hear.

"That's a dragon. Dragons are real. A dragon was here!" The words come out as an accusation, and I'm immediately ashamed. I'm not a confrontational person. I don't want Jonah to be mad at me for being mad at him when the person I'm really mad at is King Ohad for putting me through that. I can't lose Jonah, he's all I've got.

"Agatha," King Ohad calls to me.

I turn my attention to him, glad that Jonah doesn't have the opportunity to respond to my outburst.

"I apologize for frightening you," Ohad continues. "But I want you to be aware that what I'm telling you is true. There is a good chance you could die…"

I'm not listening to this. I shake my head. "I'm not going. I'm going back to Queens, to my bed. I'll wake up and be proud that I can imagine such things."

I know it's rude. I do have better manners, but I'm not the person they're looking for. I haven't even started searching for this key, and I was almost killed. I've never known that kind of fear before.

Jonah puts his arm around my shoulders and walks me a short distance away from the King. He gives me a sideways hug and periodically rubs my back. He eventually convinces me that I'm not in any danger and promises that the King won't make the dragon return.

My fear subsides, and I calm down a bit. Then King Ohad commands, "Agatha, come here."

CHAPTER 9

King Ohad's tone is harsh when he orders me to sit in the chair to his left. He might have figured out that I'm not the right Agatha, or that I lied when I told him I would search for the key. Maybe he's upset that I'm not the great warrior they were hoping for. I wish I were the person they wanted me to be.

He attempts a smile. "I'm sorry I scared you. I want you to understand what is expected of you. When we ask you to find the key and we say it's unsafe, I want you to know that it is dangerous. But Agatha, we need you. We cannot stop Stratagor Ziras. He's been searching for the key for a long time, and he's gaining power in both worlds with his promise of opening the portals."

He closes his eyes and takes a deep breath. "Agatha, imagine the war that will break out between our worlds. Think on it. Picture it. Envision that dragon and many others worse than her in your world. Imagine human armies tramping through Manahata, destroying everything and killing everyone in their path. Please, Agatha, don't leave yet. At least take the voyage before you decide anything."

The weight of what he's asking is too heavy for me to bear. My brain is making that humming noise again. He must be very disappointed, wanting a Knight and getting me.

When I don't respond, he sighs and waves his hand. "You're dismissed."

I walk stonily to Jonah, who gives me a pat on the back and whispers, "I will help you."

I shake my head. "There's nothing to decide. The King said it himself. I'm too pathetic, too young, and too...me!" I pull away from him, trying to get some air. "I can't. Look at me. I can't!"

"Let's get some air," Jonah calmly suggests.

He says nothing, just stays by my side, as we stroll around a good portion of the park, and my head gets clearer with every step. I've never been so afraid in my life. My heart is still beating fast.

It takes a long time, but eventually I feel safe again. The scare the dragon gave me doesn't leave entirely, but I can at least think again.

As if sensing my mood change, Jonah wordlessly steers me back to the King's platform. Now that I'm calmer, I think it would be best to do what they ask and take the voyage. It doesn't sound as if they'll force me to find this key. I hope it's an ocean voyage. I've seen the beach on television, but never in person, and the idea is too exciting to pass up.

"I've never been on a voyage before. I've never even been on a boat," I say to let Jonah know I've changed my mind.

He smiles at me, and his reaction is disappointing. I expected more than a smile. "Most enjoy a voyage. It will help you no matter what you decide."

I'll give them the opportunity to talk me into getting the key. I hope they're not too mad when they realize I'm not a Knight. I like this place; the faeries have been kind to me, and I like Jonah too. Ashra is fascinating, and I want to see more of it before I go home.

When we return, the King is outside on the platform in front of his palace. His thrones are back and he's in the center again. Next to him is another faerie who looks like a younger version of the King but with short-cropped hair. It's obvious that this hard, stoic faerie is a soldier because he's wearing silver armor and a short silver-plated kilt with brown leggings.

The soldier's piercing blue eyes study me with disapproval. He's definitely the meanest creature I've met so far.

"We're ready to leave, your Majesty," Jonah announces.

"Good. Good." King Ohad walks over to us. "The guards have prepared everything you need." At his words, four men appear and drop several bags at Jonah's feet. I look around for some mode of transportation. Are they expecting us to carry all of that?

"I've decided that my son should accompany you." He motions for the other faerie to join us.

I try not to let my shock register on my face. I wanted them to be more excited about my decision, and I certainly don't want this angry faerie coming with us. But I don't know how to say no to a King. I look to Jonah for help, but he only squeezes my shoulder to reassure me.

"Jonah, I believe you two have met. Agatha, this is my son, Dathid."

Am I supposed to bow to him, too? I gawk at him for longer than I should. My face gets hot when I realize my mouth is open. I quickly shut it and turn my eyes to the floor, hoping it will crack open and swallow me whole.

"Pleased to meet you," Dathid says with an accent that's thicker than his father's. It sounds similar to Scottish or maybe Australian. I'm not good with accents.

I force myself to bring my eyes up to meet his. He's well over six feet tall, and I have to tilt my head back to look him in the eye. King Ohad must be older than I thought because his son looks like he's somewhere in his twenties.

"You too," I mumble and drop my head back down. Seriously, I want the floor to open beneath me. I don't care if I plummet to my death. It would be far less painful than what I'm enduring right now.

Dathid sighs disapprovingly, if that's even possible. I need to convince Jonah that he can't come with us.

"Agatha," the King says and I glance up. "I have a gift for you."

I'm confused by his words. Why would a king give me a gift? No one has ever given me a gift before. Sometimes in school the teachers would give all the children in my class a gift, but I've never had a gift of my own. I don't want his gift.

A piercing shriek, like a hawk but much louder, makes my heart jump to my throat. I grab Jonah's arm and squeeze my eyes tight. King or not, I'm not accepting a gift of a dragon.

"Agatha, it's fine. Open your eyes," Jonah coaxes.

I pull myself closer to him and crack one eye open. It's not a dragon. It's a horse, a flying horse that's deep, iridescent purple and shimmering against the dim light of the pale lavender sky. Its wings are shaped like a bat's, only they're not leathery; they're translucent indigo and have an intricate design like that of a housefly's wings. How can wings that delicate lift something so large?

The horse lands next to the King, snorting with excitement. "Agatha, this is Lenox," Ohad says. "He is the finest of his kind, and he is yours."

Lenox puts his nose against my face and inhales sharply as if he's trying to smell my breath, but I've made the task difficult with my lack of breathing. I've never been this close to such a huge animal. I've seen police horses before but never touched one, and this guy is much larger than any of those horses.

Lenox pauses for a moment, and I'm hoping he's done. I want him to go back to the King now. Instead, the beast gives me a sharp thump to the face with his nose. I'm more startled than hurt, but I may cry anyway.

After he hits me, he walks away and jumps off the platform. His wings spread and he takes off into the air. His display of power is alarming. I hope he's running away.

Once he's in the air and far from me, I can appreciate his beauty. He flies with incredible grace and it's exhilarating watching him soar through the air. His wings are toward the front of his chest, not in the middle of his back like they show in the movies. His front legs tuck up high on his body and his backs legs drag behind him. He shrieks again and dives into the trees.

I'm about to turn my attention back to the group when Lenox emerges a few seconds later carrying something in his front feet. I didn't notice before, but his front feet are like those of an eagle. When he draws closer, I can see something the size of a large dog in his talons.

He circles us a few times and then drops the carcass of the strange animal at my feet. It looks like a cross between a giant raccoon and a rat. Lenox has sliced its stomach open with his talons and the creature's guts are hanging outside its body.

When he lands and pushes the mutilated animal toward me, the only thing that's keeping me from bolting off the platform is Jonah's firm grip on my shoulder. I stare horrified at the bloody corpse, then jerk free of his grip and run to the edge of the platform to vomit.

Dathid and King Ohad erupt into a heated discussion in their native language. This day could not get any worse. I should've gone home.

When my stomach is empty, I notice Jonah next to me at the rail. "I'm sorry that upset you," he says quietly. "Lenox gave you a gift because he likes you. It's a great honor to be given a gift by a pegasus. I fear you may have hurt his feelings."

"*I* offended *him*? I can't believe you're taking his side! How hurt do you think that thing he killed was?"

"That *thing* is a waserbee. You ate one last night. You did not seem to care how that one felt."

"Oh, I'm gonna be sick again."

"Agatha, please relax. It's customary to give a gift of meat amongst some of the curra. Didn't your cats ever gift you?"

After I think about it for a minute, I recall an instance when one of Auntie's cats left a dead bird on her pillow. Auntie thanked the cat. Now I feel bad that I hurt Lenox's feelings, even though I'm still grossed out.

I take a few deep breaths and walk over to the dead waserbee. I glance at its repulsive body and smile. "Thank you, Lenox, for such a wonderful gift," I say in a falsetto one would use when praising a dog.

I raise my hand to pat his nose but then fear makes me stop. I don't want to touch him. I don't want him to bite me. He waits, and when I move no further, he puts his muzzle under my fingers and the two of us stay that way for a long time. I'm moved by his sweetness, but mostly I'm too afraid to lift my hand.

"Now you need to eat it," Dathid says.

I drop my hand and hope he's joking.

"It's customary to share your gift with your pegasus," Jonah explains. "But if he gave it to me, I obviously wouldn't eat it. You can just let him have it."

"How do I do that?"

"You tell him he can have it," Dathid says.

I turn to Lenox and give him a giant fake smile. "Thank you again. But I had a big breakfast, so you can have it." I pat my stomach to look more convincing. Idiot, who pats their stomach?

Once he's certain that I don't want it, he picks the waserbee up in his sharp teeth and jumps over the rail. He doesn't fly this time. He just puts the animal on the ground and noisily tears into it.

"What kind of pegasus is that?" I ask Jonah.

"I don't understand your question. I'm not aware of different kinds."

"Well, aren't pegasuses—or pegasi, or whatever— they're supposed to be white, with feathers and eat oats and sweet stuff, like that."

"Oh, that's right. I forgot about that. The humans changed it. This is what a pegasus looks like."

A profound sense of loss envelops me, which is odd because I never knew I had feelings for the image I saw so frequently. "Well then, what do unicorns look like!" I blurt with a flash of anger that covers my disappointment.

"Like a rhinoceros," Dathid answers.

I don't say anything else. I've changed my mind. I don't like this place or its people, or their weird animals. I want to go back to my old boring life where everything is the same everyday.

Lenox returns quicker than I expect, and as soon as he lands, the servants pick up the bags and cautiously place them on his back. I'm glad I'm not the only one who is afraid of that thing. I want to peek over the rail to see if anything is left of the waserbee, but think better of it.

What if they expect me to ride that monster? A flash of fear weakens my knees. I dismiss the thought as ridiculous because how could the group stay together if I'm in the air? However, once we're off the platform, Jonah asks me if I want to hop on Lenox's back.

"You expect me to fly through the air on that!" I yell out of sheer panic.

Dathid laughs at my question.

"No," Jonah explains patiently. "But you may want to walk with him. We have a long way to travel."

I shake my head. There's no way I'll get anywhere near that thing. Lenox is very pretty, even cute from a distance, but he's also terrifyingly massive with sharp teeth and even sharper claws.

I tell Jonah as sweetly as I can that I'd rather walk. He doesn't push me further, and with that resolved, the King and his party say their goodbyes, and the four of us start on our journey.

CHAPTER 10

The exact moment we leave Manahata the trees turn dense and dark. No more fiery magentas and dazzling teals; these trees are deep hues of green, blue and burgundy. The towering pines don't sing, either; they resonate a soft hum, like an electrical appliance you only hear once it's off. Everything is steadily growing darker and quieter with every step of this excruciatingly long hike.

"Shouldn't we have hit the river by now?" I ask after we've walked for several hours.

"What river?" Jonah asks.

"The Hudson River," I answer with an edge to my voice. My legs hurt and I'm winded. Jonah has been guiding us in circles. We should've seen water by now.

"Agatha, you're not on Earth," he explains. "You'll see similarities between our worlds but they're not the same."

His tone annoys me further. I'm not a child and I'm not stupid. I'm tired and my feet hurt. "Why are we walking? Don't you guys have cars or trains, or even a carriage?

"Yes," Jonah answers.

"Then why don't we have one!" I stop moving. We've been walking for hours with no end in sight. "New Yorkers don't hike, especially in nature. This is crazy. We should get a car."

"We'll go a little further, then we'll stop to eat and you can rest," Jonah says patiently.

I've never yelled at anyone in my life, but his demeanor is making my blood boil. "Why do you always ignore my questions? Or answer my questions with questions? Or tell me to stop asking questions? You asked me to come here. Why don't we have a car!"

"Well, that was impressive," Dathid snorts.

I glare at him. I hate him and I want a car.

Jonah points Dathid to a small clearing in the trees. "Let's stop over there." Then he turns to me. "Sit, and eat, and rest, and then I'll answer your questions. But first, call Lenox," he orders over his shoulder when he leaves to join Dathid.

Lenox is staying close by, but he prefers flying. I search the treetops for him, but he's nowhere in sight. I don't have a clue how to get an animal to come to me. I look to Jonah for help, but he's whispering with Dathid. When Auntie would call the cats, she'd say "Here, Kitty-Kitties" really loud. I open my mouth to try it, but the words get stuck in my throat.

I don't want to call that big animal to me, but I don't want to disobey Jonah either. I always do what I'm told, but I can't make the words come out. I clasp my hands together and feel the sweat on my palms. *Just call him like a cat. Just make the attempt. Just do something!* my brain screams. Desperate to make any kind of noise, I put my fingers in my mouth and give a loud whistle; both Jonah and Dathid turn to me in surprise.

I'm proud of myself for shocking them. I shrug with a smirk. "All New Yorkers can do that."

My victory is short because Lenox actually comes when called. I need to be brave, keep breathing, and keep my eyes open. But the beating of his wings is so loud my heartbeat matches its rhythm. I lose the battle to keep my eyes open. This animal just needs to stay away from me.

When everything is quiet, and just as I'm about to open my eyes, something wet and slimy slides up my cheek.

I jump back, wiping my face and spitting. "That thing licked me! It covered my mouth and went up my nose. Its tongue is so big it coated my whole face! Yuck! I want a shower!"

I lift the edge of my sweater in a lame attempt to clean my face. Jonah and Dathid chuckle at my indignation. I forget my disgust and stand up straight. It's just pegasus spit; it won't kill me.

Lenox is in front of me with his nose inches from my face. I stare at it because it's so close it's taking up most of my field of vision. I'm afraid to take my eyes off it. He doesn't move and neither do I. Jonah said to call the beast here, but he didn't give me instructions on what to do once it arrived. My distress increases with every hefty breath it takes.

Jonah isn't helping. I'm stuck here, staring down a monster with long sharp teeth and terrifying claws. I wish I knew how to keep this thing from biting me or trampling me or just generally killing me. I search my memory for some answers, but the only thing I come up with is a reference to letting a strange dog smell your hand before you pet it. I've never done it, because why would anyone want to pet someone else's dog?

It's all I've got so I might as well try it. I slowly lift my arm, praying he won't bite it off. I'm only halfway to his face when he lowers his head and puts his nose under my fingers. He lifts his head and my hand rises with him. His warm breath blows across my face. I haven't taken a breath since I lifted my arm. I inhale deeply and remove my hand from his nose. I hope Jonah saw me touch it.

As soon as my hand is back at my side, Lenox moves and I freeze. I wish he would fly off already. He smells my fingers, and any second now he'll tear my arm off.

"Okay. Go away," I whisper.

Lenox puts his nose under my palm and lifts it like before. I gaze at my hand and then at him. "Do you want me to pet you?"

He lowers his head so I can scratch his face. I gently pat his nose a few times. He nuzzles it back up.

"Okay, I get it." I pet his face, and he moves his head so I can better reach the areas he wants me to scratch. I end up by his oversized ears that are purple on the outside and pink inside. They're long like a horse's ears but much wider and apparently very itchy. As I pet him, he purrs loudly.

I laugh. "You're a horse that flies like a bat, acts like a dog and purrs like a cat. Yeah, that's normal."

Now that I've made friends with my pegasus, Jonah returns and pulls some biscuits and prickly green fruit out of one of Lenox's packs.

"Agatha, ask Lenox to hunt some dinner for you and Dathid to eat later."

The three of us are standing together, so I don't understand why I need to ask. I motion to Lenox. "He's right here. He just heard you."

"He's yours. You speak the same language. You need to be the one to ask him," Jonah explains.

That's ridiculous. Lenox heard what Jonah said, in English, the same language I'll speak to him in. I don't argue. I just speak loudly and clearly to Lenox as if I'm talking to an old person. "Will you kill something for us to eat later? Make sure you get something for yourself. Oh, and give it to Dathid."

I have no idea if he understands me or not. But with that done, I collapse under the closest tree and examine my blistered feet. There's a particularly large pus-filled lump on the side of my big toe. I'm not sure if I should pop it or not. I poke it a few times and it really hurts, so I decide to leave it alone. It'll probably burst open on its own like the others did.

Jonah sits next to me and hands me a biscuit. He places the fruit on the ground between us and helps himself to one. The biscuit isn't big, but it's delicious. I eat two and get quite full, which makes me happy because I don't want to eat the fruit now that it's been on the ground.

I'm done first so I lean against the tree, waiting for everyone else to finish. I have a list of questions, but Jonah made it clear that I have to wait to get answers. However, he's eating the entire pile of fruit and it's taking forever. When he reaches for a fifth piece, I start the interrogation because I'm tired of waiting. "Why don't we have a car?"

Jonah slowly swallows his bite. "We don't have cars here. Ashra is not industrialized the way Earth is."

"Why?"

"There's no need. Earth is a much harsher environment. Humans needed to industrialize to survive."

"But still...a car? Why not bring a few through the portals?"

"Do you know what physics is?" he asks, out of nowhere.

"You just answered my question with a question!"

"I asked the question so I could better answer yours."

"Your mechanisms don't work here," Dathid answers impatiently.

"What do you mean they don't work?" I ask.

"What do *you* mean, what do *I* mean?"

Dathid is just annoying. This conversation is annoying, and not having a car is really annoying. "Is this something with your people? Is it a curra thing to never give a straight answer?"

"Is it a human thing to be so temperamental?" Dathid retorts.

His question shocks me into silence. No one has ever described me as temperamental before. In fact, I make it a point to show no emotion at all. Every one of my teachers has described me as *a nice girl, just very quiet.* I've been here such a short time, and yet I'm already changing. I hope it's for the better.

"I'm sorry," I say. I don't want anyone to not like me, and getting mad will definitely make them hate me.

Jonah ignores my apology. "Your concept of Earthly physics doesn't apply here. On Earth, you have natural laws that are true and unchanging. Drop something and it will fall. Push something and it will move. We don't have those laws here, and therefore, what's built based on those laws won't work."

He looks at me with sad eyes, but I can't tell if they're sincere or mocking. "Which means no cars or planes. But they do have non-motorized vehicles, like carriages and carts. Unfortunately, pine trees are aggressive and would destroy any road constructed in their territory, so we have to walk. Also, your pegasus would eat anything that pulled a cart."

I turn wide eyes to Lenox. What kind of gift did the King give me?

"However," Jonah continues. "We do have transportation for you. Lenox can take you anywhere you want to go faster than any car or plane."

A picture of me flying through the air with Lenox flashes across my brain. It's so terrifying that my heart skips a beat just thinking about it. I push the thought out of my mind and put my shoes back on my battered feet.

Jonah is next to Lenox. "Agatha, come here."

I vigorously shake my head.

"Just try it. I'll hold you the entire time."

I'm certain that if he holds me, I won't fall, but if he lets go, I'd have no way to stop Lenox if he took off. I might get really hurt. Lenox is too big; maybe if they had a smaller one, a starter pegasus maybe. They shouldn't expect a novice like me to be confident around a beast like that.

Both of them are side-by-side, staring at me. Jonah looks disappointed. I don't want to let him down, but I don't want any part of this pegasus.

Lenox's back is over my head and the thought of being up that high makes me sick. "I only have to try it? I don't need to stay up there?"

"He'll stand here and I'll hold you." Jonah puts his arms out, but waits for me to walk into his grasp.

I nod, but my feet don't move. I take a deep breath. "Okay," I say more to myself than to Jonah before I step into his arms. "As long as we don't move and you hold me."

Jonah agrees, and Lenox lifts his enormous wings out of the way. The extended wings make him look even bigger. I know he's going to take off once I'm on him. However, I don't have time to voice my objection because Jonah is already lifting me onto his back.

As soon as my legs are around Lenox, I reach my hands out to grab hold of something, but there's nothing there, just thick purple neck. I'm not close enough to his mane to grasp it, so I frantically claw at his back, trying to get my balance. My frenzied hands find Jonah's, which are around my waist. He's holding me like he promised. I clutch his wrists in a death grip.

"Gently scoot forward," he says.

Even though Lenox is standing still, the shifting of his weight as he fidgets will definitely make me slide off.

"I have to let go for one moment."

"No! I want to get down," I yell while panic seizes my guts.

"Relax. I just need to get to the other side of his wing. You don't want him to have to keep his wings up the entire time, do you?"

"Okay. But Lenox, you better not move." My threat loses a lot of its edge because of the quiver in my voice.

Jonah steps out of the way, and Lenox closes his wings. With his wings pressing down on my legs, I'm more secure like he's holding on to me. Most of the tension eases out of my body.

Jonah grabs my waist again. "Do you want to try to walk?"

"Will he take off?"

"No. And you needn't worry about flying through the air. It takes a great deal of skill to stay mounted during takeoff. You'd probably just roll down his back."

That's not reassuring. Falling to the ground from this height would surely break a few bones. However, I trust Jonah, so I agree to take a few steps.

Lenox's lengthy strides make me wobbly. It's difficult to keep my balance because I'm a couple of seconds behind his movement. I won't fall, though, because Lenox has a tight grip on my legs.

"You can let go." I'm proud of my bravery. I hope Jonah is too.

I'm so pleased with myself for trying because I never try anything. I wish someone from school could see us, but I can't think of anyone I could share this with. Lenox walks faster and I like it. It feels like I'm racing down the path, until I see that Jonah is easily keeping pace with us.

I ride for a long time and after a few hours pass, Jonah tells me to get down. "Lenox isn't made for walking. It's difficult for him."

As soon as my feet hit the ground, Lenox smells me to make sure I'm okay. I give him some good-boy pats on the head and stroke his body. When he's had enough, he takes off.

"That was fun."

"It's good to see you smile," Jonah says, making me self-conscious.

CHAPTER 11

"How much longer until we get to the boat?" I ask after several more hours of walking. I wish the light would change. The sun and moons haven't moved, but I've been on my feet for the better part of a day.

"We have another day's travel," Jonah answers. "We will go a little farther and then rest for the night."

When we finally stop, my chewed-up feet are raw, my legs are throbbing and my back is killing me. I limp to a tree and flop down. I swear, I'll never walk again. I spot Dathid looking at me with concern, but he doesn't say anything.

"Agatha, please call Lenox," Jonah reminds me.

I whistle for him. He circles with a giant bird in his talons and drops it in front of Dathid. Then he heads my way and I jump up, afraid he might land on me. Instead, he gently puts his back feet down and gracefully lowers his front feet. When he tucks his wings in, Jonah walks over to remove the packs from his back.

I plop down against a tree and take off my shoes. I don't want to look at my beat-up feet so I turn my attention to Dathid, who is unsheathing his sword and heading toward a cluster of trees. "I need some dead branches."

The noise the trees have been making all day abruptly stops, and the forest grows eerily silent. The thick pine shakes its boughs but doesn't drop any branches.

78

Dathid lifts his sword. "I'll only ask one more time, and then I'll take what I want."

He didn't ask the first time, but I won't say anything. He's an angry man. I know he wouldn't appreciate my interference, especially if I sided with the tree. I don't know why he's with us, but I wish he would've stayed in Manahata.

The tree makes a loud cracking groan, and he jumps out of the way when several sizable branches nearly fall on his head. He sneers at the tree branches, then at the tree and then smiles menacingly. "Smaller pieces, please."

The branches on the ground split apart.

"Trees! Bad attitudes, every one of them," he mutters to himself as he gathers the wood. "Especially you pines."

The tree shakes again but doesn't say anything as Dathid walks away. I'm guessing that pine trees don't talk because they haven't said or sung anything since we left Manahata.

Jonah makes a fire while Dathid cleans the bird. I'm definitely not hungry after watching him drive a spike through its mouth in order to hang it over the fire.

"Agatha, wake up. You must eat," Jonah says.

I open my eyes, startled that I fell asleep. Dathid's holding a large turkey leg in front of my face. I sit up and grab the meat. I take a bite and then remember that I'm not eating turkey. I pause mid-bite and pull the leg away.

"You don't like it?" Jonah asks.

"What is it?"

"Pteranodon."

"Isn't that a dinosaur?"

Jonah looks at Dathid, but he just shrugs. Jonah turns back to me and makes the same gesture.

"Never mind." I'm too tired to argue. It couldn't be the same thing, because dinosaurs are lizards, and whatever this was, it had feathers. I take a bite, not caring what I'm eating. It's delicious. I take the other leg and eat that one too. "What time is it?"

"We don't have time here," Dathid answers.

"Of course you don't."

"Lenox needs to sleep with you," Jonah says.

"What?" He can't possibly think I'll sleep with an animal.

"Tell Lenox to come sleep with you."

"No, that's okay. I'm good. I really don't want to sleep with a big, dirty horse-bat. That giant pegasus would definitely crush me if I sleep next to him."

"Do you have to argue with me about everything? Just tell him."

"Fine. Lenox, please come here and sleep with me."

Lenox finished his dinner a while ago and is milling around the trees, chasing bugs. At the sound of my voice, he trots over, lies down in a ball like a cat and lifts his wing in invitation. Jonah motions for me to go.

"Okay. I get it," I whisper to Lenox. "I'm not real sure about this. Be careful you don't roll over and squash me."

I cautiously sit down next to him and put my back against his side. Once I'm settled, Lenox lowers his wing. It covers most of me. I have to wiggle around until my head and shoulders are out. I lie back against his warm, soft side and am surprisingly snuggy. I rise and fall with his breathing. This must be what being comforted feels like. It's nice.

Lenox swings his head around and roughly smells me.

"Okay, okay." I giggle and raise my hands to push him away. "It's rude to blow your nose in someone's hair."

I pet his muzzle. He lets out a big sigh and puts his head down. The forest is quiet except for Dathid, who is cleaning up our little encampment. I admit he's got a great face; it's so impossibly symmetrical that if I painted him I would have to add flaws to make him look real. It's just a shame his attitude stinks.

Jonah walks over and looks at him with wide, sad eyes. Dathid stops packing the saddlebag and stands. "This detour is more than I bargained for. I wish we could've just gone straight there. I'm not sure how much more I can take."

"You seem to be holding up well."

"I'm not. I can't do this. Maybe I should head back."

Please, please, please go back. My prayers have been answered.

Jonah slaps a hand on Dathid's shoulder. "No, this is important. Your village needs you. Agatha needs you. I will be by your side."

Dathid sighs and goes back to packing the bag. He nods his head toward me. "Which one of us has it worse?" He chuckles to himself like he just said something funny.

"She's holding up better than you," Jonah says with a smile. "Give her some time. She's been through a lot, and it's only going to get more awful from here."

Dathid sighs. "I am not cut out for this."

It's Jonah's turn to chuckle. "You need more patience."

"Okay, more patience. More understanding. More selflessness. More scars," Dathid mumbles as he walks off to find his bed.

My throat burns from swallowing my tears. I'm doing the best I can. My life on Earth was always the same: school, home, school, home. I spoke with very few people and, for the most part, I was left to myself. It's unfair to be thrown into this situation and then judged for how badly I'm reacting to it. Jonah is the closest thing I've ever had to a friend, and I hope that Dathid doesn't mess that up.

I'm deep in my self-pity while Dathid finishes the chores and unfurls his wings. It takes me by surprise because I forgot he's a faerie. His wings are beautiful like dragonfly wings, long and thin, and each is at least three feet long. They have a dark bluish-black hue that glistens when they move. He flutters them incredibly fast until they're a blur, then gently lifts himself off the ground and flies up into the tree.

My fourth-grade teacher kept a hummingbird feeder outside our classroom window. That probably wasn't the best idea because the birds were noisy and distracting; the hum of their wings was so loud we could hear it even if the window was closed. We'd all run over and watch them eat. Dathid's wings make almost the same noise. I'm surprised his aren't louder. He's over six feet tall, and what's a hummingbird, like six inches?

It's strange that he chose to sleep there. I yawn. Where did Jonah go? I giggle when I picture him sleeping under Lenox.

CHAPTER 12

I awake with Lenox's wing beating me about the head and face. It is, to say the least, a disorienting way to wake up. "Okay, okay! I'm up. Stop hitting me!" I lift my arms to protect my head and he raises his wing. I spring to my feet before he decides to hit me again. It didn't hurt, but it wasn't pleasant.

"Seriously, a couple of taps and then give me a moment to respond." I'm not sure how large his vocabulary is, but he seems to understand me.

Dathid and Jonah have been up for a while. Dathid has made another fire and is currently busy cooking some eggs. I've never been camping before. I've never slept outside, either. It's nice to wake up to the fresh air, but if I never camp again, I'd be really okay with that.

"How much longer do we have to travel?" I'm trying not to whine, but my feet and legs hurt. I don't know how much farther I can go. I should've gone back to Queens when I had the chance. A boat ride is definitely not worth this pain.

"About half a day," Jonah says in such a way it suggests he could be lying to me, but not in a bad way. Like when I would ask Auntie how long something would take and she'd say *a couple of minutes* but it was over an hour. This trip will probably take most of the day. My feet blister just thinking of all that walking.

We head out, and Jonah stays by my side with his eyes illuminating the dim path in front of us. It's odd not having a change of daylight. All day and night, the sky stays its same deep indigo with stars, a distant sun, and the two moons.

He's silent until I ask, "Do the sun or the moons ever move?"

"Depending on where we are, the sky and the light will be different."

That's intriguing. I want to know more about these different areas and their different light, but Jonah doesn't say anything more about it, so I don't say anything either. Jonah never needs to talk, but today our silence is awkward like he's concerned about something. I don't question him about it because if he's worried, I don't want to know why.

We travel for several hours in silence and then stop for lunch. Lenox brings us a small woodland animal that has fur like a deer, but it's a deep shade of green with black spots. It resembles a kangaroo with large back feet and short arms, but its head is similar to a goat's, with three rounded horns on the top.

As before, Jonah makes a fire and Dathid cleans the meat. Everyone is silent and that worries me, but I still don't say anything. I wish Jonah would tell me what's on his mind.

When we sit down to eat, he sits next to me. "Agatha, what do you know of monsters?"

"Not much," I say with a mouth full of food. "They live under your bed or in a closet. Or like the horror movie ones that eat brains or just people, in general."

Jonah sighs as if he doesn't like my answer. "Do you know why you're going on a voyage?"

"Yeah, to see if I want to help you."

"It's more than that. I'm not sure you understand what's being asked of you, and I'm not sure I can explain it."

"You want me to find this key for you. It will be difficult and the journey is dangerous. I could be killed." I admit I'm not taking this very seriously. They've got the wrong girl, and this voyage will make that clear to everyone. Although Dathid might already suspect I'm a fraud.

Jonah looks at me so gravely it grabs my attention. "Agatha, I want desperately for you to locate the key."

I turn away. I've made a huge mistake. This key is important to him, and although I'm not technically lying, I haven't told the truth either. I should confess, but Jonah is still talking.

"—only if you want to find it will the Orb show you where it is." He pauses to look at me. "Your mother was killed searching for the key."

The news of my mother shocks me out of my previous thinking. I wait for some kind of personal revelation. I'm disappointed in myself for not feeling sad or angry or anything. Instead, I'm relieved. I finally know something about my parents. My mother chose this dangerous journey, and that makes me wonder if I should continue it. Maybe they're not as wrong as I think they are. Maybe they do have the right girl.

That thought makes my heart skip a beat, and my hands grow cold. If they have the right girl, then they expect me to do this stuff, to fight and to find this key. I have no skills whatsoever. I'm not good at anything. I'm going to die like my mother did.

Jonah doesn't detect my anxiety. He must need to get out what he has to say because he's talking rather fast and hasn't noticed that I've left the conversation twice.

"—Ziras knows you're here. Once I rescued you, Lord Duradin put a bounty on your head. But you don't have to do this. I could hide you where he couldn't find you."

I'm not safe as long as I'm the only one who can read the Orb. If I choose to not search for the key, I have to spend the rest of my life in hiding. Then they could find the key without me. My old simple life is looking so safe and wonderful. I desperately want to go back to it.

Images of that life and Jonah's statement mix together. The pictures and words are swirling through my head so fast I can almost feel them smacking against my brain. Jonah *rescued* me, which can only mean one thing.

"I was a prisoner," I say with an eerie calm. Which is weird because I'm screaming in my head. The blood drains from my body, and a deep bone chilling cold creeps down my arms. My history is flashing before my eyes.

Everything about my life is beginning to make sense. It's as if I was trying to build a puzzle but didn't know what the picture was. Now that Jonah filled in the gap, everything is falling into position. And I can't make it stop!

The only place I was ever allowed to go was to school. No one ever came to our home with the exception of our weird neighbors, the Millers. They weren't over often, but when they were, Auntie and Mrs. Miller would sit in our garbage-strewn apartment and whisper to each other for hours. Mr. Miller worked at my school as a janitor. And come to think of it, he moved from my elementary to my middle school at the same time I did.

"Auntie and Uncle were my jailers. I've been Stratagor Ziras' prisoner my entire life. He killed my parents and took me prisoner!"

Jonah needs to tell me I'm wrong. My brain is roaring its objection because there's no way I could be right about this. He glances at me for the briefest second and then puts his head down. The screaming is taking over my body.

"I was a prisoner? That's what you rescued me from? That's why they made me look at the Orb?"

His silence overwhelms me when I answer my own questions. "Auntie doesn't love me! That's why I never felt any love from her. I don't even think Auntie and Uncle are married. That's why he was never home. They were prison guards."

My words are getting louder and my breathing shorter.

Please, Jonah, please tell me I'm wrong. This can't be who I am. I silently beg him to make this not be true, but he just looks at me with pity. I turn away to find Dathid staring at me from across the fire with the same expression. I can't bear this burden. I can't handle the enormity of my truth.

I jump to my feet. "But why didn't the Orb work? Why am I the only one? It doesn't work for me. I'm not the right one."

Jonah sighs. "The Orb *does* work for you. You just don't know how to use it."

I take the Orb from my pocket. "This stupid ball ruined my life, killed my parents and will kill me too!"

I hate this ball. I hate Jonah, and I especially hate that stupid angry faerie. But most of all, I hate me. Why does it always have to be me!

"Make it work. Make it work for me!" I thrust the Orb in Jonah's face and yell into the trees. "I can't go home because I've never had a home. I've never had a home or parents or a life!"

I'm trapped by my own reality. There is absolutely nothing I can do to change my situation, and there was nothing I could've done to prevent it. How did I end up here? How did this happen? How did I never know? I don't know how I got myself into this situation but more importantly, I haven't a clue how to get out of it.

All I know is that it's the Orb's fault. I want to get as far away as possible from this awful piece of glass. I raise my arm and throw the Orb as hard as I can into the trees.

CHAPTER 13

Dathid flies after the Orb. I instantly regret throwing the stupid ball. I don't know what to do, so I just stand there, numb, staring into the trees—lost.

Jonah's hand rests on my back. "I'm sorry," he whispers.

My legs buckle and I crash to my bruised knees. I bend over and rest my head on the stiff, pointy pine needles covering the ground. I sob and mourn the loss of my ignorance. How dumb does someone have to be to not notice they're a prisoner?

Auntie used to say the weirdest things to me. Stuff like how she wasn't being paid enough, or that she should've never agreed to this job, or how honored she was to have the job. I thought she was nuts.

Auntie's sanity is another jolt that stops my tears and makes me sit up. "Auntie's not crazy." I say it out loud because I want someone to convince me that she actually is, but no one responds.

"Were Auntie and Duradin speaking a curra language and not a made-up one? The ball, the cats, the weird food, the neighbors, the lack of photographs. It's all making sense. Having no family, not a distant cousin or great aunt, nothing. No one. Just me and my guards. I'm so dumb."

I put my head back down, but I position my hands under my forehead this time, to protect it from the prickly pine needles. My brain shuts off as I stare at the ground and focus on the snot pouring out of my nose. I don't want to rub it on my shirt because who knows when I'll be able to change my clothes, but I may have to soon.

Jonah is rubbing my back. I don't know how long he's been doing that, but it's nice. Living with prison guards, I never knew affection. Jonah is the first person to ever hug me.

I'm brought back to reality by a piece of cloth being roughly shoved into the space between the ground and my chin. It's Dathid, sheepishly giving me a hanky. His gesture is so sweet and so awkward that it almost makes me laugh. It's enough to knock me back to the present. I wipe my face and sit up, but I can't look at anyone until I blow my nose a few more times, wishing I were a pretty crier.

With my nose as clear as it's going to get, I take a deep breath and look up at Jonah. We're both on our knees, but he's still really big. He studies my face for a moment and then hugs me. It's amazing how not-alone his hugs make me feel. It's weird that I didn't know how alone I was until I wasn't alone anymore.

"I'm glad it was you." I stay in his embrace for a long time until the embarrassment of my outburst forces me to say something. I pull away from Jonah and we stand.

"I'm sorry." I'm not sure what I'm apologizing for. I can't believe I cried like that in front of Jonah and worse, Dathid. "I never cry. I'm sorry I threw the ball. I wish I'd never seen it. I wish I had parents. I wish I had a home and a normal life, where monsters are zombies that just eat your face."

Jonah gives me a weak smile. I give him one back. I want him to know that I'm okay. "I guess I should thank you for rescuing me." That just sounds weird. He rescued me from my home. From my life. "I didn't even realize I needed rescuing."

Jonah grasps my shoulders and studies me. After a moment, he gives me another smile. "You're welcome."

He casts his dim eyes downward and studies the forest floor, then he snaps his head up. "Let's walk. We still have quite a bit of traveling to do, and moving the feet helps clear the head."

I stand and almost crash into Dathid. How long has he been behind me? Crying in front of Jonah is embarrassing, but crying in front of Dathid is mortifying. Fortunately, he's equally uncomfortable with me. He says nothing as he holds up a cloth with the Orb in it.

"Thanks," I mumble. Those are the last words Dathid and I exchange for the rest of the day, mainly because he's so far ahead of us we don't see him until it's time to eat.

Jonah gives me a push to start my feet moving. I'm lost in my thoughts. I finally know something about my parents and someone who may know more. I don't know how old I was when they died. I don't know what they looked like or what their favorite food was. Did they live here or on Earth? Sometimes I would long for them so deeply it made my chest ache. I used to ask questions about what they were like, but no one ever had any answers, so I stopped asking and tried my best to not think about them.

"What else do you know about my parents?" I ask Jonah after we've been walking for several hours.

"Nothing, really." He doesn't even turn his head to look at me.

"Do you know anything about my father?"

"He and your mother died together." He's gazing forward and appears rather bored. However, I catch a flash of regret in his eyes.

I don't want to talk about me anymore. "What will you do with the key once I find it?"

"You have to destroy it."

"How do I do that?"

"I don't know."

I glance up, shocked that he wouldn't have this significant bit of information. "What does the key look like?"

"I don't know."

"You don't know?" How am I supposed to find this thing if he knows nothing about it?

Jonah shakes his head. "I've never seen the key. I didn't even know there was one until Ziras started searching for it. I don't know what it is or how it works. I just know that destroying it will stop Stratagor Ziras. Have you ever heard of a specter?"

"It's a ghost, right? What does that have to do with the key?"

He clasps my hand. "Not quite." The contact makes me tense up. I'm still not used to someone holding my hand. Jonah ignores my reaction and keeps walking with my hand in his. "A ghost is a human who hasn't moved on because of unresolved mortal issues. A specter is created."

"Created?"

"Yes, through the dark arts. A person can turn their soul so that it never moves on."

"Ziras is human?"

"No, Ziras is a specter. He used to be human. He still looks like one but he's centuries old. He rotted his soul in order to live forever."

"Okay," I say slowly. "So there's this immortal rotten guy who made a key to a lock, but then he lost it and now only I can find it."

Jonah ignores my tone when he continues. "We're not sure who made the key. All we know is that when he tried to use it, the key was stolen from him. Unfortunately, the people who stole the key hid it a little too well. But fortunately, they also created the Orb, and only a Knight can use the Orb to locate the key."

"You're a Knight?" I say. Dathid might be a Knight, too, but I'm not sure.

"I'm a Knight Templar, yes, but it needs to be a human Knight."

"Is Stratagor Ziras a Knight?"

"No, we're not sure what he used to be. He calls himself Stratagor now. We believe the Orb doesn't work for him because he's no longer human. He kept you until you could read it."

"But I can't read the Orb either." Funny how that's now disappointing when only four days ago it was a very sane thing to not be able to see anything in a marble.

"You can. You just don't know how."

"Okay, so this Ziras guy, he's a bad ghost that looks human and he wants to open the portals. Why?"

"Power, control, fear, any number of reasons," Jonah says with disgust. "He's gaining power on Ashra by promising substantial swaths of Earth's land and resources to some of the curra who were not happy about the closure."

"But King Ohad said the humans wanted to open the portals, too."

"Some of the humans do, because he's made similar promises to them. But what he truly wants is to expand his empire."

"I don't understand. I'm human and I've never heard any of this."

"Actually, you've heard most of it. It's just been told as fiction, myths, and fairy tales. You know about all of this and most of the curra."

"But why? If we're in such danger, why is it a big secret?"

"Because all of Earth's cultures, economies and governments are based on the fact that humans are the only sentient beings in the universe. Only a select number of people are entitled to know about Ashra and the portals. Have you ever heard of secret societies?"

"No."

"Well, humans have them. Lots of them, but one of the more famous secret societies is the Rosicrucians."

"Rosa-a-whatta? That's a weird name. Why would they pick a name that's so hard to pronounce?"

"Rosicrucians," Jonah repeats.

"If it's a secret society, how do you know about it?"

"Even humans know of the Rosicrucians. The secret is what they do. The Rosicrucians are the humans who sealed the portals. They know about Ashra, but over the generations, their knowledge has deteriorated. They want the key so they can open the portals."

I make a face, but let Jonah continue his story.

"The point is, people have forgotten a lot of their history, and much of what they do remember has been distorted to the ridiculous."

"I don't understand. Earth is in a lot of danger, but these Rosicrucians want to open the portals anyway. And why would Ashra be in trouble? It sounds like the curra are going to clobber us."

Jonah is quiet for a long time. "Almost half of Ashra has been taken over by Stratagor Ziras. Some of those lands he's conquered and others were scared into surrender. The larger his army grows, the more territories he assimilates.

He's convinced his followers that he can lead them to the riches of Earth."

"That sounds like a problem for Earth, not Ashra."

"The Grucht Leisck have grown exponentially. It won't be long before he has control over most of Ashra, which is a big problem. But if he can't deliver on his promise to open the portals, many will stop following him and break free. You can see why you're valuable to him."

"Yeah," I say, feeling my importance.

"You can also see why he won't let you find the key and destroy it."

"But he can't find it without me."

"Yes, he can. He could find it tomorrow, or it might take a thousand years, but he knows what he's looking for."

"So he doesn't need me."

"You make things easier and quicker. Even though he's immortal, it will be difficult for him to keep his army loyal if he doesn't deliver Earth in a reasonable amount of time. That's why he kept you alive. But he's lost control over you. If you destroy the key, you destroy his plans."

"Is that what happened to my parents?"

Jonah studies his feet for a long time. "I don't know much about your parents. I know they died searching for the key and I know that Stratagor Ziras was responsible."

His lack of information about my parents makes me sad, so I go back to our original discussion. "What's the *groot leashk*?"

"His army of soldiers, mercenaries and slaves that has taken control over…I could name the territories for you, but let's just say they've taken over about half of Ashra. Granted, some of that is relatively remote areas, but the Grucht Leisck are getting difficult to ignore."

"Why do the Grucht Leisck follow him if he's such a bad guy?"

"They believe Stratagor Ziras' promise of land and riches."

"I think I understand." In reality, my head is spinning. "This Ziras is a smart guy with a really good plan. He told the curra about this great place called Earth, and they all want to go. But he doesn't have a key. As long as I find it before him, Earth is safe. Although Ashra may still have a problem."

"Yes, Ashra will have to face Ziras no matter what, but a good portion of his power is based on delivering Earth. If he fails to do so, he should lose a lot of his followers and be easier to defeat."

"Okay, so I'll get the key and destroy it. Problem solved." That doesn't sound as bad as I imagined. How hard could it be to find one little key?

Jonah sighs again. His voice is low when he says, "Agatha, the Grucht Leisck and Stratagor Ziras will try to stop you. All of their plans are based on the promise of delivering Earth. They will not just let you destroy all they've worked for."

"How will I keep them from killing me?" I never thought I'd ever say those words and mean them. Someone wants to kill me, actually *kill me*, Agatha Stone.

"You will be trained. You'll have defenders. We will do our best to keep you safe. But in truth, Agatha, your mother died searching for the key, and the same fate may await you."

I fall into silence. How will they train me? I'm always the last one picked in gym class. I can't run more than a few steps before I'm winded, and I don't have a spot on my body that could be defined as muscular. *They're going to kill me!*

CHAPTER 14

A change in the air draws me out of my stupor. The atmosphere feels heavier and has an odd odor to it that I can't identify. "What's that smell?" I ask Jonah, who's still holding my hand.

"The Usuóko Ocean," Dathid answers.

"The ocean!" For the first time, my heart is racing with anticipation, not fear. I never in my wildest dreams thought I would ever see the ocean. I mean, I've seen it on television but I never believed I'd see it in person. I strain to hear the waves, but it's silent with the exception of birds calling to each other.

We're still deep in the trees, so we must be pretty far away. The ground is changing, though. The deep carpet of pine needles is thinning, revealing sapphire sand underneath. My heart is pounding rapidly. I'm so eager to see the ocean that I want to run to it as fast as I can. Dathid and Jonah don't look that enthused, but I might actually explode with excitement.

When the trees finally thin out, a tall grass-like plant replaces them. It's dense, and so tall it's over Jonah's head. Dathid's in front of us, chopping the grass down with his sword. It's making traversing the grass easier but not by much because it's still thick and up to my knees. My desire to see the ocean is the only thing that's keeping me moving.

When Dathid steps out of the grassy forest, revealing the dark sky beyond, I try to run to the opening but trip. Fortunately, Jonah's reflexes are honed enough to catch me before I impale myself on the thick grassy stalks. I slowly walk the rest of the way out, but Jonah won't let go of my arm. I think he's afraid I may try to run again.

Thousands of stars sprinkled across the dark plum sky greet me as I step from the grass. It's like I just stepped off the space station. The planets are just rings of light, and the moons and sun are dim shadows of what they were in Manahata. There's no visible boundary where the sky ends and the ocean begins. The water is completely still, like a pool that's reflecting back the surrealistic painting above. Silver, mirror-like water stretches along the shore, marking where the ocean meets the sand.

A few tears drop from my eyes as the depth of being one of the few humans who will ever see such beauty reaches my soul. I'm so happy that I decided to come on this journey because I got to see this. It all seems worth it.

Lenox lands in front of me. We're on friendlier terms now, but he's still big and could hurt me by accident. He's waiting for me to do something. I reach up, pat his nose, and tell him he's a good boy. He runs off. Did I do the right thing or the wrong thing? Someone should tell me what to do with him.

I follow him to the edge of the shoreline. The silver water is so still it looks solid. There's an energy to it, like it's alive. I can't stop staring at it, almost as if it's calling to me.

Jonah and Dathid are talking about something, but I'm not paying attention as I stare out across the smooth water. It's silver, but as it goes out deeper, it darkens and reflects the evening sky. The silver just fades into an abyss. The end of the world. Everything and nothing.

Dathid claps me on the shoulder and I nearly jump out of my skin. "Lenox and I will take good care of each other while you're gone."

"Wait, you're not coming?" It's nice having a soldier with us, even if he's scary.

"We're creatures of the air."

That explained nothing. Now I'm glad he's not going.

Jonah reaches for my hand and guides me toward the water. I pull back as forcefully as I can. "Wait. I thought there would be a boat. I can't swim. Voyage means boat!"

I can't breathe. I'm pulling against him, but he won't let go of my hand. I yank harder and still he doesn't move. I stop pulling. That was stupid. Jonah hasn't moved. I just had a fight with myself. He smiles, but before he can talk me into anything, I interrupt him. "Seriously, I can't swim!" I don't want to cry in front of everybody again.

Jonah waits to make sure I'm done talking before he says slowly, "Trust me, Agatha. You're safe, and swimming isn't necessary." He takes a step, but my feet refuse to move. I've lost control of my legs. Even if I wanted to go, I couldn't. "Agatha, the water is less than three inches deep. You couldn't drown even if you wanted to."

He's right. I can at least go up to my waist. It's the ocean! When will I ever have this chance again? Maybe the boat, or some giant fish they use as a boat, will come once we're in deeper water. I squeeze Jonah's hand tightly, close my eyes and take a step.

My foot doesn't get wet.

My eyes fly open. I stare down at my feet. Have I stepped into the water? How is water not wet?

He pulls me out a few more steps.

"I'm walking on the water! This is so awesome. Look at me!" I laugh and bounce on the water. With each step, my foot sinks but there's a bouncy resistance that encourages me to jump around, which I do with great glee. I hop, and laugh, and jump around Jonah, just to watch him bounce.

"Come on, Jonah, you have to jump with me. It's not fun jumping alone!"

"Yeah, Jonah, hop around!" Dathid yells from the shore.

"You seem to be having plenty of fun without my participation," Jonah says calmly.

I bounce, laugh, and plead with him to join me.

Jonah groans. "Okay, one bounce." He jumps up and lands so hard that I shoot several feet into the air and land flat on my back in a fit of laughter. He offers me a hand. "That's why you don't ask someone three times your size to bounce with you."

"Lesson learned," I say through giggles.

We walk for what feels like forever. Dathid and Lenox have long since disappeared over the horizon, and I grew weary of the bouncing ages ago. I'm encased in nothingness: not a bird, not a boat, nothing but my own reflection on a silvery water island surrounded by all of space.

It's so empty. It makes me long for the constant noise of the city. Jonah and I haven't spoken for hours. That's just his nature, though. He doesn't need conversation. It's nice because I never know what to say.

We're companionably silent until my stomach does a flip when he grabs my arm. "The water is thin here. We should be careful."

"I'm going to drown!" I say over my pounding heartbeat.

"No, we'll stay on top of the water. But the creatures of the deep can break through here, so we have to be cautious."

"Creatures? I want to go back."

"Agatha, I don't want to explain this one. I'm here to protect you. You're safe, but we must be more careful and watchful."

"You know what? I don't really need this voyage. I'm good. I'll do it. I'll get your key." I probably could've been more convincing if my voice wasn't so shaky, but I'm serious; I'll do whatever they want if Jonah will just turn around.

"Agatha, look down."

I do and fall to my knees. The silver is gone and the water is so clear and vivid, I can see all the way to the bottom far below. It's like I'm on top of a well-lit, bottomless aquarium. There are mountains of colorfully radiant corals of every configuration that wash the surrounding water in a rainbow of light. Feeding off the coral are large schools of fish of every hue and shape imaginable. Just below my knees is a group of small creatures that look like harvest-gold cucumbers with long terracotta whiskers protruding above their wide mouths that are opening and closing as if they're trying to talk to me. They're watching me with bulbous yellow eyes, and I want to say something to them.

"Wow!" is all I come up with.

Jonah lifts me back to my feet and the cucumber-fish follow us.

"This place just gets more and more amazing. Can we swim in that? Can we go down there? Do you have scuba gear?"

"Yes, yes, no," Jonah says, keeping up with my rapid-fire questioning.

"How do you get there? What's that? And that over there?"

Jonah doesn't answer anymore, he just smiles as I keep firing questions at him.

"Do you see that?"

It takes him a moment before he realizes that I expect an answer to that one.

"What's that? It's so beautiful."

"That's a kraken."

"Wow." The kraken looks like an octopus with more legs. Its brilliant teal suction cups glow on giant orange tentacles and make it light up like a neon sign.

"Wow!" I repeat. As it swims, brilliant chartreuse lines glide down its orange body like it's moving under a nonexistent light. "They should put that in an aquarium. People need to see that."

Jonah chuckles. "You don't read a lot of history, do you?"

"What's so funny?"

"People have seen kraken. They stifled your shipping industry for ages."

"Wait, krakens used to be on Earth?"

"Didn't you ever see a movie or read a book about a giant multi-tentacled creature attacking a ship?"

"Oh. Yeah. Okay. Yes. That was a kraken? I thought it was a giant octopus."

"Any giant octopi bring down a ship lately?"

"Use any sarcasm lately?" I fire back and he laughs. "Obviously not. I'm just saying that I thought it was a movie thing. I didn't realize that they're real and that they're curra. I'd love to paint that on my bedroom wall. You know, the movies don't do them justice. They're so pretty. Hollywood made them ugly and mauve."

The kraken swims under us and I grab Jonah's arm. "Wait! How big is that thing?"

He pats my hand. "He's deep, and you're much too small for him to bother with. You can just enjoy his beauty."

I relax and watch the world beneath my feet for hours. There's so much. I could study this place forever. However, my legs grow weary and the view below becomes boring in its sameness.

"How much longer?" I whine. "We've been walking for almost a full day."

"Not much. We're almost there. Do you want me to carry you?"

His suggestion causes my whole body to tense. No one has ever offered to carry me before. I decline, but after taking a few more steps, I change my mind.

He lifts me easily into his arms and I'm asleep a few minutes later.

CHAPTER 15

"Agatha, wake up," Jonah whispers against my ear.

There's apprehension in his voice and tension in the arms wrapped tightly around me. I bury my face against his shoulder. If he's frightened, then whatever is out there must be terrifying.

He gently jostles me until I lift my head. As soon as he feels me shift my weight, he releases his grip and lowers me to the water. He won't take his eyes off the horizon. "Be very quiet. We're being watched." His eyes are shifting as if he's still searching for the danger.

He must be able to sense it or something because when I look around, everything's fine. I want to ask him what he's so scared of, but it's probably best to let him handle it. Plus, I don't want to distract him or get in his way. I wish he'd lie to me and tell me everything is fine.

He's cautiously skulking around like a cat. I'm trying to match his movements, but I'm too awkward and clumsy. When he finds what he's looking for, his eyes grow so wide they take up most of his face. He doesn't even acknowledge me when he forcefully clamps his big hand on my shoulder and pushes me forward at a fast clip.

We're practically running. Jonah easily maneuvers over the water, but I'm tripping with every spongy step. His painful grip is the only thing keeping me on my feet.

I'm trapped by the openness. There is nothing as far as the eye can see. The shore disappeared ages ago and there's nowhere to run. We're alone in the middle of the ocean, defenseless. Something brushes the side of my thigh and I jump, then trip. Jonah catches me, and we keep moving without losing a step. I think my heart has stopped, but when the thing hits my thigh again, my heart nearly bursts out of my chest. I jump again and twist in the air. I need to know what's touching me.

Jonah doesn't stop as I examine my legs and find nothing. Could we be under attack by an invisible creature? I want off this stupid ocean. I want to run, but there's nowhere to go, and that thing just touched my leg again! This time I'm ready for it. I quickly look down and discover my hand.

I'm baffled for a minute until I realize that I'm so frightened, my hand has gone numb. It's balled in a fist and has lost all feeling. When I touch it against my leg, my thigh registers the contact but my hand feels nothing. I can't open my fist or move my arm. I don't know what's going on, but it's spreading to my legs. It's in my face too, a tingling sensation that hurts. *Just keep moving.* There is nothing else to do. I don't know if someone can die of fright, but I may find out.

Jonah increases our pace. I trip again and painfully torque my knee. The pain registers to my consciousness, but it's irrelevant as Jonah propels me forward. There is nothing but the pounding of blood in my ears. We're going to die out here.

"Run!" he yells.

I'm blindly running on a blank canvass. I don't even know what I'm running from. I freeze in my tracks when the massive serpentine back of something enormous breaks the water to my left. Terrifyingly large, pointy gray fins pinwheel through the water like a saw blade. I run for my life.

Something wraps itself around my waist and lifts me in the air. I try to scream, but no sound will come out. The world blurs. Then somewhere through my fear-induced fog, it registers that it's Jonah carrying me while he runs. How is it possible to be more scared than I already was?

Jonah is sprinting alarmingly fast and then without warning, he lifts me into the air and throws me as far as he can. I land hard, but the water is soft, so I bounce a few times before regaining my footing. I look back at him, stunned and confused.

"Run!" he roars.

I don't move.

The gigantic serpent breaks through the surface, sending waves of bouncy water rippling my way, knocking me to my back. Its olive-green neck shoots up at least fifteen feet and leads to the long slender head of an eel. All I can focus on is its thin needle teeth going in every direction from its enormous gaping mouth.

It lets out a deafening shriek, and then swings its long neck toward Jonah. He leaps out of its path, but not before giving the serpent a good whack to the snout with his staff. I remember him fighting the soldiers in my living room, and it gives me some hope. But this monster is colossal. Jonah looks like a tiny mouse next to it.

The serpent recovers from its near miss. It lifts its head, focuses on Jonah, and takes another swing. This one is more forceful than the last. He leaps out of the way, but not fast enough. The tip of the monster's nose brushes his arm, sending him somersaulting across the ocean's surface.

He regains his footing while the serpent pauses to let out another ear-splitting shriek. They study each other for a moment and then the giant eel lunges directly for him.

Jonah swings his staff like a baseball bat and smashes the serpent's jaw.

The stunned monster shakes its immense head before skulking beneath the surface.

As soon as it disappears, tears spring from my eyes. I pray a boat will come and remove us from the awful water. I want off this ocean. I want Jonah to tell me it's over. I want him back over here with me.

He's standing with his legs apart and his arms stretched out wide, looking down at the water. He's so still he makes everything stop, including my breathing. My entire body stiffens with fear when he lets out a thunderous roar. It's as if an electrical shock has traveled through my body, making my heart pound in an erratic staccato. He leaps into the air and lands on the giant head of the serpent as it breaks the surface of the ocean.

Its neck extends even higher than before as it wildly thrashes about, trying desperately to shake Jonah loose. His body is wildly flailing about at a great height. He's only able to hold on for a moment before the serpent violently flings him high in the air.

A deafening scream makes my ears bleed.

The serpent opens its mouth to grab Jonah as he falls.

Another scream.

It's me. I'm screaming. I can't stop.

The eel misses, leaving Jonah hanging on one of the whiskers that surround its mouth. It violently whips about with Jonah at its mercy.

The monster jumps completely out of the water, making it temporarily airborne. Then it dives headfirst into the ocean, taking Jonah with it.

My legs collapse as they both go deep into the sea.

The serpent has the advantage in the water. It swivels its tail around and hits Jonah so brutally he flies off its head. He tumbles through the water and floats limply as if he's dead.

I claw at the water. If the eel didn't kill him, then he'll definitely drown. I can't tunnel through the thick gelatinous ocean. As soon as I dig a substantial hole, it fills in again. He's too far below. I'll never reach him.

The monster circles him a few times and dives deep. I think it's going away. But then its body grows bigger as it gets closer. Its mouth is open wide under Jonah.

I scream and pound on the water. "Wake up!"

Jonah disappears in a vortex of color and mayhem as they both exit the water. The ocean is heaving wildly, and I'm thrown on my back again. I scramble to my hands and knees to get my bearings as if my watching is somehow keeping him alive. I'm disoriented because there are no landmarks. I search the surface but there's no sign of the serpent or Jonah.

I stop and listen, but there's no noise. I've stopped screaming. The ocean is calm. I'm alone.

I tear at the water again, but Jonah's not below.

A groan from behind me causes me to spin around. Jonah's about fifty feet away, on his back. He's not moving.

I stand so I can rush to his aid, but don't. I can't travel across this water. That serpent or something worse will see me. Jonah needs me and I'm failing again. I need to go, but I can't. It's my fault he's hurt because I'm too much of a coward to help him.

Finally, he rolls over. I'm about to call to him when the serpent breaks the surface directly behind him.

Jonah swings back and buries his staff in the lower gum line of the monster. The serpent shoots high in the air and lets out an ear-splitting screech. It reaches its pinnacle, then reverses itself back into the deep. As its head passes

108

Jonah, he grabs his staff out of the monster's mouth and rolls onto his stomach.

He lies eerily still for a moment, watching until the serpent disappears under the water.

Once he's convinced it's gone, he walks over to me. My entire body is shaking violently. I throw myself into his arms and sob. I've never been through something so terrifying in my life. I've never been scared for someone else before. The newness of that feeling frightens me more than the monster. I can't lose Jonah now; he's all I've got.

He holds me tight until I let go and look him over to make sure he's alright. He's so strong, it's hard to believe anything could hurt him, but the serpent was bigger and it did. My attempt to examine him is futile because all I can see is black flowing robe and hood. I give up and ask in a voice that's shakier than I expect, "Are you okay?"

He gives me one of his best cat-like smiles. "Yes. I'm quite well. I'm sorry that scared you."

"I thought you were going to die."

He wraps an arm around my shoulder and gives me a squeeze. "I'm alright. No dying today. We've got too many important things to do."

I don't take any confidence from his words. I hate this place. I want off this water.

Jonah starts walking and because his arm is still around my shoulders, he drags me with him.

"I want to leave." I wish my voice would stop betraying me. I want to sound angry and forceful, but I sound as pathetic and weak as I feel.

"I could carry you again, but you would do better walking a bit."

Neither of us speaks for a long time. The serpent has shaken the normally unshakable Jonah, but he's trying to play it off so he doesn't upset me. I really want to talk about what happened, but I don't want to make him think about it if he doesn't want to.

"Just a few more steps and we'll be on thicker water." I can't tell if he's talking to me or himself.

Now that he's broken the silence, I have to talk. "What was that?"

"Some kind of Jörmungandr. He's gone now."

His answer wasn't helpful, but I don't ask him to clarify because he still doesn't want to talk. I don't want to think about it anymore, either. I've stopped shaking, and the queasiness is subsiding. I just want to forget it ever happened.

I'm looking at my feet, watching the ocean grow cloudier with each step. When the water returns to its previous bouncy mirror state, Jonah announces, "We're safe. We've reached the thicker water."

"So nothing can get through?"

"Nothing can get through."

"I don't like this place. Do we have to walk back?" I can't face another crossing.

"We'll have to travel across the thin water again when we return. We may not see anything on the way back. We almost made it without incident this time."

"I don't like this place."

CHAPTER 16

My knees ache and my back hurts from the unending trampoline effect of the water. I desperately want to stop bouncing. The mirrored surface of the ocean makes it impossible to see through, and that's more unnerving than before when it was totally clear. Jonah said that nothing can break through, but how can he be so sure?

We walk for a long time. There's nothing around for miles. How far will this voyage take me? Are we walking to an island? A boat? Anything at all? And if we aren't traveling toward something, why are we walking at all?

I want to ask Jonah these questions and more, but I don't want him to think I'm complaining, so I keep them to myself. Fortunately, with each new question my shaking decreases, and soon I'm so focused on the fact that we're going nowhere that I forget I'm scared.

My brain is in a loop, repeating all of my unanswered questions. Why do we have to walk out this far? Am I supposed to be thinking about the Orb and stuff? Is Jonah required to talk me into something? If that last question is true, I'm in trouble because we haven't spoken for several hours.

These questions are making my jitters come back and when Jonah touches my shoulder, I jump and let out a yelp. I'm so embarrassed by my reaction that I can't look at him.

He waits for me to recover but when I don't, he loses his patience, grabs my shoulder again and turns me to face him.

"This is as far as I can go. You must do the rest on your own." He says this so deadpan that I think I must have heard him wrong. There's no way he could believe I would go anywhere without him.

"What?" I'm already shaking my head even though I'm not sure what he wants me to do. "I'm not going anywhere alone. What if that thing comes back, or maybe one of its friends? You should come with me."

Jonah smiles and squeezes my shoulder. "It'll be fine. I won't move from this spot. It's essential that you do this part of the voyage alone."

I forcefully pull away from him as a buzzing in my ears, like a swarm of furious wasps, fills my soul. I've been tricked. "Why didn't you tell me this before we left the beach?"

"Would you have understood if I did?"

I hate it when he answers my questions with a question. "I don't understand now, so no, I wouldn't have, but you should've tried. I don't want to go alone. I don't want to be by myself."

"I'll be here waiting for you. Nothing bad will happen. This is your voyage and you need to be the one to take it. I can't do it for you."

We stare at each other for much longer than I'm comfortable with. I wish I knew how to convince him that I just want to be off the ocean and that I certainly don't want to be on it alone.

I should've never gotten into a staring contest with him because I know he's going to win. I pull my burning eyes away and examine my pathetic reflection in the silver water.

He keeps a hand on my shoulder. It's a reminder that I have to do what he wants. How did I end up here, alone, in the middle of the ocean with the Grim Reaper? My throat tightens, but I won't cry again. I can't remember the last time I cried before I came to this place. It's been years. Jonah makes me cry a lot.

"That monster will eat me." I barely choke the words out. It's the only argument I can think of and it's not a good one.

"I'll be here waiting for you. I promise, I won't move."

What am I doing? I can't swim. The thought of what's lurking below my feet is making my chest hurt. I'm not strong enough to do this, especially alone.

"Agatha," Jonah whispers, squeezing my arm. "Please trust me. I'll never let any harm come to you. I wouldn't ask you to do this if it wasn't important. I promise you, when it's over, you'll be very proud you did it. And you'll be pleased with yourself for being so brave."

Brave? There's nothing brave about walking by myself. And it's certainly nothing to be proud of. People walk by themselves every day. It shouldn't require bravery. If I weren't such a pathetic coward, this wouldn't be an issue.

I give up. I can't fight Jonah, he always wins. It's just walking. I'll go where he wants and then I can go back to the shore and get this whole stupid voyage over with.

"Where should I go? What do you want me to do?" I say it with a deep sigh so Jonah knows how upset I am. Hopefully he'll make this part quicker than it normally would've been.

Jonah turns me around to face away from him and points over my shoulder. "Walk until you find yourself."

"What!" I spin around. Now I'm just mad. "That makes no sense! Does everything have to be a riddle? Just tell me what I'm expected to do. And let's do it and get it over with. I want to be back on land. Apparently I'm a creature of the land. So just give me a straight answer for once."

Jonah shrugs his shoulders and narrows his eyes. "I'm not sure what you're asking. I gave you a straight answer. Walk that way," he points again, "until you find yourself."

"I'm right here!" I wave my arms around. "Found! Can we go now?"

Jonah's eyes slant in anger, and I stop my temper tantrum. He's very scary when he's mad. He catches himself, takes a deep breath and returns his face to the half-smile he usually wears. "I don't know how to explain it better," he says gently. "I can't go. This is your voyage. If you commence walking, maybe it will make sense."

I don't want to be on the water alone. I want to scream uncontrollably until a helicopter comes and plucks me from this terrible ocean. But no rescue is on the way, and knowing that makes me even more frightened.

My fear makes me angry and I'm taking that anger out on the only person I don't want to be angry with. I jerk away from Jonah and attempt to stomp off, but I forgot how bouncy the water is, so instead I do a ridiculous staggering hop. When I regain my footing, if not my dignity, I look back and shout, "I think I'm found now. Yep, here I am!"

Jonah's eyes slant again. "Just go."

I turn around and walk, normally this time. With each step, my confidence grows. I can do this. Nothing is jumping out at me and everything is peaceful. *Just keep stepping*, I tell myself.

Being alone has never been an issue. I prefer my own company. However, I've never done anything new and I certainly have never done anything this challenging. Thoughts of Jonah make me feel guilty about how I treated him. I look back to make sure he kept his word and sure enough, he's right where I left him. That puts a smile on my face. I know that when I return from whatever it is I'm doing, he will be in the same place, watching me.

This is what trust feels like. I've never had to depend on someone before, or more accurately, I've never had anyone to depend on before. I've been through a lot in the last few days. It's almost unbelievable that just last week I was in math class doodling in a notebook. I check to make sure Jonah is still watching me, but he's too far away to see.

My heart jumps to my throat, and my palms sweat. I can't do this alone. How long am I obligated to walk? Maybe I'm just meant to be in the peace and quiet until my head clears or something. I take a few deep breaths and concentrate on putting one foot in front of the other. My thoughts stray to Auntie, my life in Queens, and the kids at school. I'm so profoundly different from that girl I was, but I've only been gone a few days.

Am I doing the right thing by thinking about my life and stuff? I'm out here to make a decision, but I don't want to think about that. How am I supposed to embark on a journey that killed my parents when I can't even walk by myself for a few hours?

"Okay, so I have to decide if I'll search for this key." I say it aloud, hoping it will help me think more clearly. It's nice to know there's no one around to hear me sound so stupid.

"I don't want to." Admitting that is extremely liberating. It's as if the weight of the world is lifted from my shoulders—make that *two* worlds.

"Who are they kidding? I'm no hero and I have no desire to be one. Apparently, I was perfectly happy being a prisoner.

"I've been walking for two days and it might kill me. Everything on my body hurts and all I've done is walk.

How do I fight an army? I couldn't defeat a single soldier, let alone all of them. Then there are the creatures, like the dragon the King made. If Jonah hadn't chased off the sea serpent, it would've easily eaten me. I'm just one human, and not a very good one."

My lips swell and my throat hurts; tears are on the way again. "Why me? I'll fail and when I do, I'll take everyone else down with me. I can't do this."

I can't! I scream in my head as the flow of tears increases. I give into my self-pity and drop to my knees, forcing myself to cry as hard as I can now that I'm alone. The stress of the last few days overwhelms me. How can they expect someone so ordinary to do something so extraordinary?

"I can't." It's more of a plea. I curl into a ball and hug my knees. I wish someone would remove this burden from me. I'm just not strong enough.

"I can't. I'm too weak. I just can't," is what I thought I said. But the voice isn't coming from within me. And I'm no longer crying.

"I can't. I can't," the voice that sounds like mine says. It's not mocking. It's woebegone and pathetic. It sounds exactly like me.

I stay face down, curled in my protective ball, but I turn my head to the side to see the source of the voice. Just to my left is *me*. A taller, fatter version of me, but *me*, lying in the same balled-up position. It's like gazing into a funhouse mirror. It's me. It's in the same position, wearing the same clothes, only it's bigger and plumper.

"I can't. I can't," it repeats. It sobs, then turns its head and sees me. It jumps to its knees startled and shouts, "What are you?"

Immediately, another version of me emerges directly in front of the actual me. This one looks exactly like me, only it's sitting with its legs crossed.

"That's Fear," it says.

I push myself out of my balled-up position to rest on my knees as another version of me appears to my right and asks the real me, "Who are you? Why are you there? Why do you look like me?"

"Why am I not talking?" Fear shouts.

The me that's in front of me, points to the crying me and says, "That's Fear and that one over there is Curiosity. I'm Reason."

"What? No, this isn't right," snorts another me that pops up next to Fear. This one is much taller than the real me.

"Ah, Doubt," Reason says. "I was wondering when you'd show up."

"I don't like this. This is weird. I'm going crazy," Fear announces.

"If you're all out there, then who's in here?" Curiosity asks and the real me points to my chest.

"That's just weird," Doubt says, and I agree.

"I don't like this." Fear declares. "I want this to stop."

"Agatha, try to complete one thought at a time," Reason orders me before turning to Fear. "You need to be quiet. Let me think clearly. We have nothing to fear yet."

Fear stops crying and silently studies the crowd.

"Agatha," Reason says again with a wave toward the others. "You are working out a problem and each of us is helping you. What's left in there…" Reason points to my head, "is everyone who doesn't possess any answers."

A tiny version of me appears to my right, next to Curiosity. "Okay," she warbles pathetically.

Reason looks to her right and then to her left. "Agatha, do you see how big Fear and Doubt are? Now turn to your right. Over here is Curiosity, which is pretty healthy, and Trust, which is very small. Is there no one else in there that can help?"

"No," both Fear and Doubt say in unison.

Reason shrugs. "Okay, fine. We'll work with what we've got. We have a problem. We're the only one who can read this Orb."

"I can't," Fear whimpers.

"Fear, shush!" Reason demands. "Agatha, control yourself!" She takes a deep breath. "We are the only one who can read this Orb. We are in danger whether we choose to search for the key or not."

"Jonah said he'd hide us if we didn't want to search for the key," declares a small me that appears between Curiosity and Trust. This one is only about six inches tall and looks like she's starving to death.

"Hope! We have Hope!" Reason exclaims. "Good, we contain a little Hope and a tiny bit of Trust, some Curiosity and a lot of Doubt and Fear. Let's talk to you, Hope."

"We don't have a lot of Hope," Doubt mutters.

"But let's see what Hope has to say," Reason encourages.

"Well," Hope whispers, "I like Jonah."

"I don't like Dathid," Fear says.

Hope ignores Fear and keeps talking. "I like Ashra, and the faeries, and Jonah. We'll be safe as long as we're with him."

Doubt snorts. "That's ridiculous! He's just one man— or curra, or whatever. He's not here now and he can't watch me every second."

"But he said he would train us," Hope continues and grows a bit taller.

"Have you seen us? What is there to train?" Doubt asks.

"Everyone has to start somewhere. We don't need to be a superhero. We just have to know enough so that if Jonah or Dathid aren't around, we're not helpless," Hope argues.

"I don't like Dathid," Fear says again.

"I think I should search for the key. I like this place and I like everyone we've met and they need my help," announces a new me on my right. She's tall and strong.

"I knew we had Courage in there somewhere!" Reason exclaims. "Agatha, look at Courage. See how strong she is. You always relied on her, and she's here now."

"Courage isn't big enough," Doubt mutters.

Everyone is silent as we study each other.

"Are we seriously thinking of nothing?" Doubt asks.

"Quiet!" Reason orders. "Let's see who else shows up."

Fear sits up and scans the crowd with frightened eyes. "We can't do this. We're too small. We're too weak and we'll get everyone killed. We can't!"

"Yes, we can. We are not weak. We just have to be trained!" Hope fires back.

"We're weak!" Fear shouts while growing bigger.

"We can do this!" Hope yells back.

The two argue for a moment and then Doubt joins in the fray. Both Doubt and Fear grow and get stronger with each word, and Hope starts to fade.

Then an enormous Auntie appears directly in front of me and shoves Reason out of the way. "Who do you think you are!" she screams in my face, but her voice is mine. "You are nothing! You are too weak! Too stupid! And too scared to do anything! Look at this!" She snorts while she turns in a circle, assessing the crowd. "All you are is Doubt and Fear! How can someone like you take on a powerful specter, an army and Lord knows what else? You are worthless and pathetic! There's no way someone as insipid as you could ever hope to succeed! Give up now before you embarrass yourself and get the only friends you have killed!"

The big Auntie steps back as soon as she finishes spitting her rage. Reason comes forward, but the Auntie looms large behind her.

"Even though she's using our voice, those words sound different when they come from outside our brain," Reason says calmly and then points at Auntie. "These aren't even our thoughts. Get rid of her."

I try, but Auntie doesn't move. I give up and turn to the sound of Fear groaning. Another me has appeared to my left. The newest me is normal-sized but lying on her side with her knees to her chest. "She's right. I'm worthless and pathetic. I only have one friend, and it'll be my fault when he dies."

"Agatha, we don't have time for Self-Pity," Reason says. "Both of you go away. You're not helping." With that order, both Auntie and Self-Pity disappear.

Reason turns to Hope. "Hope, if you argue with Fear, you'll weaken yourself and make Fear stronger. Fear, you promised to be quiet until you were needed. Agatha, you must control yourself."

"I want to help my only friend," Courage announces.

"We'll get killed," Fear fires back, but she's getting smaller.

"I want to help my only friend," Courage says again with increased fervor.

"They'll train me. Make me strong. I can do this." Hope is regaining some of her strength.

"Jonah and the others will do everything they can to make me and themselves safe," Trust adds.

"If I'm the only one who can read this Orb, then it's my destiny to read it. Think of how the kids at school will feel when they learn about what a hero I am. I'll be famous and the world—no, wait,*both* worlds will love me. And no one will ever be mean to me again," declares another new me.

"You may be right, Ego, but we we're wanting Self-Esteem, maybe Self-Worth," Reason says. "Thank you for your input, but you can go."

Reason waits, but when no one else shows up, she says, "Agatha, I want to talk to Self-Esteem. She's in there. Let her out."

"I can't do this."

"Doubt, we've heard what you have to say. Let Self-Esteem speak," Reason demands.

A small, sickly me materializes but doesn't say anything.

"Self-Esteem, I knew you were in there. Do you have anything to say?"

"Of course not!" Auntie interrupts when she reappears. "This is stupid. You don't possess any Self-Esteem. Look at you. Look at you!"

Reason glances at Auntie and then at Self-Esteem. "I do have Self-Esteem. I'm looking at her. See how much bigger she's gotten in the few days we've been in Ashra."

Hope jumps up and down excitedly. "Imagine how much bigger she'll get if we stay and help them!"

"I can be trained," Self-Esteem murmurs. "I'm the only one who can read the Orb. And if my mother did it, then I should do it too."

With that, a sizable me comes forth and declares with conviction, "Then I've made my decision. I'm a Knight. I'll train as a Knight trains. I'll help these creatures and I'll stop a war!

Reason chuckles. "Who knew we had so much Pride?" With that, everyone disappears.

I'm alone.

I can't wrap my brain around what just happened. Did I hallucinate that or did all those Agathas really sit in front of me? When the fuzziness clears, I'm elated, almost light-headed. I'm different, like I'm changed on the inside. It's as if I now know how to think better.

I wobble when I stand. This is the first time I've ever had to give someone good news. I can't wait to see Jonah's reaction.

CHAPTER 17

Jonah wraps his arms around me as soon as I reach him. He kept his promise and didn't move from where I left him.

"I've decided to do it."

He sighs, picks me up and swings me around. I was hoping he'd respond this way because I'm getting used to his affection and I'm starting to like it. He puts me down, holds my face in his hands and studies my eyes. "Are you sure?"

I smile at him. "Well, I'd be lying if I said I wasn't scared. I'm completely unprepared, but I need to do this. So, yeah, I'm sure."

My answer must satisfy him because he smiles widely, wraps his arms around my waist and gives me another hug. "Well then, let's get you prepared." Then he throws me over his shoulder, and we laugh and giggle our way back to Dathid and Lenox.

The return journey seems faster, but I also sleep through most of it, so I'm not sure how long it really takes. I was so elated after my experience with the Agathas that Jonah and I played for a while, but then I got tired and rode most of the way on his back. Nothing exciting happened, and no creatures broke through the surface.

As we draw closer to the beach, I hear Lenox screeching for me as he paces up and down the water line. As soon as he sees me, he takes off. He reaches us in no time and circles overhead, making me feel like a woodland animal that's being hunted. When he swoops down, I wrap myself tightly around Jonah, but Lenox easily loops his talons under my arms and plucks me from Jonah's back.

The ocean flies past at an alarming speed, and I scream in terror. It doesn't matter how soft the water is; if he drops me at this speed, I'll be seriously injured. However, after only a few seconds, my fear transforms into elation, and my screams turn joyful. I've never ridden a rollercoaster before, but I imagine this is what it would be like.

Lenox is being quite gentle. I'm grateful he didn't impale me with his exceptionally large talons when he picked me up. This position is uncomfortable, but not painful, and a bit of discomfort is definitely worth this exhilarating ride.

When we reach the sand, Lenox sets me on the beach. He's such a gentle boy, which is surprising because he's so enormous. However, I change my mind when he spins around and knocks me off my feet.

He steps over me, pins me to the sand, and gives my hair and face a thorough sniffing. It's sweet that he was worried about me. The sniffing tickles and I can't help but laugh and try to push his face away. When he's satisfied that I'm alright, he gives the entire side of my face an enormous lick and then moves away so I can get up.

After I stand, I glance over at Dathid, embarrassed about acting like a kid with my pet. He's sitting on a log near the fire, watching me, but he doesn't say anything and my giddiness vanishes.

Should I go over to the fire? Should I sit next to him on the log? I don't want to do either of those things, so I just stand there looking really dumb. I wish I were better with people.

He shifts his weight and studies the fire. "So, your voyage, it was successful?"

Dathid and I have never been alone together, and we've never engaged in conversation. I wish Jonah would hurry up and get here.

"Yes," I say to my feet. I should probably add more to my answer. "I've decided to do it."

I barely mumble it out, but Dathid heard me because he lets out a long breath. "Good." I'm not sure if he's saying it to me or muttering under his breath, but with that, our talk ends and a long awkward silence ensues. I wish Jonah would get a move on; he's taking forever.

"I'm sure you're hungry," Dathid says to break the silence. "Lenox caught some *flingerts,* and I have them roasting. They should be done shortly." I don't know what to say to that, so I nod slightly and watch for Jonah.

After a few minutes, Dathid adds, "I picked some *wandel* berries for Jonah. You may like them also."

I picture Dathid picking berries and the image is so absurd it almost makes me giggle. "Thank you," I say quietly and make my way over to the log. I sit down near the fire, but not too close to him.

Lenox follows me and smells my hair again. "Seriously, I'm fine," I say as I try to shoo him away. "All good. Nothing happened." Satisfied with my answer, he lies down in a ball next to me.

"That one there has been darting up and down the beach screaming for the last three days."

"Three days!" I squeal in surprise. "We were gone for three days? I thought it was only a day, not even."

Dathid almost smiles. "The passage of time is different here."

"I thought you didn't have time. Now I'm confused."

Dathid grimaces and takes a deep breath. He opens his mouth to speak, but stops himself and then tries again. "We have time. We age. But time doesn't work here the way you think of it."

"But you said it's been three days."

"I was using Earth time to make it easy for you to understand." He starts busily tending to the meat in order to stop my questions.

I take his cue and look out over the ocean for Jonah. He's easy to spot because his eyes are glowing brightly in the dim light. He's almost to the beach, so I leave Dathid and wait at the shoreline for him. Lenox jumps up, afraid I'm going back on the water.

When Jonah reaches the shore, he tousles my hair with the affection I'm getting used to, then turns his attention to Dathid. "You've made camp. I'm surprised you did it here."

"Well, for starters, I couldn't get the pegasus to calm down. Also, I wanted to keep my eyes open for any signals." He's not much warmer towards Jonah, but he's more relaxed with him. It's funny that I make someone as strong as Dathid nervous.

"Did you sleep?"

Dathid cringes. "Yeah."

"I would've liked to have seen a faerie sleeping on the ground."

To my surprise, Dathid smiles. I didn't think he could do that since I haven't seen him smile since we met. It's a good smile, genuine. I don't like it. It makes him seem nice and maybe even approachable, which he's not.

"Well, it gets better." Dathid laughs. The laughing is even more unsettling. "Because the bloody pegasus was so distraught, he cuddled with me all night."

Jonah laughs as he sits next to him on the log. Dathid takes one of the small roasted birds off the stick he's holding and hands it to me. It's hot and I drop it on my lap and burn my leg. Jonah picks it up, puts it on a rag, and hands it back to me.

"Sorry," Dathid says. "I didn't know the temperature would be a problem for you."

I stare at him for longer than I should because I don't know what to say. I try to mumble "That's okay," but I'm not sure it actually escapes my mouth.

"From here we should head toward Gwa Twouroch," Jonah says to Dathid.

"I don't agree," Dathid says. I tune them out. They talk all through dinner about such strange things that I give up trying to contribute, and curl up with Lenox.

I must have been sleeping with my mouth open because I awake the next morning with a mouthful of wing from him bashing me in the face. I jump up, spitting and grunting. I grimace at him, but he's not looking at me. I can't be too mad because he did what I asked: one hit, and then wait. I guess he does understand what I say to him.

Jonah hands me a cup of water and some leftover meat. They've already packed up the camp, so as soon as I finish my breakfast, we're underway.

It takes me a while to wake up, and I walk for hours in a daze. A lot has happened to me in a short time. I can't keep up with my life. I'm trying to reflect and take it all in, but it's becoming increasingly difficult.

We eat lunch on the move. Jonah seems to want to get somewhere within a certain amount of time. We're not rushing, but we're also not stopping. An alarm goes off in my head. I don't know where we're going. I'm surprised at myself for blindly following Jonah. That disturbs me, but only for a moment because even if he told me, I wouldn't know where I am anyway. Either way, though, I want to know.

"We're on our way to Cromsmead, the village of the elves. Cromsmead elves, to be exact," Jonah answers after I ask.

"Why are we going there? When do I get to read the Orb? How do we get the key?"

"Agatha, when you ask a question, do you expect an answer?"

"When you answer a question with a question, do *you* expect an answer?" I respond.

Jonah smiles at me. I think he likes it when I fight back a little bit. Auntie never let me fight back. *My way or the highway* was her favorite expression.

"Don't worry about the key, it's not time yet. You don't know how to read the Orb, so don't worry about that, either. And we're headed to Cromsmead so you can receive your training."

"Training!" I shout excitedly. "I'll be trained? Trained to do what? Read the Orb?"

"Trained to be a Knight."

"A Knight! I'm going to be a Knight? Like with swords and jousting and stuff like that?"

Jonah smiles. "Yes, stuff like that."

A flash of fear makes my heart flutter. I shouldn't have agreed to this. "But I don't know how to do anything even close to that."

"That's why you'll be trained."

I'm not strong. I can't do the things Knights do. I'm afraid of everything. How could someone like me be a Knight? I stay in my doubts for a long time and almost crash into Dathid. He's always far ahead of us, so I usually never see him outside of camp. How long has he been here, waiting for us?

Dathid glares at Jonah as if he might hit him. "Well?"

Jonah looks at me. Am I supposed to answer? What could "Well?" mean?

"Agatha," Jonah says in a tone that suggests I won't like whatever he says next. "We have a choice. We can go through Smivler's Gorge or we can walk through Montmort. Montmort will take about a week longer, but it should be uneventful."

"I don't want to walk for a week," I whine. "My body and especially my feet are in a lot of pain. I want to get to wherever we're going as quickly as humanly—or curra-ly, possible."

Dathid groans but Jonah ignores him when he continues. "We can go through Smivler's Gorge. It would only take about two days. It's beautiful. You'll like it, but that means we'll have to go through Gwa Twouroch."

"Gua Torooch?" I repeat. Why is his tone so dire? They want me to go to a beautiful place, the likes of which I've never seen. How bad could this Gwa place be?

"Gwa Twouroch loosely translates to *Cave of Thought*."

"Cave of Thought? What's that?"

"Well, it's what I said. It's a cave. Not a very long one. But when you go through it, whatever you think about materializes."

My face lights up. "That sounds fantastic. Really! Anything you think about happens? Like if I think about ice cream. Bam! There it is? Can I eat it? Will it taste good?"

"Well—" Jonah begins.

"So if I think about this guy, Corey, at school, he'll actually be there? What if I think about pizza? Could we have pizza?"

Dathid gives Jonah an *I-told-you-so* look while Jonah waits for my questions to stop. I ignore both of them. I really want to see this cave.

"This is not a good idea," Dathid mutters.

"She can do it. I want to get somewhere safer as fast as we can."

I stop my questions. There's something they're not telling me. A chill creeps down my spine and freezes my feet in place. "There's a giant spider in there that'll eat us. That's the part you're not telling me, right? Some horrible creature that sucks your guts out."

Dathid throws his hands up. "And that just proved my point."

"Agatha, if you think there's a giant spider in there, then there is one," Jonah explains slowly. "That's the problem we have with going through Gwa—the Cave of Thought."

"Oh, okay. So think happy thoughts. I can do that." This sounds pretty easy. I don't know what they're so upset about.

Dathid frowns at me. "Have you ever been in a cave before?"

"No," I respond, trying to match his condescending tone.

"Gwa Twouroch is large," Jonah says to me. "We can all walk through it easily. There are well-maintained paths and steps. It's just dark."

"Oh. Okay, that doesn't sound so bad." I'm being honest. I can't wait to think of things and make them appear.

"If I coach you on what to think about, do you think you could listen to me? Think about what I say?"

"Yeah. Sure."

"All right, then we'll take the shorter route." Jonah turns down the path that leads to Smivler's Gorge.

"Great," Dathid mumbles. "I'm going to be eaten by a giant spider."

CHAPTER 18

It takes another two days to leave the woods. They don't end gradually like they did at the beach. One moment we're surrounded by trees, and the next we're in a vast desert. Well, sort of a desert; it's more pebbles than sand. It's filled with low-lying, brightly colored plants and gigantic cadmium red and burgundy rocks. Many of the rocks are piled high in odd gravity-defying arrangements. Just looking at the mammoth boulders precariously heaped on top of one another makes me nervous. Walking next to them is both awe inspiring and heart stopping.

It's peculiar how these rocks managed to arrange themselves in this way. Some look freshly assembled and jagged while others have eroded away to form inexplicable shapes. We just passed one that looks like a donut on its side, if the donut was three stories high.

I'm liking this part of the journey because I can clearly see where we're heading. In the far distance is a wall of mahogany red rock, jutting up and down as high as the skyline of Manhattan, only stretching out farther. It's comforting in a way. It's familiar, even though it's rocks and not buildings. I wish I knew what a gorge was so I'd know exactly where we were going.

The sun is setting over the wall of rock, but the sky is brighter. When the trees, ended so did the night. A pink line, like a jet trail across the noon sky, marked night and day. I prefer the blue, even if the setting sun makes it kind of pink.

It only takes about an hour before I admit that this part of the journey is the worst yet. It's hot and extremely dry. There's no path, but the plants are spaced far apart, so it's easy to traverse the gravelly ground. My sneakers are worn through. They were cheap shoes to begin with, and they were never meant for hiking. I feel every stone under my feet, not to mention the tiny pebbles that love jumping into my shoes.

I don't know how long it takes us to arrive at Smivler's Gorge, but I've been staring at it for days. It's just a split in the rock. From far away it's a hairline crack in the mammoth skyline wall but now that we're up close, I can see that the opening is wide enough for the four of us to walk comfortably side -by -side and still leave room for the numerous plants and trees growing in it.

"Wow!" jumps from my mouth. With those few steps, I've entered another world. I spin in a circle, studying the cliffs on both sides. This is how tourists must feel when they visit New York City for the first time. The walls are so high that staring up at them makes me dizzy.

"It gets even more beautiful the further we go in," Jonah explains.

I want to climb the honeycomb rock face, sit on one of the frightening overhangs, and study the unusual striations that range from gleaming orange to blood red. The vertical cliffs on both sides are so tall they make me feel very small and inconsequential. I'm not worthy of seeing something this astounding.

The trees have long branches with poofs of tiny bright leaves at the ends that remind me of poodles. They add to the splendor by singing a low-tuned song that sounds like something I once heard coming out of a church. We follow the dirt line traveling down the center of the gorge, but just off the path are dense exotic plants with broad multicolored leaves that are bigger than I am.

I yawn and Jonah looks down at me. "Are you fatigued?"

"Yes, and I'm starving."

"Dathid, do you think it's safe to camp here?" Jonah asks even though he's already taking off his pack.

"Sure," is all Dathid says before dropping his bag. He might be tired too.

Jonah makes a fire and we eat dinner from the food the faeries packed. I sit on the ground with my back against the gorge wall and study my surroundings. Jonah soon joins me.

"I wish I brought my brushes with me," I say to him. "This place gets more amazing with every new spot we visit. I want to paint it."

Jonah smiles at me. "Tomorrow you must tell Lenox to meet you on the other side of the gorge."

"Why?"

"Because the gorge will get narrow and the footing will be less stable. Plus, you won't be able to convince him to walk through a cave."

"Why am I the only one that can talk to him?"

"Lenox is your pegasus."

Why do I have a pegasus? Why is he mine? Why am I the only one that can talk to him? I want to ask Jonah all of these questions, but I'm afraid of the answers, so instead I ask, "What language does Dathid speak? What's that accent?"

"Gàidhlig."

"And what language do you usually speak?"

"English. I'm from Brooklyn."

I'm surprised by his answer. "Do all Knight Crawlers speak English?"

"No, we speak the language of whatever region we are residing in. Knight Crawlers do not have a land or a language."

I may have discovered something, but I hope I'm wrong. "Okay, well, why does Lenox speak English if he was raised with the faeries?"

"Because Lenox is yours."

"So, when he was given to me, he just suddenly knew English?"

"No, he was trained by the Wiltonshire elves. He knows a dialect of Naga-Nuru that the elves speak."

"Naga-Nuru?" I repeat. "Then how does he understand me?"

"Because he was taught English and trained for you."

"What?" It's more of an accusation than a question. "How is he trained for me? I thought you just found out about me! How could you have a pegasus ready for me?"

Jonah puts his hand up to stop my questions. "We always knew about you. But we weren't sure what happened to you. Preparations were made, in case you survived. There were many pegasus trained in various languages in the hopes of your return."

I should be honored that these people are excited about me coming back, but his revelation fills me with doubt. I don't know anyone here. I just blindly followed Jonah. Could that night at Auntie's have been an elaborate ruse to trick me into coming here?

"That first night when you came into my room, why didn't you just take me then?" I whisper.

"Agatha, I was more shocked to see you than you were to see me. I never thought we would locate you. More to the point, I never thought I would be the one to find you. I

135

thought—we all thought that if you returned, you would be with Lord Duradin. It was our hope that you would be incorruptible or at least salvageable, and that we could release you from his grasp." His words trail off as he becomes lost in his own thoughts.

He takes a breath and continues after a brief pause. "That night, I was rescuing a gremlin that was being hunted by your neighbors."

"Mr. and Mrs. Miller were trying to kill that thing!" His expression grows weary but he doesn't comment, so I continue with my questions. "So that thing, that gremlin...what happened to him?"

"He died that night."

"Oh," is all I can think to say. "Was he a friend of yours?"

"No. He was a young gremlin who fell into a trap."

"Oh," I say again because I can't think of anything else. I never knew anyone, who knew anyone who died.

Our silence continues for much longer than I'm comfortable with. "So that's why you didn't take me that night? Because the gremlin was dying?"

"No. I would've sacrificed him for you. I honestly didn't know what to do. I knew I could get to the faeries and back before Lord Duradin could give your foster mother orders. So that's what I did."

"So you were ordered to take me?" I've exchanged one set of jailers for another.

"Yes and no. As I said before, we never expected to find you. King Ohad was making arrangements for a rescue mission and I was sent back to assess the situation. Unfortunately, Lord Duradin was faster than we anticipated. I made a judgment call."

"So, you took me." The words are faint. I'm saying them to myself. I don't know what to say or even what to think. What would a rescue mission have looked like? I probably would've thought I was being kidnaped. However, if a threat was introduced first, like Lord Duradin, I would've willingly gone with my hero, even if he was the Angel of Death.

Jonah watches my mood sink. "Agatha, I didn't abduct you." He sounds upset that I would accuse him of that. "You have always had choices. You can choose to leave now. You can choose to stop and go into hiding, or you can choose to continue."

I don't want to talk anymore. I get up and head over to Lenox. "I thought I had choices with Auntie too," I whisper into the air.

Lenox is already curled up for the night. He lifts his wing when he sees me approach. At least I never have to question *his* motives. I lie in the comfort of his embrace while tears roll unchecked down my face.

I wake up the next morning lying on the ground with Lenox standing over me, smelling my hair. I must have been out cold because I don't remember him getting up.

"Lenox, let her sleep," Dathid orders, but Lenox ignores him.

"I'm up. I'm up." I groggily push at his nose. Usually, I wake up lying with him, but he seems to have been awake for quite a while, as does Dathid. "Where's Jonah?" I ask.

"He went up ahead. He should be back shortly. You need to eat." He hands me a biscuit and some fruit.

I was out of line last night. I might have permanently damaged my relationship with Jonah. I wish he'd hurry up and get back here so I can apologize. I eat my breakfast and watch Dathid efficiently break down our small camp when a long shadow appears on the gorge wall. I look down the path, hoping Jonah has returned, but there's nothing there, not even a bright light to make a silhouette.

It's definitely a shadow and it definitely is moving toward us. I brace myself because whatever it is, it will be upon us in a matter of seconds. Then without warning, the shape becomes three-dimensional and Jonah appears. It's so sudden that I jump and let out a small squeak. My face gets hot when Jonah and Dathid look at me questioningly. I focus on my fruit and hope they forget I'm here.

"'Bout time you came back," Dathid says.

"I went all the way to the opening. It's clear. Did you check above?"

"No. I was letting her sleep. She's only been up a short time. We can start out and I'll go up and have a look."

Why do they always talk about me like I'm an object? They do that a lot for expedience. If they talk to me, then they need to explain what they're saying. I agree that can get tedious. When we first started out I didn't want to know, but since this journey seems to be unending, I want them to include me in the discussion.

Of course, I'd have to tell them that and that might make them mad. I just need to get over it. They know what's best.

Jonah is quiet this morning. That's not unusual, but today I'm taking it personally. I want to talk about last night. I can see he's distracted because he keeps looking around. I lose my nerve. I shouldn't talk to him now anyway, because Dathid is directly in front of us. He's usually so far ahead I never see him, but today I could reach out and touch him.

I stop dead in my tracks when he unfolds his long wings. I know he's a faerie, but his wings are always so neatly tucked up along his back, like a backpack, that I forget about them until he unfurls them. Without a word, his wings flap furiously until they're a blur, and he starts the long climb up the gorge.

He ascends a good distance up the cliff when Lenox takes off after him, thrilled at finding a playmate. Lenox is faster and more agile than Dathid and makes a game of circling him and then dodging him when he tries to shoo him away. Lenox bumps Dathid in return. I'm not sure they're still playing when Dathid gives Lenox a solid push. Lenox responds by putting his muzzle under Dathid and giving him such a shove that it sends Dathid tumbling high into the air.

When he recovers, he hovers for a moment and then calls to Lenox. Lenox speeds toward him at a remarkable rate. As he passes, Dathid grabs his tail. Lenox doesn't like having a passenger and increases his speed as he climbs straight up the gorge walls. When he's almost to the top, he abruptly turns and throws Dathid free of his tail. The momentum shoots Dathid out of the gorge, and Lenox chases after him.

"He's going to be mad when he returns," Jonah chuckles, and we continue down the path.

Now that we're alone, I can't keep the words in any longer. "I'm sorry about last night. I was just tired. I know you didn't kidnap me and I'm not your prisoner. This is just a lot."

"I'm sorry too. I'm not trained to teach thirteen-year-old human girls, and sometimes I don't know how you'll react to things."

"It's just a lot," I repeat then change the subject. "So, I'm like...famous here?"

Jonah nods.

"I always thought it would be wonderful to be famous, but the reality of it is unnerving. It's because I can read the Orb?"

"Yep, you're the Keeper of the Key," Jonah corrects.

"But I don't have the key."

"Not yet."

I think about his cryptic response. "So what do I have to do once I get it?"

"No one really knows. Your mother was the Keeper of the Key, but she never had it either. It's assumed that when we locate the key, we'll know how to destroy it."

"Wait a minute!" I shout. "I'm supposed to find this key, and when I do, *then* we figure out what to do with it?"

"Yes and no," Jonah explains calmly. "My knowledge of the key is limited. There are others who know a lot more, but no one has ever seen it. So we're not exactly sure what it is or what to do with it."

I don't like Jonah not knowing, but to be fair, he's not really in charge of the key or me or any of this. He's just the lucky guy who happened upon me. It's weird to think that an entire world has been searching for me, waiting for me, and preparing for my arrival.

These people who are in charge, are they even right? Does the Orb lead to a key? And if it does, would that key unlock the portals? So far, they seem to know so little, and yet they're asking me to risk a lot.

"Agatha," Jonah says as if he's reading my thoughts. "We know the Orb will find the key. We know that we have to keep the key away from Ziras. It could be that simple. We will take this one step at a time. First, you need to be trained."

That gives me some relief, but I don't want to talk about it anymore. The footing is getting rockier and more unstable, so I turn my attention to that. We travel in silence for a long time and eat our lunch on the move. When the passage gets narrower, we stop so I can call Lenox.

After I whistle for him, he appears above us almost immediately. He's very high up so it takes me a moment to see that Dathid is clinging to his tail again. Lenox is descending amazingly fast, and Dathid's joyful cry is echoing through the gorge.

Lenox dives toward the gorge floor and turns just before he smashes into the ground. Dathid, however, violently hits the dirt and rolls a few times before coming to a stop in a cloud of dust.

I'm about to run to his aid because Lenox might have seriously wounded him. But when the dust clears, he's sitting on the ground with his legs straight out in front of him, covered in a layer of dirt, all disheveled and laughing. Why is being smashed in the dirt funny?

"That was a lot of fun," he says with a wide grin.

Lenox lands gracefully a few feet away, then promptly gives Dathid a powerful shove to the ground. He laughs harder. He stands slowly and by the time he's back on his feet, he's reverted back to his overly serious self. "There's nothing up there."

"Good," Jonah says with a smile.

Dathid and Jonah engage in a brief conversation. I'm not sure what it's about because they're talking too low, but it might be provisions since they're packing Lenox's saddlebags.

"It's time to tell him to go to the other side," Jonah says to me when they're done.

I point to the small bag Dathid's holding. "Is that enough?"

"It'll do."

Once Lenox goes, almost all of our supplies go with him. I hope he comes back. I'm pretty confident he will when it takes a lot of coaxing before he'll leave me. But he flies overhead and keeps an eye on us.

The path grows increasingly narrow, and soon the plants thin out until there are none. Eventually, the walls are so close together we have to walk single file. Jonah is too big to fit through easily, so he ends up flattening himself along the gorge walls with only his hand sticking out, holding his staff. It's wondrous watching him shrink and elongate his body like a shadow in changing light.

Jonah leads the way, and Dathid follows behind me. The footing is rocky and treacherous and I fall down several times. Sometimes Dathid catches me, but usually he doesn't. I have to climb over enormous boulders that are lodged in the canyon and worse, jump down from them. I even have to crawl under one, which is terrifying. After we climb over yet another colossal boulder, I'm met on the other side by a deep crevasse that makes me freeze in fear.

"You'll have to jump," Dathid explains from over my shoulder.

"I can't." My voice sounds pathetic, even to me. I'm not an athletic person and the jump is well over six feet long. There's no way I'll make it.

Jonah easily crosses the chasm by elongating his body and materializing on the other side.

"I can't," I repeat to Jonah. My entire body is shaking.

"You won't fall. Jump to me. I will catch you."

"I can't." My hands are involuntarily balling into fists. My feet are numb. There's no bottom to the crevasse. It's just deep, dark nothingness.

"Agatha," Jonah asserts in a firm tone. "If you say you can't, you'll be right. Stop fighting fear, and ignore it. Listen to me. Jump!"

I try to move, but I can't. I remember Reason telling Hope not to argue with Fear and just ignore her. *Ignore Fear*. Jonah won't let me fall. I have to do this. I have to jump. *Stop thinking and jump*. I close my eyes and leap into the air as hard as I can.

I miss by a lot. My feet never come close to the edge. I scream when gravity starts to take me. Jonah grabs my wrist, wrenching me to solid ground and his comforting embrace.

"Are you alright?" he asks to the top of my head.

A surge of joy bursts from me with a giggle. "Ouch," I cry and pull away, playfully rubbing my shoulder.

He smiles at me. "Walk ahead a few paces so Dathid can cross."

Dathid's wings are too wide to expand in the narrow passage, but he's able to leap to the other side easily. Once everyone crosses safely, Jonah flattens himself against the wall and passes me in order to lead the way.

"That's really creepy, you know," I say to him.

"He can't talk when he's like that."

"Why?"

"I should've known that a question would follow. I don't know, ask him."

Our progress is slow and silent. I have to leap over several other crevasses, but none as wide as the first one, and my confidence grows with each jump. Dathid helps me over the boulders, but my legs are shaking and tired. I'm worn out from the difficult journey, and my whole body hurts.

"We'll be stopping up ahead," Dathid reassures me.

Once we slither under another huge boulder that's wedged firmly in the gorge, the walls open a bit so the three of us can stand together. Jonah materializes again.

"I wish I could do that," I say to him.

"It's convenient," Jonah responds, then looks at Dathid. "Let's make camp here. She can rest. We have plenty of time."

Dathid agrees as he swings the pack off of his back. He removes some biscuits and fruit and hands them out.

I sit on the ground, holding my food, but I'm too weary to eat. Jonah takes my dinner away and tells me that it's all right to sleep. I'm not sure if I lie down or if I fall over, but I'm asleep before I hit the ground.

CHAPTER 19

I awake sometime later in the dim light of the canyon. It's so disconcerting not having a change of daylight. I have no idea how long I've been asleep but it wasn't long enough. I sit up and Jonah hands me the food he took away earlier.

"Agatha, I told you how Gwa Twouroch works but I need to explain to you how to control it."

"Okay." I'm very much looking forward to this part of our journey. Finally, something fun.

"First, you should know that you won't be alone in your apprehension. Faeries don't like being underground."

I look up at Dathid. He shrugs his shoulders. I have no clue what that means, so I turn my attention back to Jonah.

"This should be reasonably easy, but it's essential that you control your fear. Every one of us will have a random thought. When that thought appears, replace it with another thought."

"So like, if I think of how many spiders would live in a cave like that, I instantly think of ponies and then the spiders go away and then the ponies are there?"

"Exactly."

"So don't think about spiders."

"No!" His reaction takes me by surprise. He sounds afraid. Maybe Jonah doesn't like caves either. He clears his throat and mellows his tone. "In order to tell yourself not to think about something, you first must think about it. So don't think about it. Think ponies."

"Okay. So I won't think about spiders or snakes or Ziras."

"Agatha, stop thinking about things you don't want to think about. What did I tell you to think about?"

"Ponies." I wish I would've said something different. I run images through my head, but I'm only seeing cartoon ponies. I might have seen a television show once that had ponies. Or was it a book? I should've said cars. I've seen a lot of cars.

"Yes, ponies." Jonah seems delighted with the pony idea; maybe ponies make him happy. I picture Jonah with one of the cartoon ponies, and a laugh escapes my throat. I cover it with a cough and no one's the wiser.

"—think about the different types of ponies you can imagine," Jonah says when I tune back into our conversation. I probably should've been listening. He's treating this like it's important, but he's overreacting. This cave sounds incredible. "—think about the things ponies can do, and all the pony facts you can remember," Jonah says, still talking.

I really should pay attention. However, I have no idea what ponies do. I want to switch to cars, but Jonah has been going on about the ponies for so long, I'd feel bad changing it now.

"Do you think you can do that?"

I wasn't listening again. Fortunately, because I never pay attention in school, I've honed my *make the teacher think you care* skills. I squint my eyes and tap my chin with my forefinger a few times. Then I look at Jonah and shout, "Pony!" I giggle at my own humor, but Jonah doesn't think I'm funny. He must be very frightened of this cave.

146

"All right, I guess we go," Jonah grunts to Dathid before he turns to me. He puts his hand on my shoulder and looks me in the eye. "Agatha, the cave is short, so we won't be in there long. Just keep your thoughts under control."

The canyon snakes along as we climb to where the gorge walls meet. The cliffs have been growing closer together all along our journey, but now we've reached the part where the top of the gorge closes in on itself, leaving a triangular hole at the base.

I saw a commercial once for caves in Pennsylvania. I thought this would be like those, giant openings with walkways, handrails, and lights. But it's not like that at all. It's dark and spooky. What if I can't control my thoughts?

Jonah looks at me. "Ponies."

"Ponies, ponies, ponies," I repeat, trying to hide my apprehension.

The cave is so dark it's like walking into a black hole. I force myself to not be afraid. Once we're inside, Jonah stops and bangs his staff on the floor a few times to make it glow. It illuminates a good portion of the cave, and the bit of anxiety I had vanishes.

I thought it would be as narrow as the canyon, but the roof is several stories high and it's wide enough for us to walk next to each other with room to spare. The walls and ceiling of the cave are covered with numerous stalactites. Some of them are so immense they reach the floor, making peculiar columns and chambers. I'm more intrigued than scared, although I'm not looking forward to going any deeper into the dark hole.

I nearly jump out of my shoes when a loud rumble echoes from the depths of the cave.

"Sorry. Sorry. That was my thought," Dathid says with a laugh. "Had to get that one out, I guess. It's gone." He looks around at us but doesn't make eye contact. His expression changes to one that's even harsher than usual. "Ponies, right?"

A few paces away, a cute black and white spotted pony appears. It's so sweet, with its poofy mane and big brown eyes that my heart melts. I'm glad we decided on ponies. They're so adorable.

My eyes travel over the pony and then back up to the extraordinary ceiling. I follow its assortment of contours until my eye catches a small stalactite that reminds me of a bat. I wonder how many bats live in here?

A massive whooshing sound rushes past me as a flood of bats whip toward us. I scream and jump around when they hit my face and body. Bats are everywhere. I'm frantically spinning and screaming. I'm being pummeled by flying rats. I'm both revolted and terrified. I hate creepy, crawly, dirty rodent things!

Jonah fights his way toward me through the overabundance of bats and wraps himself around me, shielding me from the swarm.

Over my screaming, Jonah shouts, "Ponies! Ponies!"

I clench my eyes tight and chant, "Ponies. Ponies. Ponies."

The bats dissolve as quickly as they materialized. This was a bad idea. I don't know what made me think I could do this. I'm afraid to stop talking, so I keep repeating myself. I want to make sure those bats are gone.

When Jonah lets me go, I open my eyes to see that the entire cave is packed wall-to-wall with ridiculously colored ponies. They're real, but they're cartoonish in both hue and proportion. I can't even get the stupid ponies right. Neither we nor the ponies can move because there are way too many of them. The tears threaten to start. I thought this would be fun.

"It's alright, Agatha. It's good. We can work with these ponies," Jonah says reassuringly. "Just keep talking. Ponies."

We can't take a single step. The ponies are pressed against us and although Jonah is trying to push them aside, there's nowhere for them to go. Dathid unfurls his wings and lifts himself over the herd. It's a good idea, but he only makes it a few feet when the ponies spook and kick.

He tries to land, but a pony now occupies his previous place. He flutters around searching for another spot but there's not a single space. He finally gives up and just lands, ending up on all fours, on top of several ponies. However, as soon as his weight is on them, their fear turns to anger and they thrash about. The other ponies follow suit and soon the entire pack is agitated, biting and kicking at each other and us.

"Happy ponies," Dathid says.

"Happy ponies," I repeat and the ponies calm down.

"Agatha, climb up on the ponies like Dathid," Jonah orders.

It's difficult, but there's nowhere to fall, so I'm not scared. I'm afraid of hurting the cute little ponies, and my suspicion is confirmed when I crawl to another one and it screams and kicks as if it's in pain. Soon the entire herd joins the fray.

"Happy ponies!" Dathid and Jonah say in unison.

"Happy ponies," I repeat and they settle down.

It's difficult figuring out the best way to climb from pony to pony. I'm trying not to feel foolish for packing the cave with so many. I'm trying not to think of anything at all while navigating over the sea of furry bodies. When I travel a good distance from Jonah, his glowing staff comes up beside me and I notice his shadowy form attached to it. It's comforting having him here, even if he can't talk to me.

"Happy ponies," I repeat.

It's taking a long time to maneuver over the herd. They're quiet and content, even though two people are climbing all over them. But crawling on all fours over the shifting mass is difficult; my arms are shaking and my badly bruised knees are sore. I'm trying not to notice my pain and doing everything I can to concentrate on keeping the group happy.

It's slow going, but Dathid and I are making progress. We're about halfway through when Dathid looks at me and slowly says, "One pony."

"One pony," I repeat and then slam to the ground when the ponies vanish. The fall isn't far, but I wasn't prepared for it, so I give myself a good jolt. I don't spend long on the floor because I've just hurt myself and I'm struggling to keep my thoughts together. I don't want to think of anything that's wrong.

When I get to my feet, the little black and white pony from earlier has returned. "One pony!" I shout and laugh.

Jonah materializes next to me. "One pony." His tone implies that he wishes he'd thought of that earlier.

With the cave free of ponies, the walk is easy. The path is wide and the footing is good. I'm following the pony, which is leading the way, and letting my eyes wander around this amazing place. I've never been in a cave before and I haven't seen many pictures of them either. This is an entirely new experience and it's surprising that I'm enjoying it so much because usually, I don't like new things.

This cave has so many twisting and turning alcoves that I really wish we could explore. We pass one particularly interesting stalactite that has stretched all the way to the ground in an exquisite rotating pattern that's breathtaking. I take my mind off the pony for a second when my eyes follow the multifaceted column up to the top of the cave and back to the other stalactites above us. I'm transfixed by the bulky yet delicate formations jutting from the ceiling in the most intricate arrangement.

The image above me blurs when Jonah yanks my arm so forcefully he lifts me into the air. I'm confused and both, physically and emotionally hurt, that he would do that so unexpectedly. My face stings, but I can't figure out why. Jonah is propelling me forward when an explosion erupts to my right.

It's a stalactite, falling from the ceiling. Chunks of rock pummel me. I tumble to the floor. Another stalactite crashes next to my head. Jonah grabs the back of my pants and tosses me to my feet. It's raining rock. I glanced up at the stalactites and wondered what would happen if they fell. It wasn't a real thought, just a brief flash. Now we're running for our lives as more and more stalactites fall.

CHAPTER 20

"Ponies! Ponies!" I scream. The stalactites dematerialize. I smash into a pony because the cave is once again packed.

I can't even do one stupid thing like control a random thought. This part of the journey should've been easy and fun, but I'm messing it up. Dathid is right. I'm too stupid to do this.

I'm diving deep into my self-loathing when I'm loudly interrupted by a deafening thud that knocks an involuntary yelp from me. It sounds as if something huge is moving toward us.

The ponies disappear and my blood chills, sending shivers down my arms. I don't know what's heading our way because I don't know what I thought of. Whatever it is, it's big. I'm so frightened I can't concentrate enough to make the ponies come back.

When the exceptionally large and malicious Dathid appears, the shock on the real Dathid's face is almost comical until the giant Dathid swings his sword at him. The real Dathid draws his sword too and deftly blocks the hit, but the gigantic Dathid is undeterred, striking again and slamming the real Dathid to the ground. He rolls over, slices the ankle of the giant and jumps to his feet.

I'm so overcome with embarrassment that I can't stop gaping and make the ponies come back. I can't believe I thought of a giant Dathid. "I'm going to die," I say aloud.

It's an expression, *die of embarrassment.* I don't mean it literally, but without warning, my air stops. I can't breathe. I'm choking. I wildly slap at Jonah, who is engrossed in the fight between the two Dathids.

He forcibly grabs my arms and shouts at me. My panic is making his words incomprehensible. I'm going to die in this strange world, in this strange cave, with these strange people.

"Agatha!" Jonah screams, his voice wavering with terror. "You are alive! You are alive! Ponies. Bring the damn ponies back! You are alive!"

My knees buckle and Jonah holds me up by my shoulders and shakes me. My vision tunnels and dims as Jonah's voice warbles.

"You are alive! You can breathe!"

I'm alive? It's a question, but my air comes back in a rush.

"I can breathe." I gasp and cough. After a few more breaths, I push away from Jonah and announce, "I can breathe and I can bring the ponies back!"

The multitude of ponies returns. Giant Dathid looks around, baffled, and sheathes his sword. The real Dathid wordlessly folds over and collapses against a green pony. He lies there motionless until, finally, he stands and rubs a hand down his ashen face. He slowly sheathes his sword and shakes himself off. A lavender sky appears above us, and the cave gets brighter. I didn't think of that, so it must be Dathid's thoughts.

I jump when a door slams.

I know that noise. Uncle's home. I'm in trouble.

The cartoonish ponies explode into mounds of paper, broken furniture, and clothing. *Ugh, that smell.*

The trash pushes me into a corner. I'm struggling to swim to the top but I'm being buried alive. Jonah reaches out to me, but the wall to my bedroom closes him off. I fall to the garbage-strewn floor. Am I shaking from fear or the rumble of tons of trash piling up throughout the cave?

I've trapped myself in a small cell. Auntie's television is the only noise when the rumbling stops.

"Hello," Uncle calls out.

"She's in her room, pouting," Auntie yells back.

"Stay calm. They're not really here," I whisper as I sit on the floor next to my bed. "This is not my room."

On the wall that blocked out Jonah are drawings, depictions of my experiences in Ashra that resemble my paintings. It's done exactly in my style, all jumbled together and random. But I didn't paint them.

"I'm in a cave," I whisper through pants of air. "Uncle is not here. He is not mad. I've done nothing wrong."

"You better have brought her Highness some dinner because it's all I've been hearing about," Auntie yells.

"I never said anything." I want to shout at her but I'm barely whispering. My hands are shaking. I wipe the sweat from my forehead just to make them do something.

"I said I would! Seriously, Liz, you need to do something about these cats. Cats were never part of the arrangement. You can't smell that?"

I've locked myself in a room made of the debris scattered around Queens and collected by Auntie. The top of Uncle's thinning red hair is visible over the wall to my left as he walks up to the giant Dathid.

"You need to go. You don't belong," Uncle orders and the giant Dathid disappears without argument.

Uncle walks past the real Dathid as if he doesn't exist and stops in front of a half-wall of newspapers and magazines. He glares down at me on the floor. I bow my head and try to think about what I could've done to make him mad.

154

"I'm not in Queens. It's not my birthday. This isn't real."

He plops down a bag of fast food and a milkshake. "What are you mumbling about?"

In the bag are two cheeseburgers and a small order of fries. It's a standard meal but the cookie-dough milkshake is special. Uncle doesn't know that, but Auntie does. She must have told him to get me that milkshake for my birthday. Sometimes Auntie remembers me.

"Auntie is my prison guard. I thought of the dinner and the milkshake. She did not remember," I whisper.

"How about a thank-you?" Uncle snaps.

I lower my eyes. "Thank you, sir."

He's looking at my paintings on the wall. My chest tightens with the exposure. I don't want people to see my work, especially Uncle. "What's this?" His face contorts with anger. "How do you know of this?" He's glaring at me with rage in his eyes.

I shake my head. "I don't know how I know."

"What's she doing now?" Auntie yells.

"Have you seen what she's been up to?" Uncle shouts back. "Get your butt off that recliner and get in here. You're supposed to be watching her."

"Calm down," Auntie yells, obviously not getting up. "It's just those stupid stories she draws. She fancies herself an artist. It keeps her quiet."

"Liz! Get over here!"

When Auntie and Uncle fight, it's always bad for me. I shouldn't have painted those things. I shouldn't have made such a big deal about dinner.

"Excuse me," Dathid says, pointing to the bag. "May I?"

Uncle loses interest in the wall as he stares, bewildered, at Dathid, who is cautiously reaching into the bag to pull out a long French fry. He smells it and then bites it in half. Uncle is shocked out of his hostility. "Who are you?"

Dathid nods his head at the fry and offers the remainder to Uncle. "Dathid, and you?"

Uncle looks so small staring up at Dathid. And old. Uncle always seemed so large and scary, but now he's an ordinary old man.

"Paul Johnson. How did you get in here?" Uncle's anger returns hotter than before. "Liz! Did you know she has a guy in here?"

"These are delicious." Dathid offers Uncle a fresh fry. Then he takes a sip from the straw and makes a face. "That is not. How can you drink that?" he asks me.

I almost smile, but then Uncle shakes his head. "Agatha," is all he needs to say to make my stomach drop.

"I'm sorry," I whisper. "I don't know how he got here."

"Don't try to explain your way out of this!" Uncle yells.

I press my lips together. The more I say the worse this will be. If I stay still and silent they'll forget about me.

"What's she doing now?" Auntie pushes herself between Dathid and Uncle. She slowly eyes Dathid up and down, and with a smile that is disturbingly flirtatious adds, "Never mind. How'd a mouse like her find this one?"

Dathid offers her a fry.

These three don't belong together. Dathid should go. I'm in a lot of trouble. He shouldn't be here.

Dathid takes another gulp from the shake.

"I thought you didn't like it," I say.

"Now it's Pheihl Ale," he says with a grin. "I can think of stuff too."

156

"I don't know what you think you're doing, but this is not right," Uncle says. "Your friend needs to leave! And never come back, or I'm calling the authorities. I'm going to the store to get some paint. You are repainting this vulgarity tonight. You are not an artist. You are nothing. Do you understand me?"

I nod. "Yes, sir."

Dathid meanders over to the wall. He traces the sea serpent with his fingers and studies Lenox. Him looking at my art is worse than Uncle. I've exposed the deepest part of my soul and now he's entitled to judge it. Uncle criticizes everything I do, so I'm used to it. No one else has ever seen it.

"This is good. You have talent."

The compliment shocks Auntie and Uncle silent. Some kind of energy runs through my body. I don't like it, so I take a deep breath to make it pass.

Dathid kneels next to me. "You need to stop this. Remember the pony."

I nod. A painting of the spotted pony appears on the wall.

"I think we need to call someone," Auntie says. "This girl is out of control! It's that school. I knew it was a bad idea."

"One pony," Dathid says softly.

"One pony," I repeat.

The trash explodes and Auntie screams. Dathid wraps his arms around me and shields me from the papers and garbage flying everywhere. When it settles on the ground, it disappears. All that remains is the little black and white pony standing sweetly where Uncle used to be.

The wall to my room disappears and Dathid lets me go.

Jonah rushes to my side. "Are you alright? I could hear, but I was locked out." He picks me up in a big hug and squeezes me tight.

"I'm good. Very good. Me and the pony are good."

The purple sky reappears and Dathid walks far ahead of us.

I focus all my attention on the pony as we travel through the cave in silence. I keep a hand on it and stroke it frequently. His name is Munson, after my third-grade teacher, Mr. Munson, because they have the same hair. Mr. Munson had wild hair that would start out under control in the morning, but by the end of the day, it was a cloud of brown frizz surrounding his head. Other than that, I'm not sure why I chose that name, but it was the only one I could think of without really thinking too much. I'm doing everything I can to keep my mind focused on Munson.

The sky fades out and it's obvious that Dathid has left the cave. I'm sad I have to leave Munson behind. I'll miss the little guy.

"Is there any way I can make him real?" I ask Jonah.

"He's as real as your thoughts."

I say goodbye to my pony and walk out of the cave. I'm glad I thought of ponies instead of cars because I enjoyed my time with Munson. Plus, if I packed the cave with cars, I might have killed us all. I glance back to have a last look at the tiny pony, but he's already gone.

CHAPTER 21

The light is much brighter on this side of the gorge. The sky is similar to Earth's vivid cerulean blue with frothy corn-silk clouds, although there are still two moons. The dimmer moon is somewhat more visible and so are the dim purplish outlines of the other planets. It's not exactly like Earth, but it's comfortingly familiar.

We're on a dirt path in a meadow at the top of a hill. In the distance is a liberal smattering of farms and houses dotted over the rolling hills, connected by intersecting, tree-lined cobblestone streets. The trees and grass are an intense green. Are they truly more vibrant than normal trees or do they seem more brilliant because I've been in such dim light for so long? Paved roads and blue skies..."I like this place."

Dathid is sitting on a tree limb with his back against the trunk and his head in his shaking hands. I don't know what's wrong, but I'm guessing the trip through Gwa Twouroch was rough for him, too.

Lenox lands in front of me and starts his inspection. He thoroughly sniffs my hair before giving me a good thump to the face with his nose.

"I wish you would stop with the head bashing." I try to be stern, but I'm just too happy to see him. However, some of my exuberance soon diminishes when he gives my face a big sloppy lick. Once he's satisfied that I'm in good shape, he checks on the other members of our party, and Jonah removes the packs from his back.

"Let's make camp here," he shouts over to Dathid. "We saved some time by going through Gwa Twouroch so we don't need to hurry."

"No," Dathid says in a gruff voice. "I can go on." He jumps down from the tree and slowly walks toward us.

"Well, let's at least take a rest. We could use one." Jonah says it in such a way that we know it's an order, not a request.

I can't face Dathid. First I showed him what a monster I thought he was, and then I bared my soul.

"Agatha, ask Lenox to catch us some lunch, and then go ask the trees for some wood."

I should be happy that Jonah gave me the excuse I needed to leave, but seeing how shaken Dathid is makes me want to stay. I give Lenox his instructions and slowly walk to the trees; Jonah never said I couldn't listen to their conversation.

I watch as Jonah puts a reassuring hand on Dathid's shoulder. "Are you alright?"

"Yeah, I am. That giant was just…bizarre." He shakes his head like he's trying to clear it. "It was like contemplating suicide. Do I have what it takes to kill myself? That thing…that was me. Was it me? Would it kill me?"

"I can't comprehend how that was for you. I'm sorry you had to endure such a trial."

"I've fought in many battles and have killed more enemies than I care to remember. I've held my dying friends in my arms…" Dathid's words trail off when he gets lost in his memories.

He raises his stricken face to Jonah. "*Was* that me? I mean, it fought like me. I had a difficult time trying to figure out how to outmaneuver myself. I couldn't control my thoughts." He's talking rapidly, but then he abruptly stops and glances pleadingly at Jonah.

Jonah stands with him in silence while Dathid relives the encounter in the cave. When Dathid returns to the present, Jonah whispers, "No, that wasn't you. That was a little girl's interpretation of you."

"That's just it," Dathid says loudly, becoming more animated. He pulls away from Jonah and paces. "It wasn't all her. Initially it was. She made it appear, but I fueled it! I made it attack. Those were my thoughts. That was my violence!"

Jonah lets him pace. Only when Dathid slows his steps does he speak. "Dathid, you're a warrior. You've been through a lot and you are under tremendous stress. You have fought in countless battles over countless years. You swore an oath to protect her. You did just that, even if that meant battling yourself."

Dathid stops moving and stands with his head down. Jonah puts a hand on the back of his neck. "You did what you had to do in an extremely abnormal situation. You would battle anything she thought of, including yourself. You did the right thing."

Jonah gives Dathid a push to start him walking. They slowly make their way over to the pile of packs on the ground. Jonah digs through one and pulls out a small flask that he promptly hands to Dathid. He takes a long swallow, then follows it up with a short gasp of air.

Dathid passes the flask to Jonah. "I had a moment of blind panic when she locked you out. I think she forgot I was there. I wasn't sure I could get her back. Never had to do anything like that before."

Jonah takes two swigs from the flask. "I could hear you guys, but I couldn't get through. It was an impressive feat of mind control that she could so completely lock me out. You did well battling that."

Dathid shakes his head. "Have you ever eaten a French fry? The smell of the food overpowered the smell of whatever that place was."

"That was her home?"

Dathid grimaces with disgust. How far down into humiliation can I sink? Not only did he see my paintings, but he saw how I lived and how Auntie and Uncle treated me. He doesn't even like my favorite foods.

"I was ready for spiders," Dathid announces.

"Is that what that thing was in the beginning? I *thought* I saw a giant spider."

"Yeah," Dathid says with a laugh. "I was preparing for it and then there it was. I'm glad I made it disappear before she saw it."

They both laugh and then Dathid lifts the flask and shouts, "Happy spider!"

I'd been watching from the shadow of the trees. I turn away, sad and embarrassed. This is what I deserve for eavesdropping. I sulk over to the trees and choose one that has some dead wood. It's not singing, so I'm self-conscious when I have to speak to it.

"Excuse me," I whisper.

The tree doesn't acknowledge me. Dathid and Jonah are sitting against the packs and Jonah is drinking from the flask. They're not paying any attention to me, so I get a bit braver.

"Excuse me," I repeat in a firmer tone.

"Agatha Stone!" the many-voiced tree says.

I'm taken aback that it knows my name until I remember that the village knows I'm on the way. It's reasonable to assume that the tree would know too, but it's still unnerving.

"Hi, um." I stop when I lose my nerve. Demanding wood might be rude, so I decide to make conversation first. "What kind of tree are you?"

"What kind of tree are *you*?" the tree repeats.

"I'm not a tree. I'm a human."

"I'm a human too."

I understand Dathid's judgment of trees. I'm already getting tired of this.

"You're not human. You look like a maple."

The tree gasps and the other trees laugh.

"I am no maple!"

The tree's indignation would've been more intimidating if its voices weren't so high pitched. It almost makes me giggle. "Well then, what are you?"

"I'm a palm tree."

"You are no palm. I once knew a Yucca that was very good at world history. I know you're no palm."

"I'm a palm! In fact, I'm a Royal Palm," it says, shaking its branches theatrically. The other trees erupt in laughter. "Make that a Queen Palm."

Just my luck. I pick the tree that wants to be a comedian. I turn to see if Jonah and Dathid can see me, and I'm horrified to discover them watching me struggle with this useless tree. I'm already irritated, but now a hot flash of pink stretches across my cheeks.

"Give me your deadwood, you stupid maple, or I'll grab an ax and chop all of you down!"

The laughter abruptly stops and the tree next to the one I've been talking to drops all of its deadwood. It's a lot more than I need, so I gather what I can and leave the rest. I thank the tree that helped me and make a face at the rude one.

When I return, Jonah has me stack the wood in a neat pyramid, and I help him light the fire. I'm proud of myself for doing another thing on my list of things I thought I'd never do.

I sit with my back against one of the packs, hypnotized by my fire until a dead animal drops at my feet with a loud splat. I jump up in revulsion as Lenox lands noisily in front of me. I barely acknowledge him because I can't stop staring at the nauseating carcass. It looks like a sheep, except that it's almost perfectly round and doesn't appear to have legs. Its overabundance of wooly fur is impossibly white without a trace of black or beige on it. I think the head might be different too, but I don't know enough about sheep to say for sure.

Jonah and Dathid are more shocked than I am when the sheep thing plops in front of us. They both look around and then at each other. "It's already dead," Dathid says with a shrug. Then he drops to his knees to clean it.

Jonah turns his attention to me. "You need to explain to your pegasus that if he poaches domesticated animals, the farmers here will put a bounty on his head. His kind aren't welcome here."

"What is it? Is it a sheep?"

"No, it was bred with sheep a long time ago, which is why they're so similar. It's a *kaddamoll*. The farmers here breed them for their wool."

I don't ask any more questions because he wants me to talk to Lenox right now. It takes a while for me to get Lenox's attention because he's a good distance away, watching something flying through the trees. I explain the situation to him, but I'm not sure he comprehends or cares about what I'm saying.

When I rejoin the group, the sight is so gruesome that a bit of vomit rushes up my throat. Dathid has removed the head of the kaddamoll and has hung it by its back legs over a tree limb. There's a bucket under the deflating kaddamoll, collecting the muddy brown fluid that's leaking from the stump of its neck.

I turn away to find Dathid digging through the packs. After some serious searching, he removes two cups. He dips them in the bucket and then casually strolls over to me. "Here," he says, holding out the cup to me. I can see the light brown chunky liquid sticking to the side of the cup and I'm afraid to grab it.

"Here," he repeats, bringing the cup closer to me.

I force myself to reach out and take it. My fingers touch the warm, gummy slime and I almost drop the cup. I stand with the tepid cup of sludge in my hand, and Dathid nonchalantly walks away. He picks up the bucket and gives it to Lenox, who dives into it with loud slurping noises. If I vomit, it will match what's in the cup.

He returns to find me still staring at the cup. "I take it you've never eaten an herbivore before."

I stare blankly at him with wide eyes that refuse to blink, and shake my head.

He smiles at me for the first time. He's a handsome guy even when he frowns, but when he smiles it's disarming. Dathid being nice makes me feel wrong for keeping my guard up around him. The smiling is much more disconcerting than the frowning.

"They don't have meat or bones like the carnivores. They're just fluid."

I shake my head again. The camel-colored muck inside the cup has swirls of teal and pink with small brown chunks floating just below the surface. I don't want an animal to die for nothing, but I can't bring myself to bend my elbow.

"It tastes really good," he says, trying to be encouraging. "You probably ate something similar to it at the Feast of the Faeries. I guess no one told you what it was."

165

I continue to stare at the cup, trying to will myself to drink its contents. I appreciate his efforts, but I can sense his growing discomfort. I want to end the awkwardness between the two of us and drink the putrid swill, but my arm refuses to move.

"I don't understand. Is it the fact that it's raw, or that it's a liquid?"

Just the question makes my stomach flip. I want to answer. I want to try to have a conversation with him, especially after the incident in the cave. I can't believe he's being so nice, particularly now that I've shown him that I think he's a monster.

He puts his hand over mine and we hold the cup together. "If I held the cup for you, would it be easier?"

The contact shocks me out of my stupor. "No," I say meekly. "I can do it."

Dathid lets go. I close my eyes and raise the cup to my mouth. *Drink!* I command myself.

I take a sip and prepare to throw it up, but it's delicious. Dathid's right, I ate something similar to it in Manahata. I'm really glad no one at the party told me what it was. It's sweet and creamy, with a caramel nutty flavor that's similar to drinking a caramel sundae.

He smiles wide. "I told you it's good."

I finish the rest of the cup without incident until I glance up and see Lenox licking the decapitated corpse hanging in the tree.

"Lenox, stop that!" I yell, but he ignores me.

Dathid casually cuts down the shriveled kaddamoll and brings it back to the mound of packs.

"We're taking that with us?" We've never taken any other remains with us before.

"Yeah, the farmers here primarily breed them for the wool. Although this one was killed, its wool is still valuable. We will take it to the village and find its owner."

As I watch Dathid work, I'm ashamed by what I did to him in the cave. "I'm really sorry about what happened earlier," I say to my feet.

He looks up in surprise and then shakes his head. "You've got nothing to be sorry about. You did quite well. Many people go into the cave and never come out. Or if they do manage to get through it, it haunts them forever. So no harm done, you did fine."

It's surprising he can be so calm. I'd be devastated if someone thought of me that way. Maybe Dathid is just a quiet guy with an unfortunate propensity to frown. I'm ashamed to admit that he has, in fact, been rather nice to me. He's done all of the cooking and most of the cleaning and has never asked me to help. I'm embarrassed to remember that I never offered my assistance, either. He's actually never done anything mean to me, except maybe be a little impatient. But I've been comparing him to Jonah and that's unfair; Jonah is the personification of patience and calm.

"Thank you," I say shyly.

"You're welcome." He nods and walks away.

"I just want you to know…" I blurt out but then lose my nerve when he turns back around. I take a deep breath and force myself to speak. "I want you to know that I don't think of you that way. I mean…" I pause again because my courage is waning. A few tears threaten to seep from my eyes, and my embarrassment amplifies. "I mean, I don't think you're mean. You've really been very kind to me. I want you to know that I did notice. I'm not used to people taking care of me. And, well, I want to thank you because you've done a lot and I shouldn't have thought what I did and I'm sorry."

Now it's Dathid's turn to be self-conscious. "You're welcome. You don't need to apologize for a random thought. I was also having some trouble, so I guess we're pretty equal. I'm not good with people in general and I've never had any dealings with humans."

He slides a hand across my back to give me a sideways hug then pushes me forward a few steps. "Come on, you can help me pack."

CHAPTER 22

"They're on the way. They just crested a hill by the Saldeven's farm," Dathid says to Jonah. We'd barely started down the dirt path when he spotted the carriage heading our way. He doesn't look happy about it. Of course, I wouldn't know what a happy Dathid looks like.

I'm so excited I'd jump up and down if my feet didn't hurt so bad. "Finally, something with wheels. I'll never walk again! Seriously, I swear on this day, that I'll only ever walk to the corner store and back, that's it. I'm not made for hiking, or for that matter, exercise in general. And I'm never doing it again."

Jonah laughs. "It's good to see some of your fight back."

He shocks me into silence. Sometimes I forget that he listens to me when I speak. I hope I didn't make him mad, but he's laughing, so I think I'm good.

It takes some time for whoever's driving to reach us, but we see them every time they come to the top of a hill. As far as horse-drawn carts go, this one is different from the carriages in Central Park. The wagon itself is linen-white with an open top and tangerine interior. The two matching orange horses at the front both complement the cart and add to its showiness.

"I've never seen horses that color before. It doesn't look weird or anything, just unique. Are there other horses where we're going and are they also interesting colors?" I ask, but no one answers. It's not until the carriage is almost in front of us that I notice the horns on the horses' heads.

"Those are unicorns!" I shout at Dathid. "You said unicorns were rhinoceroses!"

I slap him. He jerks away, which makes the contact with his elbow all the more gratifying.

He laughs at me. "I guess I lied."

The carriage pulls to a stop, and a petite older woman with a poofy, red bouffant hairdo jumps down from the driver's seat. In New York, only the more mature ladies wear long skirts with frilly jackets. However, this woman's suit looks like something women wore over a hundred years ago.

"Well, I'll be! I've never met a Knight Crawler. It's surely a pleasure," she says with an accent that's hard to decipher. She fans out her full sage-green skirt in an elaborate curtsy to Jonah. "The Queen welcomes you. Mrs. Albína Cutty. Honored to meet you, Sir. I will be providing your transportation to the castle. I was informed that English is the preferred language." As she dips down, she stretches out her hand and Jonah bows over it.

"Jonah. The pleasure is mine."

This is so official and proper. I hope she curtsies for me too. She probably won't because I'm a kid and not important like Jonah, but still a curtsy would be fun. Although if she does curtsy for me, do I curtsy back? Jonah bowed, so would I bow too? Now I hope she doesn't curtsy because that would be weird.

Mrs. Cutty is much stiffer when she turns to Dathid. Her curtsy for him is lower than Jonah's, but instead of lifting her hand, she holds her skirts and bows her head. "Your Royal Highness, it is truly an honor."

He tenses and gives her a slight bow. "The formality is unnecessary," he says with a frown, transforming back to grumpy old Dathid.

Mrs. Cutty steps in front of me and I can't stop staring at her sharp-featured face. Everything about her has a keen edge, from her narrow body to her long face and angular chin that accents her downward-sloping nose. Even her ears are pointy. I can't decide if her face is beautiful or threatening.

I'm about to stretch out my hand to shake hers when she curtsies so low, she touches the ground. I'm proud of myself for getting the grandest curtsy, but it's embarrassing.

"Agatha Stone, we are a grateful people," she says, with great reverence that adds to my discomfort. She stays on the ground, so I guess I'm supposed to say or do something.

"Mrs. Cutty, please," I say in a rush, growing increasingly mortified. "We don't do this kind of courtesy thing where I'm from. Please get up. That's unnecessary."

She rises looking perplexed. "Please, Miss, call me Albína."

I grab her gloved hand and shake it, which shocks her speechless for a moment. "Pleasure to meet you, Albína," I say too exuberantly.

She pulls her hand back and yanks more amber frills from her cuff before adjusting her perfectly tailored clover-green jacket. I'm about to apologize for manhandling her when she turns ghostly white and gasps. Lenox has walked up behind me. He's pressing against my back to get a better look at the unicorns.

As soon as the unicorns see him, they spook and almost break their rigging. Before anyone can move, Jonah

171

nonchalantly whispers some soothing words, and the unicorns relax. One even falls asleep.

I pet Lenox's neck until the tension eases from his muscles. He's still interested, but he's behaving for now.

"Goodness," Albína says, staring up at Lenox. "I've seen these before, but only the babies and only from a distance. They certainly do stop one's heart."

Jonah and Dathid load Lenox's packs into the back of the carriage. "Agatha, tell Lenox to stay here until you whistle for him. It should only be for a short time. He can't fly over the unicorns so it's safer if he stays until he's called."

Lenox doesn't take the news well. My heart breaks when he drops his nose to the grass and blows out a deep sigh. I do my best to comfort him, but it doesn't help. "I promise. As soon as I get to where we're going, I'll call for you. Okay?"

He keeps his head low and ignores me. I'm holding up the group so I have to go. I hop into the front seat and wish Jonah would've sat with me, but he's in the back next to Dathid. I've never ridden in a carriage before—or in a car, for that matter.

My feet are so badly blistered they're bleeding, but that pain is minimal compared to my legs. My back is sore and my arms ache. I can't imagine why my arms would hurt from walking, but I guess my body is mad at me for doing this to it. I'm glad it's over.

I try to sit back and relax, but the ride is too stimulating. Albína is chattering away to Jonah about things I don't understand, so I take the time to study the countryside. However, my eyes keep going back to the unicorns. Actual unicorns!

As far as I can tell, humans got the unicorn right, except for the color. These two are radiant orange—not an offensive traffic cone orange, but like everything else here, they're more vibrant than their equine counterparts on Earth. Their vivid lemon manes and tails bounce when they trot, and they have a puff of showy yellow fur on the backs of their ankles. Their horns are painted in an elaborate paisley pattern with appliquéd jewels of various colors highlighting the centers. I'm not sure I like the effect, but other than the horns and their color, they're just like horses, only bigger.

We trot down the lane and when we pass a farmhouse, Albína puts her hand on my leg and starts explaining. "That's the Bracknaugh farm. You'll be meeting them soon. You'll like them. One of the last to come over. From Northumbria, I think."

I don't know where Northumbria is, but I listen intently to Albína's explanation of each farm we pass. Cromsmead feels so homey to me. It's like Earth, but about five hundred years ago. The sky is blue, the grass is green and the kaddamoll graze on every hilltop. It's so quaint. I wish I could paint it.

When we turn a corner, I literally gasp when a giant castle appears before us, seemingly from nowhere. I saw glimpses of its vibrant peaks when we would crest a hill, but I thought it was the entire town, not a single building. The castle is gigantic and rivals anything I've ever seen in pictures.

The enormous jade-green castle walls are trimmed with glittering ruby and emerald colors surrounding sparkling windows and elaborate balconies. Its glittery appearance is enhanced by the acres of shimmering amethyst roof tile pitching up and down like a stormy sea. The skyline is pierced with more ornate, knife-like towers than I can count. And completing the wedding-cake structure are small cylindrical turrets penetrating evenly throughout the massive stone walls that surround the entire enclosure.

I gawk at the castle for so long that I'm not aware we're passing through a village until we're halfway through it. It's a tiny town poised in front of the castle wall. All the buildings are low to the ground with timber framing and thatched roofs, and are plain compared to their flashy neighbor. It's weird that such a large castle would be built in such a small town.

The town is giving me a strange sensation that I can't explain until I notice that there are no people in it. It looks to be recently occupied. All the buildings have well-maintained signs hanging above their doors in a language I can't read. Everything is cared for and neat. There are filled water buckets, and clothing hanging on a line, but there's not a soul in the village. It's eerily quiet with the exception of Albína's chatter.

When we reach the castle wall, I'm so happy I almost applaud when I see it has a moat with a thick drawbridge over it. As we cross, I gaze into the crystal clear cornflower-blue water and see large colorful fish swimming around. I look down both sides of the wall but it's so wide I can't see an end on either side.

I glance up and my heart skips a beat when we pass under the heavy and sharp iron gate that's suspended over us. The wall is thicker than I imagined. We're traveling through a narrow passageway that has been artfully cut through it. It's all beautifully carved with gruesome battling figures and small holes fashioned throughout the tunnel. I wish we could stop so I could examine it better.

The end of the tunnel has a slight bend and when we turn the corner, a loud, excited cheer rings out when we exit. It startles everyone in the carriage, including the unicorns.

CHAPTER 23

The swirl of noise and color pulsing through my body is making my heart beat erratically. I pray the ear-splitting roar is the ground cracking open so it can swallow me whole. *Run!* my brain screams, but I'm frozen like a statue. Hopefully the frenzied crowd won't notice me if I sit still enough.

Is this a parade? Can you have a parade with only one vehicle? There's a band playing and people are dancing in the street. It's definitely some kind of block party. Is this for me?

Little pointy people are flooding the street, shoving at each other to get a closer look at the carriage. They're not tiny like Santa's helpers, but they're small, like jockeys. They're dressed in overly elegant attire that doesn't match their rowdy behavior, but does highlight my dirt and remind me that I'm still in the black sweater and jeans I've been wearing for longer then I care to remember. I'm dirty and smelly, and I haven't combed my hair in over a week. Worse, I'm being compared to the beautiful Dathid and elegant Albína.

I close my mouth and plaster on a smile. Although my eyes betray me, I'll pretend to enjoy their admiration with some meek waves. The happy faces of the villagers passing by makes my stomach knot, so I turn my attention to the colorful architecture. I'm surprised that the village is inside the castle's walls, but then again, I don't know much about castles. Everywhere my gaze travels there are flowers, streamers and wreaths covering every surface. This can't all be for us. I want to ask Albína if elves normally decorate this way, but she wouldn't be able to hear me over the music and cheering.

We slowly progress through streets clogged with celebrating elves and eventually make it to the castle steps. I want to study the colossal building, but I don't want my admirers to think I'm being rude by ignoring them. I wave continually and count twelve towers before I get distracted by the massive gargoyle statues that are tucked into various nooks along the enormous jade-colored walls. I want to study the exquisite artistry longer, but Albína stops the carriage and everyone hops out.

Jonah smiles down at me. "Did you enjoy that?"

I half-heartedly smile back and am about to tell him how I really feel, but he turns away before I can answer. "Are you ready for this?" he asks Dathid.

Dathid's teeth grind together and he takes a deep, unsteady breath. "I knew this was part of it, so let's get it over with."

"What are we getting over?" I whisper to Jonah's back.

He doesn't have time to answer because a dark-haired elf, who's only slightly taller than I am, is charging down the stairs. His ultramarine blazer and lightly ruffled melon shirt are conservative by the elfin standards I've witnessed so far.

"Hello! Hello!" the strange little man shouts. When he reaches the bottom step, he collects his dignity and says formally, "I apologize for my tardiness. Cypus Turehart, at your service. It is truly a pleasure, Sir Agatha." He says this last part to my feet because his bow is so grand, his upper body bends parallel to the floor.

I think *Sir* is a title. And I think it's for men. Does this guy think I'm a boy? Albína's curtsy was amusing, but the bowing and the waving, and especially the cheering grates on my nerves. I've been invisible my entire life and now everyone is staring at me. I wish they would've warned me about the parade because I'm still so rattled from that ordeal that I may vomit on Turehart's shiny red boots.

I jump when Mr. Turehart rises with a clap of his hands, but no one notices me because he's already bowing to Dathid, who looks mad, uncomfortable, and bored, all at the same time. This bow is quicker than the one I got and when it's over, the elf gracefully leaps and spins in the air. "Her Majesty is waiting. Follow me."

We climb the stairs and enter the great hall. It reminds me of the gymnasium at my school, only because it's a giant rectangle and that's really where the similarities end. The fireplaces at each end are so massive they look like rooms unto themselves. It's funny that such tiny people would have such an enormous room.

The floors are a combination of shiny cobalt-blue stones and intricately woven rugs that change the vibrato of our shoes echoing through the chamber. I don't know where to look first as we walk around a colossal U-shaped table that fills the entire space. An ornate red and gold damask tablecloth covers the table and on it are colossal candelabras of various metals, colorful bouquets of flowers and more plates and flatware then I've ever seen in my lifetime. Who lives like this?

My eyes are traveling all over the room trying to find a place to focus. There's so much excess that I can't take it all in. The huge chandeliers are made of some kind of shiny coral red metal that's clashing with the tapestry behind it. That tapestry makes my eyes stop.

Depicted in amazingly fine needlework is a proud gilded elf standing with her foot on the neck of a fallen faerie, her sword piercing his heart through his open chest. I glance over at Dathid, but he's staring straight ahead. He seems tenser than usual, but it's hard to tell with him.

I catch Jonah's eye and direct him with a look to the tapestry. He glimpses over at it and then gives me an odd squint. I have no idea what that means.

I'm concerned for Dathid. Would these elves hurt him? That's such a weird thought. They're so jovial and truly ecstatic we're here. Neither Dathid nor Jonah are upset about it, so maybe the tapestry is old, but they should've taken it down anyway.

We exit the great hall, walk down a long corridor and enter a gallery that's almost as large as the room we just left. The room is practically empty except for the two soldiers who are flanking a set of beautifully painted double doors and watching Dathid closely.

I want to see his reaction, but I'm afraid of drawing any more attention to him. The doors open automatically. Mr. Turehart abruptly leaps to the side and bows as we walk past. It's such a gracefully undignified maneuver that I would laugh if I weren't so nervous.

This new chamber is considerably smaller than the other rooms we've seen thus far but unlike the other rooms, this one is packed with elves. The pressure in this place makes sweat drip down my neck. Everyone is staring at us. I want Jonah to hold my hand. Things are always safer when Jonah holds my hand.

I don't look at any of the faces staring at me. Instead, I focus on the two luxuriously dressed windows that we're walking toward at the far end of the room. With each step, the air tightens. When we stop, I pull my attention away

178

from the curtains and try not to notice that sitting between the windows, on a ridiculously ornate throne, is the Queen.

Her strong pointed features are even sharper on her pale, slender frame. She doesn't have the warmth of King Ohad. In fact, she seems cold, like if I touched her, she'd be physically chilly. I drop my eyes to the hem of her aquamarine gown. Should I make eye contact, or will she behead me for looking at her?

I cautiously raise my eyes up her lapis-blue robe but stop when I come to the neckline. There are so many jewels on the collar of that robe it's shocking her boney physique can hold it up. I skip over her face and choose to travel up her long wavy white hair until I come to the simple silver crown with jewels in varying shades of blue.

My knees almost buckle when it dawns on me that I've just given a Queen a thorough once-over. I can't breathe. She watched me do it, too. I bring my panicked gaze to her face and find her staring at me. The world tilts for a second and then an eerie calm washes over me. I like it until the room starts to fade. I wobble a bit and then remember to breathe. The room comes back into focus.

The Queen's attention fixes on Jonah, who gives her a bow, but Dathid just nods his head. I've already made such a fool out of myself that I'm afraid to move. Bow or nod? I'm not sure. She's staring at me again so I shrug my shoulders.

I can't believe I just shrugged my shoulders!

The Queen smiles like she's enjoying my discomfort. Her eyes turn from humor to suspicion when she glances at Dathid. Are they going to hurt him?

When she returns her attention to me, she asks in a heavily accented voice, "Agatha Stone, do you know who I am?"

The accent is so thick I can barely understand her. "No, ma'am."

"Do you know why you are here?"

"To get the key." I'm not sure if that's the right answer.

The Queen frowns. "Yes, in a broad sense, you are here to find the key. But do you know why you are in Cromsmead?"

"No, ma'am." The light-headedness is back. I've already made such a bad impression, I don't want to pass out, hit my head and bleed all over her shiny floor.

"I am Queen Ekecheiria. You are here to receive your training."

I turn my feet awkwardly and stand on the sides of them. I keep my eyes on my twisting hands. "Oh, yeah, right. I knew that."

The Queen turns back to Jonah and speaks in yet another language. This one is different from what Dathid speaks. Am I supposed to learn all these languages? I speak English good enough, and my Spanish is getting better, but that's it. Every new curra we've come upon so far has spoken a different language.

They're talking about me. It's rude when people discuss you right in front of your face. If she doesn't think I'm the right person for the job, she should just say so.

"She has tremendous courage and an eagerness to learn. Agatha is open-minded and a quick study," Jonah answers in English.

The Queen scowls but recovers. "Good. Good." After a moment, she smiles brightly. "Well, as you can see, the people of Cromsmead are celebrating your arrival. Tonight we have a grand party scheduled. Albína will be your secretary, as she's one of the few who speaks English. If you need or want for anything, all you need to do is ask."

And with that, we're dismissed.

CHAPTER 24

Albína weaves her arm through mine and chatters away as soon as we leave the Queen's presence. I'm not listening to her, I'm reliving my encounter with the scary royal. The Queen knows I'm a fraud. What will they do to me when I fail?

I push those dark thoughts down and force myself back to the present where Albína is still talking and guiding me through a maze of hallways. I turn to ask Jonah what he thought of the meeting, but he's gone. Dathid's not here either. I rip my arm out of Albína's grasp and spin in a frantic circle.

She grabs my shoulder. I try jerking away, but she's surprisingly strong for such a tiny person. I call for Jonah while fighting to escape from Albína's superhero grip.

Just as I break away, I catch a glimpse of her ashen face. Her mouth is open and her eyes are huge. I follow her horrified gaze behind me and see Jonah's long shadow sliding along the wall. My relief at seeing him is dwarfed by the realization that I didn't break her grasp; she let go. I can't even defeat an old lady. How will I battle a powerful specter?

As Jonah moves across the floor, Albína steps behind me and gasps loudly when he materializes.

"Are you alright?" he asks as soon as he can speak.

"Yes." I already feel foolish for getting so upset. "I didn't see you. I didn't know we were separating. Where did you go?"

"I apologize. I was distracted by Dathid. I didn't think how our separation would affect you."

My instincts were right. Dathid's in danger. I wish they would tell me stuff so I wouldn't have to figure it out on my own. They should trust me more. If they would've explained that we were splitting up, I wouldn't feel so stupid and childish now.

"No, I'm sorry. I should've known better." I'm embarrassed about freaking out when it's obvious he's worried about Dathid.

"Albína is escorting you to your room."

"But what about Lenox?"

"Oh, Lenox!" Jonah throws his hands in the air. "I forgot about him."

Whatever is going on with Dathid, Jonah is obviously concerned and preoccupied with it. I'm getting worried, too.

"Have your stable master meet us on the roof," Jonah barks at Albína. Then he gently grabs me by the shoulders. "I have to go back for a moment, but I'll join you in a few minutes so we can retrieve Lenox. Are you good with that?"

"Yeah, I'm okay now. I just got worried when everyone disappeared. I can handle Lenox by myself if you need to be with Dathid."

"Very good," he says and leaves.

I stare after his departing shadow, willing the tears to stay put in my eyes. Usually he hugs me and makes sure that I'm really okay, but this time he just left. I lied when I said I thought I could handle things and now I'm stuck. I wish I knew what was going on.

182

Albína's waiting for me to do or say something. We gawk at each other for so long we both grow uncomfortable.

"What would you like to do, Miss?" she asks.

That's when it dawns on me that without Jonah, I'm the one who has to orchestrate Lenox's care. I have no idea how to take care of an animal, especially a giant pegasus.

"Well," I say, in order to say something. I should've made Jonah stay with me. I remember some of what he said and repeat that. "We need to speak to the stable master. Can you tell him to meet us on the roof?"

"Certainly, Miss," Albína chirps and then barks orders in her native language to the others around us. Everyone scurries off until it's just Albína and me in the hallway. I like being the boss. No one has ever listened to me before. I wonder what else I can get them to do.

Albína is leading the way up and down a maze of hallways, happily babbling about what rooms are where and who is in them. I have no idea what she's talking about, but she likes to talk so I let her prattle on.

When we reach the roof, I can see all the surrounding farms for miles. From this viewpoint, Gwa Twouroch is just a green-covered mountainside. This view is so homey and familiar, which is weird because I've never been anywhere that wasn't covered in a multitude of buildings and concrete.

The rooftop on this section of the castle is flat and made of thick timbers that don't make noise when I walk across them. It has towers on both ends that form a barrier to the north and south, and in between the towers on the edge of the roofline are two sidewalls of staggered heights. It starts over my head, drops to my waist, then shoots back up again. It looks like square teeth.

I whistle for Lenox, and Albína jumps with a startled yelp. Then she shuffles behind me a second time when Lenox comes bounding in from above. It's funny that a woman so much older than me thinks I'm her protector, especially after she won our last battle.

Lenox lands and does his inspection. After I'm thoroughly sniffed, he turns his back and walks away. This is new and perplexing behavior. He might be angry that I didn't let him come with us. I try to face him, but he keeps turning his back to me.

"You're mad at me? I wasn't the one who decided to leave you behind. It's unfair that you're upset with me."

Lenox doesn't answer, but he does bend one of his oversized ears toward me. I don't know how to get him to not be mad, but I wish he'd get over it because Albína is watching.

"I'm sorry. I don't know how to ride you, and the unicorns thought you would eat them. Did you really want me to walk the entire way?"

Lenox tilts his head, but he still doesn't move.

"Listen, I'd gift some meat to make it up to you, but I'm not good at killing things, so you'll just have to accept my apology. I'm here to learn how to ride you so it won't happen in the future. Will you please forgive me?"

He flips his head back to face away from me and doesn't move. I stare at the back of his head, wondering what else I can do. Finally, he turns toward me.

Out of options, I hold out my arms and softly say, "Come here."

Lenox moves his whole body to face me. He walks over with his head low like he's in trouble. I pat him on the neck a few times when suddenly he lifts his head and pushes me to the ground.

"Do you feel better now?" I ask as I get to my feet.

I give him more pats and notice that Albína is shielding her body with the door we just came through.

"Albína, he won't hurt you. Come here and meet him. You'll see. He's quite sweet."

She steps unsteadily from behind the door and cautiously walks toward us while he watches her with interest.

"Lenox, this is my friend Albína. She's afraid of you, so be good."

He studies her as she approaches. I stroke his face. "He's really nice. See?"

She's just a few feet away when he lets out a loud hawk-like screech that makes me jump and sends her fleeing out the door. This time she closes it behind her.

"What was that, pegasus humor? That wasn't nice. Now I'm mad." I stalk toward the door.

Lenox follows with his head low.

"Albína, I'm sorry," I shout through the door "He was kidding. He won't hurt you. I guarantee it." I quietly listen for a response with Lenox waiting behind me.

He puts his head on my shoulder trying to make amends. "I'm not the one you need to apologize to," I say with a quick stroke to his velvety nose.

A few moments later the door opens. It's not Albína, but a short male elf yelling in Naga-Nuru.

I wait for him to stop and when he doesn't, I try explaining and then gesturing that I can't understand him, but nothing works. He just keeps shouting. Eventually, I walk away from him mid-tirade in order to search for Albína.

She's just inside the door. "Please come out here. I need your help. Why is this man screaming at me?"

The elf rages at her. I'm surprised when she fires back. She seemed so demure, but now the two of them are engaging in a lengthy argument. The fight seems to be escalating rather than diminishing.

Finally, I put myself between them, throw my hands up and order, "Stop!"

The shouting ceases so suddenly, I have to look at both of them to figure out what just happened. They're staring at me as if they expect me to say more, but I didn't think they would listen to me in the first place, so it takes me a moment to think of what to say next. "Who is this man and why is he yelling?"

The elf starts to speak again, but I ask him to stop and he does. I like being in charge.

"This is Mr. Galnoy, the stable master," Albína explains. "He says take your Wiltonshire demon somewhere else."

"Oh." I wish Jonah were here. I'm defeated already and I haven't even done anything yet. How can these people admire someone who can't even take care of a simple thing like sheltering her pet?

I pat Lenox on the nose and move toward the door. I keep my head down because I can't look at the mean Mr. Galnoy. As I pass Albína, I let her know what our next step should be; maybe one of the farms will take Lenox in. "I guess we'll go speak to the Queen."

Albína translates what I said and then Mr. Galnoy races in front of me, putting his hands up in a motion to stop me. He's talking quickly, but his tone has mellowed and he even smiles a few times.

"He says he apologizes for his bad manners." Albína translates, but makes a face to communicate that she doesn't believe him. "He's never taken care of a pegasus before and was just startled."

"Well, can he take care of him?"

186

Albína and Mr. Galnoy speak for a few minutes. Then Albína says, "Yes, Lenox will have to live here, and his meals will be delivered.

Before Albína can translate, Mr. Galnoy starts speaking again. Albína says something back and then she says to me, "He's not allowed to hunt while living here. And he must be kind to his caretakers."

Albína's translations are a lot shorter than the actual conversations she and Mr. Galnoy are having. She's leaving a lot out. Once the arrangements are made and I'm confident Lenox will be well taken care of, I reluctantly leave him in Mr. Galnoy's care.

CHAPTER 25

Albína happily prattles on about castle life as if the ordeal on the roof had never happened. She walks us through so many corridors, upstairs and then down, that I'm thoroughly confused and totally lost when we finally reach a room that might be mine. There's got to be some mistake though, because there's no way this room is for one person. It's huge.

The room is a maze of alcoves just like the castle. The entire place is awash in bright reds, deep greens, and royal blues in patterns I've never seen before. The whole effect is both beautifully intimidating and pleasantly cozy.

Behind the sitting area, in the center of the room, is a stone fireplace with a roaring fire. Beyond that is a canopy bed draped in thick soft fabrics of midnight blue with heavy gold fringe and so many pillows I can barely see the bed.

My eye travels up to the ceiling that is painted with a beautiful sky and small multicolored birds flying around big fluffy clouds.

"Those birds are moving!"

She looks up. "You don't have birds on Earth?"

"Yes, but those aren't real birds. They're painted and they're moving. How are they moving?"

"Those aren't real birds. You don't need to be frightened."

"How are they moving?" I ask again. "Seriously, I need to know. It's paint on a ceiling. There's no television screen or projector."

Albína speaks slowly as if she's talking to a frightened child. "Those are Latuus Birds. When they stop moving it's time for sleep, and when they sing, you wake up."

I give up. I've seen a lot of weird things in the past few days and this is just another oddity. Flying painted birds are what they have here, and I'll have to get used to it.

The room is round, so we might be in one of the towers. "I have a balcony," I announce as I gaze out the French doors to the enormous patio. "A gigantic room, in a castle, with a balcony. My life has changed so radically in less than a month."

I rip open the doors and dive onto another of the inviting sofas that matches the two inside. I flip to my back and stare up at the unmoving blue sky. This is what happy feels like. I laugh even though nothing is funny.

Noises from below make me walk over to the rail to investigate. The sidewall matches the up-and-down pattern of the wall on the roof, only this one is shorter so I can easily see over it into the surrounding village.

Elves are dancing in the street. There are tables set up with food and drinks, and a band is playing in front of a clothing shop. Everyone is having a fun time. This must be the celebration the Queen was talking about.

I walk back inside. "My room at home could fit on the bed. Heck, the entire apartment could fit in this room and we'd still have space left over for those giant sofas."

Albína ignores my comment. "Would you like a bath, Miss?"

"Yes!" I answer a bit too excitedly.

Albína leads me into one of the alcoves on the other side of the bed and my heart does a little leap. I might have

189

done a few dance steps, too. "I can't tell you how thrilled I am to have a fully functioning bathroom. I was worried that I'd have to use an outhouse like they did in the olden days."

She chuckles like I made a joke.

When she asked if I wanted a bath, I didn't think she meant an actual bath. I've never been in a bathtub before. This one is the size of a small pool and has its own alcove with arches. Exotic painted sea creatures swim across the walls and ceiling. I watch one swim over the stained glass window and dive to the bottom before swimming out of the casement. How is that possible?

She rummages through the cupboard and pulls out two glass jars, one with light green powder and the other with pale yellow. She measures out two scoops of the green powder and throws it into the tub. Then she adds a scoop of the yellow and the tub instantly fills with water.

I'm speechless. Three scoops of powder fill a gigantic tub with water in under a second. I want to ask her about it, but it'll be like the birds; it's just what they do here.

She pulls out some fluffy towels and a thick fuzzy robe. "Well, you're all set," she says. "There's a tray of toiletries in the corner. Did you need anything else, Miss?"

"No, I'm good. Thanks." I'm anxious to try out the tub.

"Very well. After you get in, close the curtains to keep it warm," she says over her shoulder as she leaves.

I run my finger through the water. I was expecting it to be thin like drinking water, but it's lighter, almost fluffy. The tub is wonderfully deep. When I sit the water reaches to just above my shoulders. It's difficult to scrub the dirt of the past few days off me because my body wants to float around, but I manage.

Once I'm clean, I give in and let the water push me wherever it wants. I end up floating on my back just below the surface with my arms outstretched. Only a small portion of my face is out of the water. I'm surprised I'm so relaxed because I don't know how to swim and water usually makes me nervous.

My body unwinds as the fish swim overhead, through the window and over the curtain. I wake up some time later and briefly panic, but settle down quickly after I remember where I am. I jump out of the tub; maybe they could install a shower for me.

Albína is waiting for me outside the door. "Sorry. I fell asleep. How long was I out?"

"Not long, Miss," she says as she walks into the closet and pulls out an elaborately embroidered gown and holds it up for my inspection.

"I'm not wearing that!" I blurt out a bit too harshly before I can stop myself. "I'm sorry." The gown is pretty, but it's also fussy, and big, and uncomfortable. "I'm more of a jeans and sweatshirt kind of girl. Do you have anything close to that?"

She puts the dress down and stands quietly, tapping her finger against her mouth. "There are pants used for riding and warring. Would you want that?"

"Yeah, thanks. That would be nice. I like to be comfortable." I'm glad she didn't force me to wear the gown.

Albína rushes from the room and returns a short time later with a more fitted version of the men's breeches, tall brown boots, an embroidered purple jacket and a yellow frilly shirt. I'm much happier with this selection, even if the clothes are still too flashy for my taste.

CHAPTER 26

"You're very pretty," Jonah says when I meet him at the steps leading to the Great Hall.

I'm so rattled by his compliment that my entire head gets hot. I lower my gaze to my feet. No one has ever told me that before.

The hall is packed with all kinds of strange creatures and tons of elves. As we walk the length of the enormous room, all eyes turn toward me. I'm probably going to trip or do something equally as embarrassing. It's hard enough just remembering to breathe. I regret the breeches because I'm the only female not in a gown. I should've done what Albína suggested.

Jonah steers me to the raised dais in the center of the U-shaped table. The Queen is sitting in the middle and on her left is an elf who I assume is her husband. On her right sits a beautiful elf who looks so similar to the pale Queen that she has to be her daughter. Next to the younger elf sits a miserable Dathid.

He's even more handsome in his fine clothes. He's wearing a black velvet jacket trimmed in gold with a high collar that circles his neck. His dark appearance is a stark contrast to the brightly clothed and frilly elves. He smiles at my defiant wardrobe choice, which makes me happier about my decision. I'm glad it brought him some joy because he's so despondent.

Jonah walks me up to the Queen and bows. I still don't know how to act with royalty, so I stand there like an idiot. The Queen smiles and then Jonah sits me next to her husband. "Your Majesty, this is Agatha Stone. Agatha, it is my pleasure to introduce you to His Royal Highness, King Terek."

The King stands for the introduction. We're the same height. "The pleasure is mine," he says with a joyful smile. "It is customary to shake one's hand in human. Is it not?" He holds out his hand and I shake it.

I want this dinner over with already. The King matches my silence with a beaming smile. He's much friendlier than his wife. He pulls my seat out for me and as soon as I sit, the food is served. It's obvious that I made them wait. I hope they aren't too mad about it.

The King pours a bright yellow liquid into my goblet, and Jonah takes it away. "My pardon, your Highness. Many human cultures don't allow their children the use of mood-altering substances."

King Terek laughs. "Of course, of course. My apologies. I have so many questions. You know, the humans and the elves lived together for so long. Now, we've all but forgotten about them."

I give the King an awkward smile. I'm so intimidated by being in front of such a large crowd and having to make conversation with a King that words can't even form in my head, let alone come out of my mouth.

Terek takes a bite of food and with his mouth full asks, "So, Agatha, where do you hail from?"

"Um," I say, trying to force the words out. "Um, New York?" It sounds like more of a question than an answer because I don't know how specific I'm supposed to be. "Queens. America."

The King chuckles. "New York. You don't say. There you were, under the faeries' noses this entire time. That Ziras is a clever one."

He turns his attention back to his food, and we quietly eat the delicious meal. Before I've even finished, more food is piled on my plate. I don't know if I'm supposed to eat it all. I'm already full, so I ask Jonah for help.

"They'll keep serving you until you stop. It's rude to have a guest with an empty plate."

That's the last time I'm able to talk to Jonah because King Terek begins his questions. I can answer some. I'm thirteen years old, lived with my foster parents, and so on. But for others, I have no idea. I've never been outside of New York. I've seen some of its landmarks on field trips, but that's really all I know about Earth.

"So, do humans remember the elves?" I've been dreading this question and had hoped he wouldn't ask it.

"Um…" I say, trying to give myself time to formulate an answer. The elves are clearly a proud people, and their culture is an aristocratic and formal one. "Um…" I say again.

"Sort of…there are stories, but they're kind of jumbled up. I also don't know a lot about what other cultures might have to say about elves. But in some of the stories I've heard, elves live in the woods and have arrows and things like that. Usually they wear green clothes of some kind. Oh, and they're magical. We remembered the pointy ears and they sort of got the height thing right."

The King waits for more but when I don't say anything else he adds, "Really? I heard we are tiny and work as slaves for a fat man, making toys for spoiled human children."

My heart skips a beat. "Yeah, there's that, too," I mumble.

King Terek laughs loudly. "Maybe I'll make you a toy later. Make you feel more at home," he says with a wink.

The Queen calls for the entertainers and I'm saved from any more conversation. I watch everyone not seated on the dais push the tables to the walls. Then an odd assortment of painted creatures that are just a bit over three feet tall bound into the center of the room. They have two sets of arms on each side of their stout body and a thick fleshy tail that they use as a third leg.

They juggle all kinds of objects and even each other, performing mesmerizing and dangerous acrobatics that make me jump with fear. Their show is so exciting and terrifying that I have to cover my eyes a few times. I enjoy every minute of it and clap loudly when it ends.

As soon as the performers have cleared the center area, the band plays a heartfelt song. No one moves, but all eyes simultaneously turn to the dais. My heart drops to my feet. Happily, it's not me they're watching but Dathid, who has just stood and is holding a hand out for the Queen's daughter.

They walk gracefully to the center of the room and perform a beautiful and formal dance. Everyone is watching them closely, and I'm surprised that Dathid dances so well. He and his partner would be perfect together if they both weren't wearing expressions that said they would rather be anywhere else.

Everyone in the room can feel the tension between them. It's obvious that the elfin princess doesn't like the faerie prince and he doesn't care much for her either. It was mean of whoever it was, most likely the Queen, to force them to do this dance. Although a glance at Her Royal Stuffiness confirms that she isn't happy about it either.

Others join the dance floor, and Jonah grabs my hand. "Miss Agatha, would you do me the honor of the first dance?"

I'm glad I'm sitting because the blood leaves my head so fast I get light-headed. I try to be sneaky about taking a few deep breaths, but when I see the humor in Jonah's eyes, it's obvious I've failed.

I shake my head. "No." A flat refusal is rude, so I add more words to soften it. "I don't dance. I don't know how. Not like that. Not to music like that."

Jonah smiles. "Well, you must learn sometime and there's no time like the present. It's a party. You have to dance." He pushes his chair back.

I don't want to get up because standing leads to walking, and walking leads to dancing. But I acquiesce because I can't disappoint Jonah.

He finds my hesitation funny. I glare at him. Considering how terrified I am, he should be happy I haven't thrown up on his shoes. I'm going to humiliate myself. This dance is done as a group. I have to switch partners at particular times and there are so many moves, there's no way I can do them all. Fortunately, I stalled long enough for the song to end by the time we reach the dance floor.

I giggle with relief. "Oh well." I shrug and turn to go to my seat. Unfortunately, Jonah doesn't let go of my arm, and another, livelier song begins.

He escorts me onto the floor and holds my hand out while bracing his other hand on my shoulder. He slowly steps to the side and pulls my wooden body along with him.

"Relax. No one is expecting you to know these dances. They're thrilled that you're making the attempt. Just enjoy yourself."

I put my free hand on his waist and stare straight ahead at his stomach. I try really hard to have a good time, which is a lot of work, which is not fun. It's easier to watch my steps, so I concentrate on the floor. I can't see Jonah's feet under his robes. Does he even have feet? I find my answer when I step on one. I step on the other a few moves later. He spins me, and I elbow my neighbor by accident.

Jonah tries to hide a laugh while I profusely apologize. "I hit that guy in the head. It's not funny." I don't finish the sentence before he loses his battle to not laugh and that makes me giggle too. "You're supposed to be the better person. Are you laughing at my bad dancing or that poor guy?"

Once I accept that I'm really bad at this, my body relaxes. Now that I'm calmer, it's easier for Jonah to spin me and stuff, and I get the hang of it. I think I'm doing alright, until the third spin.

On that particular move, Jonah lets go of me and I'm caught by an elf. I tense up, but my new partner seems happy about our pairing so I give him my best smile. After a turn around the floor, I relax again. My new partner is about my height, which makes moving much easier than it was with the giant Jonah. Plus, this elf is quick enough to keep me from stepping on him.

My new elf friend spins me around a few times and then shouts, "*Sonti!*" as he jumps.

I jump too, but I'm far behind everyone else, which makes him laugh. His mood is infectious and soon I'm laughing, too.

"*Sonti!*" he yells again, and this time, I'm more prepared. I almost jump on cue. By the third time I've got the hang of it, but I get spun again and end up with a different elf.

This elf seems more nervous to be dancing with me than I am dancing with him. He does his best to guide me, but we're both relieved when the song ends. I attempt to curtsy to my partner, but it's harder than it looks. I give up about halfway through, which is a good thing because on the way up, I'm stormed by a group of women corralling me into a line.

Once they have me properly placed in the line of women, we curtsy to the line of men across from us. I didn't know we were going to do that, so I'm late and only get my knees bent when the music starts.

Everyone moves the same way, so it's easy to know what to do. However, soon the tempo increases and I struggle to keep up as the women around me guide me through the steps. I'm beginning to enjoy the dancing and when the women and men join together, I'm actually having fun dancing with my partner.

I dance for a long time through multiple songs and various partners. When one of the elves makes a gesture that suggests he's offering to get me a drink, I gesture back that I'm looking for someone and shout, "Jonah" over the loud music.

Jonah smiles when I reach him. "Having fun?"

"Yes," and I mean it.

"Stay here and rest." He hands me a mug with blue foam on the top, from one of the passing trays.

"What is it?"

"Swillen Beer."

I take a small sip, then follow it with huge gulps until I finish the entire mug. "That's sooo good!"

Jonah smiles and takes the cup away. We stand next to each other and watch the dancers on the floor. I'm so enthralled with the activity around me that I don't notice Dathid until he's in front of me, more dour than ever. He has the Queen's daughter next to him. Why does he spend so much time with her when they obviously don't like each other?

"Agatha," he begins formally. "I would like to introduce you to Princess Elaeria, my wife."

CHAPTER 27

It's true that someone's mouth can literally fall open if you surprise them hard enough. I don't know why, but it's bizarre thinking of Dathid as having a wife. He doesn't seem like the type of guy to have a family, and most definitely not an elf family.

I'm staring at them like an idiot, so I shut my gaping mouth and mutter a quick "Hi." I do a little wave that adds to the awkwardness of the moment.

Princess Elaeria starts speaking in English, but it's heavily accented and difficult to understand. I don't have a lot of experience with married people, but I would think that Dathid should've mentioned a wife or a family at least once during the time we were together. Why is he married to an elf? Why does it seem like he's in danger if he's married to the princess? What's the deal with that awful tapestry? From what I've seen so far, the elves and faeries hate each other. And it doesn't seem like there's a great love story happening here.

I'm so lost in my thoughts that it doesn't register that Dathid has said something until he moves to leave. I have no idea what he said, or what to say to him, so I just quietly watch them go. As soon as they're gone, I turn my wide eyes to Jonah.

"Not here," he says.

"Well then you better take me somewhere, because I have lots of questions and I don't know how long I can hold them in."

Jonah grabs me by the wrist, leads me into a secluded alcove and closes the curtains behind us. The alcove has a bench carved into one of the sides, and Jonah sits, taking up the whole thing.

"Are you married?" I demand as soon as the curtain is closed.

"No, Knight Crawlers do not marry."

"Why didn't you tell me? Why are they married? They don't even like each other."

"I didn't tell you because I thought you had enough to deal with without worrying about Dathid."

"Why should I be worried? Why are *you* worried?"

"Well, I'm sure you've noticed that faeries and elves do not get along. I'm worried because Princess Elaeria's former betrothed is not happy with the match and neither are most of the elves."

"I don't understand. Usually when people are married, you can tell. Seriously, how are a faerie and an elf married?"

"They didn't marry for love. They don't even feel enough emotion to hate each other. Theirs is a marriage of alliances."

"I'm confused. Why wouldn't she marry the guy you think wants to hurt Dathid? He seems to have plenty of emotion."

Jonah takes a deep breath. "With Ziras gaining power, many of the curra are joining forces. The Cromsmead elves and the Manahata faeries have been battling over their border for generations. A marriage between the two kingdoms was the best solution for a quick peace."

"That's weird. Why would anyone agree to that?" Then a thought occurs to me. "Will I be forced to marry someone?"

"No, you get to choose if you want to marry or not. Now, let's get back to the party before we're missed."

We don't stay long because it's late. When we get back to my room, Jonah follows me in and adds wood to the fire. He kisses the top of my head and turns to leave.

My insides jitter like I drank too much coffee. I close my eyes and focus on breathing. There's nothing to be afraid of. It's just new and different. I clasp my hands together and say to his back, "Jonah, will you please stay here tonight?"

"All right," he agrees without a thought.

It's stupid to be afraid. "I'm sorry. It's just I've never been anywhere before. I've only ever slept in my own bed. I mean, since before I met you. But after you, I had you and that makes it easier. Wait. I'm not making sense."

"You don't need to explain. Will you be all right for a little while? I have to go back and support Dathid, but you get ready for bed and I'll come back as soon as I can."

The sky is still bright even though it's the middle of the night. The sun doesn't move across the sky, so it's always sunny. This is selfish. I need to get a grip and go to bed.

"I'll send Albína up to sit with you. When I come back, I'll sleep under the bed. You don't need to be alone."

"No, that's okay. I'm good. You go enjoy the party. Dathid needs you, and I'm sure Albína is having fun. I've always been alone, so this isn't a big deal. I don't need a babysitter."

Jonah looks offended at my suggestion. "Maybe *I* need the company."

I'm surprised by his comment until I realize he's joking.

"I'll be back as soon as I can," he says and walks out the door.

For the first time since I came to this strange world, I'm alone. I feel every bit of my solitude. "Albína will be here soon. Stop being a baby."

The sheer size of my enormous room makes me uneasy. A wave of homesickness washes over me when I think of my comfy little room in Queens. "You're just not used to it. Get a grip."

To ease my fears, I learn my new space. First I try out one of the sofas and am pleased that it's even more comfortable than it looks. The elves certainly know how to do luxury. However, I can only sit for a minute because my anxiety makes me jump to my feet.

I pace the room, then explore one of the many doors on the far wall. I open the first one slowly and find another bedroom. That's weird that my bedroom would have a bedroom. Then I notice the little room also has a door leading to the hallway. Why does this room have a door to my room?

This second bedroom is considerably smaller than mine, but it's still lavish. Someone has recently moved in. There are gowns and women's clothing on the bed, and crates with various items littered everywhere. Who's staying here? It occurs to me that spying on this person is wrong, so I close the door and hope that it locks.

Next to the little room is an alcove with a narrow door that leads to an empty closet. The only things in the space are the clothes I wore here, the gown I refused to wear and a nightgown. I assume the nightgown is for me, so I change into it.

Auntie's Orb is sitting on the dresser in the corner. Someone put it on a pretty silver candlestick. I'd forgotten completely about it. I'm relieved I didn't lose it with my carelessness. I pick it up and try to see whatever it is I'm supposed to see. I stare at it as hard as I can for as long as I can, but nothing happens. Frustrated, I put the Orb back on its stand and leave the closet. How mad is everyone going to be when they figure out I can't read it?

Pushing my dark thoughts aside, I leave the closet and walk past the bathroom to another door that opens into a small bare room. There are empty bookshelves along two of the walls and a bench seat under a picture window. There's an old delicate desk in the center and that's it. The room gives me the creeps, so I quickly close the door.

I turn around and jump when I find Albína behind me.

"I'm sorry, Miss."

"No, I'm sorry. I'm a little edgy," I say, but that scare knocked some of the wind out of me.

"Are you getting to know your room?"

"Yeah, I found the closet." I wave to my nightgown.

"Whose room is that?"

"That's mine, Miss."

"Oh, sorry! I peeked in it."

"No worries. Think nothing of it. Got to get your bearings." She pulls the bed covers down.

I climb in and she hands me a cup of warm liquid that tastes like flowers. I drink it all and lie down. It's odd having someone stand over me while I'm in bed. It really gets embarrassing when she pulls the covers up and tucks me in.

She hums to herself while she closes the heavy window drapery, and the room gets dark with the exception of the light from the fireplace in the center of the room. Then she settles in the chair closest to the fire and pulls out some yarn from a nearby basket.

"You don't need to stay, Albína. I'm okay." I'm mortified that I need a babysitter and feel guilty that she's missing the party.

"I'm sorry, Miss. Sir Jonah told me to sit with you. So sit I must."

"I'm sorry you're missing the party."

"'Tis nothing. It's truly an honor to be serving you. I don't mind missing the tail end of a dying party."

I stare at the ceiling. "Where'd the birds go?"

"It's time for sleep."

I have no idea what that means, so I repeat, "Yeah, but where'd they go?"

"To the clouds for sleep."

I still don't understand, but my head is growing soupy and I'm wondering what was in the drink she gave me. I blink a few times, then everything goes dark.

CHAPTER 28

I wake up with a start in a strange place with birds singing loudly overhead. Nothing is familiar. I'm in a huge bed and the noise from the birds is deafening. When Albína comes out of her room, the past few weeks flood back to my foggy brain.

She smiles warmly at me and places a full breakfast tray on the bed, completely oblivious to the screaming birds. Then she bids me a good morning and calmly proclaims, "*Vido cluana.*"

The birds shut up. I need to remember that phrase.

"Did you sleep well?" she asks.

"Yes. Thank you. What time is it?"

"It's time to wake up. You've a busy day ahead of you."

I remember that Jonah promised to sleep under my bed, but he couldn't have slept through that racket. I bend over and peek, but he isn't there.

"He left a bit ago. Scared the life out of me when he came out from under your bed like that."

"Yeah, he does that," I say with a shrug and a mouthful of food.

When I'm done with my breakfast, Albína holds up another riding habit. This one has chocolate brown breeches and a royal blue hunting jacket. I appreciate her efforts to find me clothes that are close to what I like, but they're still far too bright for my taste and I look ridiculous in the sherbet-colored frilly shirt. However, I'm not complaining because the alternative is far worse.

She ushers in three women who measure me for new clothes. I make a point of showing them my jeans and sweater so they'll know my tastes. The women are appalled at my clothing choices, especially my love of dark colors.

When we're done, Albína escorts me to the rooftop where Lenox smells me thoroughly. I'm happy he misses me, too. "You seem to be doing okay," I say, scratching his itchy ears.

Albína is anxious to leave, and not just because she's afraid of Lenox; my training starts today and we're late. At least, that's what I surmise from the tension in her face and her constant reminders that we should be leaving soon. I promise Lenox I'll be back, but he's purring so loudly it adds to my guilt when he watches me leave.

She walks me a good distance to another tower in the castle. I'll never learn my way around the twisting, turning structure. If I ever lost Albína, I wouldn't even be able to find my way outside, let alone back to my room.

When we climb about halfway to the top of a massive stone spiral staircase, she stops and knocks on a door that's on the wall in much the same way a large picture might hang. It's mid-step, and has no threshold and a rather sizeable step up.

"Who is it?" says a gruff male voice through the door.

"Pardon me, sir, it's Albína. I've brought you Agatha Stone."

"Come in," barks the voice, sounding upset at the disruption.

Albína opens the door, and I help push her up into the doorway, then she helps pull me through. Once inside, I gape at the bookcases reaching to the top of a very high ceiling and covering the curved walls of the overstuffed room. The cases are brimming with so many old dusty books that it gives the impression that they'll either collapse under the weight or explode into a barrage of paper.

It's difficult to find the source of the voice because the man it belongs to is hidden among the tables scattered throughout the room that are piled high with books, pots, bottles and various bric-a-brac, as well as a thick layer of dust. On the wall across from me, a fire is burning in the fireplace with a black cauldron hanging over the flames. Sunlight is pouring through the only window, and I'm distracted by the airborne dust sparkling in the sunlight.

The room has an unusual odor that I can't decide if I like. It smells of old flowers, burnt meat and something sweet, not to mention the smell of books, which I love, and dust, which I don't.

I peruse the room for much longer than is socially acceptable, but eventually find a tall human male standing behind a table at the other end of the room. He's wearing brown trousers, an old shirt that used to be white, and over all of it he has a lab coat with a multitude of stains and holes. He's clean-shaven, but on top of his head is thick white hair that points in every direction.

Evidently, I have to learn some chemistry and I have one of those teachers who's more interested in what he's doing rather than imparting any wisdom. His head is down because he's busy reading a book while holding a bottle in his hand. Albína and I wait patiently while he reads and then pours a splash of thick gray liquid from the bottle into the bowl on the table. He mutters something to himself, then picks up the bowl and tosses it into the trashcan on the floor.

He glances up at us and says rather brusquely to Albína, "You may go."

She wastes no time bolting for the door. I want to leave, too.

The old man walks over and studies me from my head to my toes and then back up. He doesn't like what he sees, but I refuse to squirm under his disapproval.

"How old are you?" he demands.

"Thirteen." I try to make my voice sound more forceful but fail, and now I'm mad at myself.

"Where you from?"

"Queens."

"Huh." He looks me in the eye for an uncomfortable moment. "An American. Figures." He walks back to his table. While his back is to me, he keeps talking. "Hail from Toronto myself. Like it better here." He finishes with a point to the window then turns around, surprised I didn't follow him. "Come here. We need to start."

I stand my ground. "Who are you?" I say with some force that makes me proud.

The man is genuinely stunned by my question. "They didn't tell you?"

I shake my head.

The old man snorts. "Elves, arrogant little pissers. Think that everyone knows their heritage." He walks back from around the table. "Well, I guess we need chairs." He's looking up so I question if he's truly hunting for a place to sit.

"Ah, there you are. *Talush ba dio*," he says and moves his arm as if he's picking up a chair. I glance at his hand and then follow his gaze: two chairs are gently floating down from the ceiling.

"That's so weird," I whisper in awe, more to myself than to the strange man. Moving painted birds and fish swimming across walls are magical, but right now I'm watching real magic being performed. I'm trying to act natural, as if chairs fly around all the time back on Earth, but my wide eyes are giving me away.

The chairs land softly on the floor, and the man motions for me to sit. I hesitate. What if they go back up?

"Go ahead. They're not going anywhere," he says as if reading my thoughts.

I gently take a seat, and the eccentric man sits across from me. We stare at each other for an uncomfortable amount of time. I'm not sure if he's still studying me or if he's thinking of what to say. Finally, he sits up straight, puts his hands on his knees and announces, "I'm Doctuir Kyrbast. Everyone here calls me Kyrbast. You may call me Kyrbast also."

He stops talking. Am I supposed to call him Kyrbast right now? I wait to see if he'll add more, but when he doesn't say anything else, I ask shyly, "Why am I here?"

He smiles as if I've said something funny. "That's the answer everyone wants to know."

I'm not sure that's an answer. It sounds like he just threw some words together to make it sound like he answered, when really he didn't say anything that made any sense. This man is obviously a little off. I can't imagine what the Queen thinks I'll learn from him.

We're staring at each other again. I cross my arms across my chest and stretch my feet out. We may be here awhile.

Kyrbast cocks his head to the side and rubs his chin. "I'm what you would call a Wizard."

This news makes me sit up. I'm talking to a real live wizard. Mr. Duradin was a wizard, but I didn't know that until after I left. I'm disappointed he doesn't have the big hat and gray robes, though.

"You're here for training. I'm here to teach you some basic wizardry."

"Am I a wizard, too?" This training just got a lot better. He smiles and shakes his head. "No, you're a Knight. Knights learn a little bit of everything."

I huff. I don't want to be a stupid Knight. Knights fight and die and stuff. Wizards do fun things like making stuff fly around, like he did with the chairs. I'd much rather be a Wizard. Maybe someone else can be the Knight and I can stay here and do magic.

CHAPTER 29

"Can I be a Wizard instead?" I'm proud of myself for asking.

Kyrbast shakes his head. "You are destined to be the Keeper of the Key, the Reader of the Orb, the Lost Knight. Did I remember all your titles?"

I've heard them before, but never all together, and it makes my head spin. Kyrbast winks like it was a joke, but it's not a joke. They expect me to be worthy of those titles.

"You okay?"

I nod, and then shake my head.

He smiles. "Well, that answered that question."

I shake my head for a second time. I have to add words before I nod again. "I'm not any of those things."

Worthless, stupid, lazy, ungrateful. Auntie's words echo around my brain.

"Where'd you go?" he asks, snapping my attention back to him.

He was talking but I didn't hear what he said. I shake my head. He chuckles. I add words. "Sorry."

He groans. "What I said was…you were born to be a Knight. Knights are courageous, strong of mind and body, selfless and inquisitive."

I'm about to shake my head but I stop myself and study my feet. I don't want to talk about this. I just want to see some magic tricks.

212

"Your mother was a Knight. Your father was a *Tutotor*, a leader. You are a Knight."

The mention of my parents snaps my head up. "Did you know them?"

It's his turn to shake his head. A burst of energy makes him jump from the chair and lights up his face in a happy smile. He raises a finger in the air and says, "I know what we can do!"

My energy doesn't match his. I stay in the chair and halfheartedly watch him run around the room gathering items. He moves pretty quick for an old guy.

He runs past me and abruptly halts in front of the bookshelves. He spreads his hands out dramatically and asks in a rush, "Do any of you have a portrait potion?" Then he leaps back as three tomes fall from the high shelves and land with a thud.

I jump to my feet when all three books open and rapidly flip through their pages.

"I wish books on Earth did that."

"They can," Kyrbast says as he casually picks them up and puts them on a nearby counter. He grabs at his hips and then his chest in a motion that suggests he's searching for something. When he doesn't find it in his pockets, he looks around at the various tables. "Oh!" he shouts and then races to a bench by the window to retrieve a wand. He brings it back to his table, waves it around and says, "*Tiseek e zar.*"

All the books, beakers, papers and dust that are piled in front of him fly briskly to another already overstuffed station. It's a wonder that a wobbly stack of books—precariously placed on top of a beaker that's on top of a pile of test tubes—doesn't smash to the ground.

"One of the drawbacks of Wizardry," he says to the air. "You never really clean. Just *swoosh!* and you've got what you need." He emphasizes his words with a few waves of his wand before he puts it down. Then he looks at me with surprise. "Well, come here. Might as well start now. You'll like this."

I jump out of my seat and rush to his side. I'm going to do a magic trick!

He gathers a few empty beakers and some test tubes from various tables. Each of them has a different colored liquid or powder in them. One test tube in particular smells terrible, so I push it as far away as I can.

Kyrbast reads aloud from the book. I lean in and try to read along, but it's in another language with odd letters. He puts an empty bowl in front of me, then places a graduated cylinder in front of that. Then he hands me a test tube with white liquid in it. "Pour four milliliters."

My fingers are shaking with excitement but with a little patience, I'm able to get the measurement right. He hands me several other powders and liquids. I measure them all and pour them into the bowl.

"Okay, stir that up well." He takes out a small knife. "You're not going to like this part. We need five drops of your blood."

I reflexively jerk back, but after my initial shock wears off, I hold my hand out.

He holds the knife up. "Do you want to do it, or do you want me to?"

I turn my head and close my eyes. "No, you do it."

My entire body clenches when he grabs my hand and cold slices across my finger, followed by heat and then pain. I writhe under the pressure of him squeezing the blood out. I want to open my eyes, but I hate blood, so I wait until he covers my wound with a bandage.

"All done," he announces. I open my eyes, and my stomach flips when I see my blood in the bowl.

I study the bandaged finger. "You don't have magic that will heal this?"

He smiles. "No magic works better than your own body. I have a few salves that may help, but it's only a small cut and it should heal fine on its own."

I'm disappointed. What good is magic if you can't do really important things like heal wounds?

He reads aloud from the book again and stirs the potion. As he reads, white smoke pours from the bowl and billows up to the ceiling. Color penetrates the smoke and, slowly, a woman's face takes shape. She has bright brown eyes and a long angular nose. Her dark blonde wavy hair is falling forward because she's looking down. She's smiling and talking, but no sound is coming out.

"That's my mother," I whisper.

"Yes, you were young when you last saw her. It looks like she's talking to you while you're in your crib."

"What's she saying?" I ask in amazement. This is my mother. I know her. The blood drains from my head, and my hands grow cold. I'm numb from the inside out. I don't remember her. I never knew what she looked like or any story about her life. But here she is, *my mother*, gazing down upon me. I'm whole, as if a part of me was missing and I never knew it. I stare at her, unblinking, until my eyes burn and the smoke dissipates. I'm losing her all over again.

"Don't worry. We can create another," he says to console me. "I will make you another more permanent one that you can take with you. Those take longer and are a lot more complicated. I thought you would enjoy doing that one yourself."

I have no words. I had a mother. I mean, I always knew I had one, but in the sense that everyone has one. But now I saw in her own eyes that she loved me. My mother loved me.

"Well, I guess that's enough for one day," he says after an awkward cough. "We have a lot to learn, so make sure you rest up tonight." He pulls one of the ribbons hanging on the wall.

We stand in awkward silence for a long time until I say in a shaky voice, "Thank you."

He smiles. "It was my pleasure. You look like your mother."

I've never heard that before. It causes a chill to run through my body. The pressure builds in my nose and my vision blurs. I push down whatever feeling is about to erupt. I won't get emotional here. Instead, I give Kyrbast a wobbly smile and whisper, "I look like my mother."

He's about to say something else when we're interrupted by a loud knock at the door. "Your escort has arrived," he says and walks away to do whatever he was doing when I came in.

I jump down from the doorway. Albína isn't here. Instead, there's a male elf in a military uniform waiting for me.

CHAPTER 30

This elf is the same height as I am but twice as wide at the shoulder, which makes him look even shorter. Even without the uniform, there's no mistaking he's a soldier.

"Hello, Ms. Stone. I am Matban Tadin," he says with a bow. One of those names is a title and the other is his name, but I don't know which is which. He flashes a brilliant smile. "An honor to make your acquaintance." His words are short and clipped, and the smile does nothing to soften the tough military countenance.

"Yeah, you too." I press my lips together. I wish I would've been told that Albína wasn't picking me up. I'm still reeling from seeing my mother. I'm not good with new people, and this guy looks like a talker.

"I'm your escort." He holds his arm out. I know I'm supposed to grab his elbow, but I don't like all the touching, especially strange men I've just met. He looks at me expectantly, and I grab his elbow because I don't want to make a big deal out of it. "Are you enjoying your stay so far?"

"Yes." I need to add words. "Everyone has been very kind to me."

"How are you and Albína getting on?"

Why does he care? *He's making conversation.* I need to be nicer. It's just that the uniform and the mannerisms make me feel like I'm in trouble. "She's very nice. I like her."

"Good to hear it. So you're friends with a Knight Crawler? That's exciting. How long have you and Sir Jonah known each other?"

I want the conversation to stop now. I want to think about my mom and process meeting a Wizard. I want to shoot him a snarky glare and tell him there's no time on Ashra, so how should I know, but I'm not that girl. Instead I ask, "Do you want me to tell you in days?"

"Sure." He grins again. "I understand some of Earth's time references."

"How do you know about them? And where'd you learn English?"

The smile disappears. "I only semi-understand your time references, but I've been told they're common in Earth languages. As for your second question, many of the higher-ranking officials speak American."

"Why?"

He chuckles. "That's unfair. I've answered several of your questions, and you haven't answered mine yet."

I stare at him blankly. I can't remember the question.

He raises his eyebrows. "Jonah?"

"Oh right. Jeez, I don't know. Like a month, maybe? Do you know what a month is?"

"Not really," he says with a shrug. "Just making conversation. What about Dathid? The same time?"

I'm surprised that he didn't use Dathid's title. Elves always use titles. "No. I met Jonah first and then Prince Dathid a few days later."

"How'd you like Manahata?"

"It's very pretty and the food is good."

"I guess that's why you're a Knight. I'd be scared to be in the heart of Manahata."

I snort. This guy doesn't look like he's scared of much. "Why?"

He gazes at me with wide eyes, like he's trying to communicate telepathically. It must have worked because I remember their conflict. "Oh. It's not like that." I shake my head for emphasis.

"Really? What's it like?"

Maybe I can help him understand that the faeries are not that bad. He doesn't need to be afraid of them. "Well, it's surrounded by the buildings of Manhattan, but they're like a shadow. King Ohad said I could walk right through them. And I guess I did when we walked to the ocean. It's kind of like a rainbow—they disappear when you get too close to them."

"That sounds fascinating! I'd love to walk through a building. So it was just you and Sir Jonah and Dathid walking all by yourselves?"

"No, we had Lenox."

"Lenox. That's right. I haven't met him yet."

We round the corner leading to my room. I'm glad this conversation will be over soon. "I love him. He's so sweet and cute."

"Well, no wonder you could feel safe in Manahata when you have a friend like Lenox."

I shake my head. I want him to understand that I felt safe the entire time. "I didn't get him until we were about to leave."

He stops and looks at me. "See, you *are* a Knight. Brave and strong."

"No," I laugh. "It's not like that. They're very nice." Maybe it will help the peace if I tell him what they're really like. "They had a party. It was fun."

His eyebrows knit together. "But what about all those soldiers flying about?"

We start walking again. "I didn't see a lot of soldiers. It was a party."

He gives me a sideways look that lets me know he thinks I'm crazy. "The entire time you were there, you didn't see any soldiers? That can't be. Look how many we have, and Cromsmead is much smaller than Manahata."

I shrug. "It was all pretty overwhelming. I guess I didn't notice."

"You look like them," he says. It almost sounds like an accusation, but he's smiling, so I guess it's a compliment.

I blush. "What! Faeries are gorgeous, and tall, and glamorous. I don't look like them."

"Well, you do. Is that why Dathid decided to join you?

I'm grossed out by the implication that Dathid accompanied us because he was attracted to me. He's way too old, somewhere in his twenties. Yuck! He's good-looking, but eww. He couldn't have implied what I think he did. It's probably a language issue. It has to be.

Matban Tadin hasn't said anything since he asked that weird question. Maybe's he's embarrassed after seeing my reaction.

"I don't know why his dad made him join us," I answer honestly. "Dathid probably wanted to see his wife."

Matban Tadin makes a face. *Yeah, that was stupid.* Dathid didn't come here to see his wife. But that's a good question; why did he come here?

"Had you ever talked with the faeries before?"

I tune back in to our conversation. "Before what?"

"Before you were in Manahata?" he says with a laugh.

"Before that, I was in Queens." I thought everyone knew that. But maybe I'm not as gossiped about as I feel.

"Are there faeries in Queens?"

It's my turn to furrow my brows. "How could there be faeries in Queens? That's on Earth."

He laughs. "Oh, that's right. I got caught up in our conversation. That was dumb."

I'm happy we're in sight of my door. This elf makes me uncomfortable with his questions. I don't think it's appropriate for him to talk to me about faeries.

"So the first time you ever saw a faerie was in Manahata?"

"Yeah, when I went through the portal." I want to add a snort, but that's rude. How could I have met a faerie before I was on Ashra? I don't think this guy is too bright.

"And you and Jonah were friends on Earth?" His tone is no longer overly friendly and neither is mine.

"We were on Earth together for a day."

He must have read my face because the big grin is back. "Yeah, a day because you've only been friends for a month."

"Right. Well. Bye." I shut my door on him. If I never speak to that guy again it will be too soon.

CHAPTER 31

"What's wrong?" Albína asks when I look at her with a mix of relief and confusion. We're sitting across from each other eating, quietly on Lenox's rooftop. I'm not hungry but if I don't eat she'll give me a hard time about it, so I play with my food and occasionally take a bite.

"I'm not sure." My conversation with Matban Tadin replays in my head. It left me feeling bad, but I don't understand why. He didn't ask anything inappropriate, though the Dathid question was weird. It was just a talk between two acquaintances trying to be nice to each other. So why do I feel like I've done something wrong?

"I met Matban Tadin," I say, wanting to judge her reaction.

"Oh, I heard." She places her elbow on the table and rests her chin in her hand. "What's he like?"

Short is the first word that comes to mind. It's a mean word, but I've decided I don't like him. "He seems nice enough."

"I know his husband Wymon. Very handsome." She's grinning from ear-to-ear. She obviously really likes him. I'm not going to get any answers from her.

"Is Matban a title or his name?" That's a safe enough question.

"It's his title. He's second to Ceržent Solara."

"Whoever that is."

She smiles at me. I change the subject. I had a weird conversation with a weird guy. I need to get over it. "I saw my mother today."

"How wonderful! Tell me all about it."

I don't understand why seeing my mother makes me so sad. It should've made me ecstatic. "I'm sorry, I can't. Not yet."

She pats my hand. "I understand. I'm happy for you."

I wish I understood. I've missed out on something important. I never knew my parents. I always told myself that it wasn't important. Lots of people don't have parents and they're just fine. But it's not fine. Something fantastic should've been in my life, but it was taken away before I ever knew what it was. Now that I've had a tiny glimpse of what my life would've been like with a beautiful woman smiling down on me with love shining in her eyes, I want it back. I want it more than anything I've ever wanted.

After lunch, she takes my mind off my troubles by filling me in on the castle gossip while escorting me to the far end of the keep. It works only because I'm tired of being depressed and not because I care for gossip about people I don't know.

This side of the castle is deserted and quiet. Albína's voice reverberates down the empty corridors until she suddenly stops both her mouth and her feet at the only door in the hall.

"I can't go any farther, but you need to go in," she whispers. "Master Sarpedon is waiting for you."

"Who is Master Sarpedon and why is he waiting for me?" I whisper back.

"I'm not allowed to tell you. It'll be all right. He's another of your teachers."

Why are we whispering? Just a second ago, Albína was practically shouting. And we're the only people on this side of the castle. I don't want to meet this new teacher. I already met one today, and one a day is plenty. Plus, it's disconcerting that Albína has to wait outside.

I don't say anything to her as I obediently walk through the door. It's a small foyer that's well lit by two torches hanging on the wall. There's no one in the little room, but there's another door a few feet in front of me. In the center of this other door is a life-sized skull and crossbones that reminds me of a pirate flag. If Master Sarpedon is a pirate, then shouldn't he be called Captain Sarpedon?

The skull door is locked. I knock. The skull makes a clicking sound as the crossbones separate and the mouth slowly opens. It's meant to be scary, but it's cheap funhouse stuff.

I take a deep breath to alleviate some of the pressure building behind my eyes. Why can't I just meet this guy and have Albína next to me and not have to go through whatever this stupid show is about?

A loud scream makes me jump. The skull is growing out from the door. Its eyes are burning red and it's chanting loudly. I stop breathing. My feet freeze in place. I hope by not moving it won't notice me. When the skull keeps creeping forward, I leap back to the door I just came through, but it's locked and won't budge. I'm trapped with the evil skull breathing down my neck and malevolently chanting at me.

"This isn't funny!" I pound on the door. "Open the door! Albína, open the door!" I'm screaming at the top of my lungs, and the skull is so loud I know Albína can hear us. Why doesn't she answer?

Then it stops, and the silence is like a presence. I press myself against the door, trying the knob again, but it's still locked. The room is eerily silent. I'm afraid to breathe. The quiet is worse the than the cacophony. I don't know what the skull is doing. It could be right behind me.

I slowly turn my body to face it, but I keep my hand on the knob, willing it to twist and free me. The skull is back to being the benign funhouse door I thought it was. I take an unsteady breath. The skull doesn't move, so I take a few more. I'm panting and sweating, and pressed so hard against the door my back hurts. I want to scream for help, but I don't want to wake the skull up again.

I refuse to faint because the skull will eat me if I hit the ground. My guts seize and my heart stops when the knob on the skull door turns. Not again. I don't know how to fight a door. I brace for the worst as the skull door slowly creaks open. I almost collapse when a tall man peeks his head out.

"Well, the door didn't kill you, so I guess you're a Knight," he says, as he swings the door open.

My head swims when I see the man's impossibly triangular face, a shape that's emphasized by the small pointy beard on his chin and his large flat nose. The sharp angles of his face are softened by the shock of thick curly hair on his head that only slightly covers his pointy ears and small circular horns. He's wearing the jacket and frilly shirt of the elves, but his bottom half is a goat's.

I press my back so hard against the exit door that I'm surprised I'm not passing through it.

The man's piercing gold eyes scan my horrified face. "You are a Knight, yes?"

I don't move, I don't speak and I don't breathe. My vision blurs as I stare at his furry legs and hooves. I wobble, but steady myself before I hit the ground.

"Ah, you've never seen a satyr before."

I shake my head and regret it when the world blurs with the movement.

The man smiles; somehow he thinks this is funny. "Well, you've got nothing to worry about." He crosses his small goat legs and leans against the doorframe. "We satyrs are a fun lot. Most find us rather charming, and I promise, you've got nothing to fear."

"Are you Master Sarpedon?" I whisper in a shaky voice. I wish Jonah were here to witness my bravery. I can't believe I got those words out.

The man snorts. "Well, that's a first. No one has ever accused me of that before." He chuckles to himself. "My name's Gurador. Master Sarpedon is waiting for you inside. I assure you, I'm much better looking and a lot more entertaining."

Gurador moves aside and gestures for me to come in. I don't want to leave my door. I don't want to go any further into the funhouse. I can see the disappointment in Gurador's eyes. I'm here to be a Knight and save the world, but I can't even walk through a doorway.

I wobble past the satyr trying to keep as much distance as I can from the scary skull door.

"Once inside there will be no talking," Gurador whispers as I pass.

I'm in a horror movie. I want Jonah with me. Everything is better and safer when he's around. Gurador is directly in front of me, holding a torch that is the only light in the narrow hall. The flickering flame is casting eerie, moving shadows across the intricately carved passageway. I'm definitely in one of Auntie's late-night horror movie marathons.

The only good part is that the elves have taken great pains to make every inch of Cromsmead visually interesting. Whenever I'm scared or unsure, I can always go to the happy painter place in my mind. Now is no different. The intricately carved, gruesomely distorted figures covering every inch of the walls and ceiling take me away from this haunted house. Even as I follow the satanic creature down a dark hall with his torch light flashing images of bloody battles and the dismembered bodies of horrifying monsters, I can't help but wonder who carved these exquisite images.

When the passage ends at a plain black curtain, I'm disappointed with the person who decorated this place. A simple curtain at the end of such an exquisite hallway is just offensive. I'm glad when Gurador pulls the ugly drape away.

He steps aside and motions for me to go into the room. I take a deep breath, force my feet to move, and enter a massive oval-shaped room that resembles a theater. Two enormous chandeliers hang from the ceiling, and the torches scattered about make it almost cheery. The reason this place reminds me of old movies is because everything is black and white. The walls and ceiling of the hallway I came from were black. The floor has a continuous black-and-white checkered pattern with a complicated mosaic around the edges.

The long sides of the oval-shaped room have rows of black leather seating that are staggered so that everyone has the best view of the center floor. In front of the seats are white stone arches with more of the gruesome faces carved at the top. On the floor where the arches open are stone balustrades that separate the seating from the center area. The only color in the room comes from the embroidered flags hanging on each column. Every one of them is different.

I stop a considerable distance away from the strange figure sitting on the floor in front of the stage in the center. The creature is wearing a red robe and has its hood pulled low, so I can't see its face. However, I can see long slender hands covered in bright red gloves that don't match the red of its robe. Around the figure's seated posture is the edge of a scarlet pillow the same color as the gloves. I look around for another pillow for me, but there isn't one. I let out a sigh. I didn't want to sit with it anyway.

Whatever that fiendish creature is, it looks threatening just sitting there, and I can't even see its face. Gurador gives me a shove, but my feet are welded to the floor.

"Come here, child," the thing on the floor whispers. It's male, with a strange accent that adds S's where they aren't needed, making it difficult to understand. Especially because its voice reverberates, almost like two people are talking at the same time.

My knees are shaking. My feet melt to the floor. I shake my head even though he can't see me.

"Come here. I have been waiting for you. You have nothing to fear."

Meet him and leave. I ball my shaking fingers into fists to hide them and shut my brain off. I charge forward until I'm in front of Master Sarpedon.

Sometimes when I sit on the floor, my body sways a bit, but he's a statue. His hands have been raised in prayer since I entered. They've got to be tired. I stand before him in awkward silence for so long that my fear disappears and is replaced by annoyance. It's like some game is being played, but I don't know the rules.

"So, are you going to say anything? Do I need to do something?"

"Sit," he commands slowly in his strange accent.

I sit cross-legged on the floor in front of him. From this angle, I can see his face. What I thought were red gloves are actually his hands. They're bright red with a faint gold diamond pattern traveling down the backs of them, and on each finger is a stubby gold claw at the tip.

The cushion he's sitting on is the same shade of red but with a larger diamond pattern. It could be part of his body. Is he sitting on it or is it wrapped around him somehow? I study it for long enough to realize I'm being rude, so I snap my head up to look at his face.

I'm braced for the worst, but I'm pleased to see a kind, gentle face. It's scarlet like the rest of him, with ancient reptilian eyes. Two ridges follow the path of his slender gray eyebrows. He has a nose similar to Jonah's, in that he really doesn't have one. It protrudes from his face and has two small slits in front for air to pass, but it doesn't go back in like a normal nose. Below the small airway is a long, thin gray mustache that hangs down to the upper part of his chest.

Under the mustache is a large mouth that's stuck in a permanent smile. The chin is a distinct end to his face and has a thin long beard in equal length to his mustache. I've seen similar features on a creature on Earth, but I can't place it.

"Satisfaction in harmony be upon you, Sir Agatha. I am pleased to meet you. I am Grand Master Sarpedon. I will be instructing you in the ways of the Knight."

His speech is excruciatingly slow. I give him a wave and mumble, "Hi."

"Are you afraid of serpents?"

That's a strange question. Why would he open with that? I answer my question when my blood turns cold, and the room blurs for a second. He's a snake. A huge snake. My eyes practically bulge out of my head as I stare down at the pillow, which is actually his tail and has to be at least ten feet long.

He's a snake.

And I'm dinner.

CHAPTER 32

I pull my eyes away from the tail and back up to his serpent face. I jump to my feet and back away until I hit the railing in front of the chairs. I don't know how fast this thing can strike me. It hasn't moved since I got here. I'm being played with like a mouse. I need to run, but I'm locked in.

Master Sarpedon chuckles. "I guess that answers my question."

I'm annoyed that he finds my fear funny. I scan the room for anything to use as a weapon, but it's bare.

"Good. You have excellent instincts. Gurador removed all weapons from this room in case this was your reaction."

He's so calm. His tone drains the adrenaline from my veins. I'm defeated and foolish. I wouldn't even know what to do with a weapon if he handed it to me. Exhaustion hits me so hard I wobble on unsteady legs. I might be falling under a spell or something. My stomach's in knots and I'm dizzy.

"I'll wait. Your reaction is normal. Climb over the rail and sit in the chair. You will be much more comfortable."

I leap over the rail and flop into the closest chair. Why are there so many? Who sits in them? I'm not asking any questions or speaking to the snake. I'll wait here until it either kills me or lets me go.

I find a loose thread on my blazer and pull at it. When I accumulate enough, I wrap it around my thumb and turn the tip purple. I free my thumb, pull more thread, and wrap up two fingers.

I don't know how much time passes, but I've made a nice-sized hole in my borrowed jacket, and my entire hand is tied up in a messy knot. Sarpedon hasn't moved since I first saw him. He hasn't looked around or dropped his hands, not even when he spoke to me, or when I jumped.

The heavy tiredness eases. My breathing and heartbeat have returned to normal, and my nausea and dizziness have disappeared. I cave. I can't take the silence any longer. "I don't like to sit."

"Then stand."

I get up, muster my courage and hop over the rail. "What I mean is, why am I here? Are we just going to stare at each other?"

Sarpedon drops his hands and uncoils his long tail. His body rises only a few inches as he stands at his full height. Now he really looks like a snake. The dizziness returns. I flex my fingers to stop them from shaking. I'm not running away. I have to stand here and do whatever he wants so I can leave. I hate snakes, especially giant talking ones.

I jump and let out a yelp when a door slams in the hall. If another snake comes in, I'm done. I'm ready to make a dash for it when Jonah steps out from behind the curtain.

The rush of relief is almost as overwhelming as the panic attack. I race to Jonah and fly into his arms. He gives me one of those hugs I'm getting used to. I needed this comfort. He holds me tight and waits until I move away from him before he speaks.

"I'm sorry I'm late. You were not supposed to come here without me. Stay by my side. Everything's fine."

He grabs my hand and takes a step toward Master Sarpedon, but my legs refuse to move. I'm not going anywhere near that thing, with or without Jonah.

He smiles at me, drops my hand and walks over to Master Sarpedon. When he reaches him, Jonah salutes him by putting his right hand over his heart and making a slashing motion down and away from the front of his body. Standing at attention, he quietly says, "*Jwi héxé en koitep.*"

Master Sarpedon makes the same salute and says in response, "*Nan lapè în sül avètk,*" Their hand motions form an X, and I wonder if they know that.

Jonah drops to one knee and Master Sarpedon has to raise his hand to reach the top of Jonah's bowed head. He mutters some strange words that might be a greeting or a prayer, and then Jonah rises. They face each other. Jonah grabs Sarpedon by the shoulders, and Sarpedon reaches up to do the same but can only reach Jonah's elbows. It's some sort of hug. It only lasts for a moment before they both drop their arms.

"Sir Jonah, I am so pleased to see you. How fare you?"

"Well, Master. How do things fare here?"

"Stable for now."

They both want to say more but won't in front of me. They turn their attention my way and my face gets hot.

"She is very brave," Sarpedon says.

"Yes, she's been through a lot over a short period of time and has adapted well."

Now my face is burning. I'm not used to praise. What am I supposed to do?

"Do you feel confident enough to come over here now?" Jonah asks.

I slowly walk over. I still don't want to talk to the snake.

While I'm making my way to them, Jonah says, "She's more at ease if she can ask a dozen questions at once."

232

Sarpedon smiles wide, making his gentle face turn wicked. "Curiosity, the weapon of the brilliant. Ask your questions."

My brain refuses to form words. I twist my sweaty hands around each other. *Think!* I command my dying brain cells. I blurt out the first question that comes to mind. "Do you have feet?"

Sarpedon's eyes widen in surprise, but he quickly recovers. "No, I have what humans describe as the torso of a man and the tail of a serpent."

My eyes immediately go down to the long tail extending from the bottom of his robe. I force myself to look at his face, only to find he's studying my face as well. He's waiting for more questions. Now that Jonah's by my side, I feel a lot safer and definitely calmer. Jonah would never let anyone harm me. My confidence is back, so I let the questions fly.

"What are you called? What species, breed or whatever? Are you venomous? How come I've never seen your kind in a book or movie or something? How tall are you? What is this place?"

Sarpedon looks to Jonah and then back at me. I try to read his expression, but his face never changes. "Now, repeat your questions back to me, individually and in the same order you asked them. Only this time, leave me room to answer."

He's talking down to me like I'm a child. I didn't want to ask the questions in the first place, but he made me. Now I have to repeat them and try to keep my voice calm and the tears from falling. I take a deep breath to steel my courage and do my best to remember what I said.

"What is your species called? I know that's not exactly what I said before, but that's what I meant and I asked it more concisely now that I've had more time to think about it."

"I am a Nüwa."

"Are you venomous?"

"No, we are not snakes. We share common features," he says and then adds, "Besides, my teeth fell out ages ago."

"Oh, I remember," I say, after too long of a pause. "How come I've never seen a Nüwa in the movies or books and stuff?"

"My homeland does not have a portal. We had to travel a great distance to get to one. It led to the human area of Asia. Although we were not prolific on Earth, our culture influenced the human Asian cultures. In other words, if you were born on the other side of Earth, you would be more familiar with our kind."

"Oh, okay," I say, trying to remember my next question. I want to get this right because I don't want this mean creature to chastise me in front of Jonah again.

"How tall are you?" I almost forgot that one.

Sarpedon pauses for a moment, then speaks in that way that makes me feel like a child. "Well, if you are asking my height, I would say in—you are from America, correct?"

I nod.

"In American measurements, I am about eight inches below six feet tall. Now, if you are asking my length, I would be just over fifteen feet long."

I listen to his answer, which of course leads me to another question. "Can you change your height? Can you stand on different parts of your tail?"

"That was not one of the questions you asked before. You need to control your thoughts better."

I'm dragged here and held captive by a monster, I get talked down to like I'm a simpleton, and when I relax, just a little, he reprimands me. Asking these stupid questions is invasive. I should've worked them into a conversation and not just interrogated him. But he's the one who insisted that I ask them in the first place. "Well, if an answer leads to another question, when am I supposed to ask it?"

Sarpedon raises one of his eyebrows at me. "If you ask questions one at a time and wait for the answer, you can then easily ask another question. Your style of rapid interrogation leaves many questions unanswered."

I don't understand what he's telling me, so I don't know what to do next. "So are you going to answer it or should I ask the last question?"

"Yet another question?"

I've had enough. I am never coming here again, no matter how much they push me. I take a deep breath to make sure my voice is steady and ask the last question. "What is this place?"

"This is the Temple of the Knights. You may have heard of it as the Knights Templar. The Temple was replicated many times on Earth, but this is the original Temple."

"Like a church?" I cringe when I remember that I'm not supposed to add any questions.

"No, most temples on Earth are used for worship, but this Temple is used for the high functions of the order of the Knights Templar."

I'm confused and speak before I think. "You named yourself Knights of the Temple and then built a temple to be knights of?"

"Are you always so literal?" Sarpedon asks.

I shrug because I don't know if I'm supposed to answer that.

Sarpedon continues. "This is our main meeting place. We call it a temple. This is not the Temple we are referring to in our name."

I wait and when he says no more, I lose my patience. This snake enjoys confusing me. No matter what anyone says, I won't be taught by him. "Okay, then where's the temple?"

"You're standing in it."

Now I'm just mad. "Does everything here have to be a puzzle? I'm really tired of getting half-answers and riddles, and then getting ridiculed for being stupid when I don't understand."

"With patience, you will find more answers and fewer questions," Sarpedon says.

I don't want him to talk anymore. I shift my weight back and forth, and take turns standing on the sides of my feet. Then an idea hits me. "Ashra's the temple!"

Both Sarpedon and Jonah nod.

"Why is Ashra a temple?"

Jonah chuckles and Sarpedon sighs because I just asked another unauthorized question.

"I will answer only one more question. Think about it and then ask what it is you truly want to know."

I don't hesitate. "I want to know about the height. Can you change your height?"

Sarpedon is stunned by my choice, and Jonah laughs. Their reaction makes me defend myself. "You'll eventually tell me about the temple. It has to be part of this training. But if I don't ask about the height thing, I may never know."

I finish with my voice strong. I'm proud of myself for shocking him. It's probably rude to ask such a personal question, but they should've given me a book on these creatures instead of letting me figure it out on my own.

Sarpedon looks at me with what might be admiration. "You are clever. I am built to be this height. I am not a snake. I do not slither along on my belly. However, if the need arises, I can raise or lower myself for short periods with effort on my part. Have I answered your question satisfactorily?"

I smile back at him because I'm relieved to be done. I think he wants to answer the other question too, so it's only polite that I give him the opportunity. "Yes, you can tell me the Temple thing now if you want."

Jonah chuckles.

"You will have to be patient," Sarpedon says. "I only wanted us to meet. You will begin your training on the morrow."

Jonah bows and salutes. "Satisfaction in harmony be upon you, Master."

Sarpedon bows and returns the salutation. Then Jonah grabs my hand and leads the way out of the temple.

CHAPTER 33

"Where have you been?" I ask Jonah as soon as the door to the Temple closes and we're alone in the hallway.

"I've been making arrangements for you."

"What kind of arrangements?"

"Well, we've been deciding how much time we have. How much training you need. Who will be giving you that training? What should be done about security? That type of thing."

"Security? Why would I need security? Am I safe here?"

"You're as safe as you can be. You need not worry. The elves are fierce warriors. They can protect you."

I'm satisfied with Jonah's reassurance, primarily because I don't want to think about it. If he isn't worried, then I won't be either. "Master Sarpedon gives me the creeps."

"Yes, I tried to warn them about humans and serpents. I was supposed to be there, but I was delayed with the Queen. I wish they would've waited, but Master Sarpedon wanted to test your reaction. You did well."

I smile at Jonah's praise even though my first meeting with Master Sarpedon didn't go well at all. "I don't like him. It's not just the snake thing. He talks down to me like he knows everything and I'm intruding on his important stuff."

"Master Sarpedon is very wise. He most likely does know everything. He's also very important. We—especially you—need his help. I would suggest you stop taking offense and just listen. He's trying to help you."

"I can't believe you're taking his side. He was mean and rude and condescending."

"Listen, the council shouldn't have let you go in the Temple and meet a Nüwa without preparing you first. You reacted bravely to something most humans would've run screaming from."

"I wanted to."

Jonah laughs and then catches himself when he realizes I'm not joking. "You stayed and faced him. When I arrived, you two were talking. That's very courageous." Pride makes me walk taller as Jonah continues, "Master Sarpedon is a dear friend of mine. He's been my teacher and mentor for a long time. He has no experience dealing with humans, or with anyone of your age. I admit he can seem a bit condescending at times."

Jonah pauses to make sure I'm paying attention to what he's about to say. "Master Sarpedon, of all the people here, has your back more than anyone. He has no political gains. His main interest is keeping you alive. He'll always act in your best interest."

I give him a skeptical glance and he starts walking again. "Give him a chance. Nüwa are kind souls, and Master Sarpedon will be your biggest ally."

I sigh. "All right, if you say so," I agree, not really believing him. "Can you have a word with him about treating me nicer?"

"Meet with him again and if you still have problems, I'll intervene."

With our conversation at its natural conclusion, we walk in companionable silence through the twisting halls of the castle. I'm replaying in my mind my encounter with Master Sarpedon. I never knew I was afraid of snakes. Of course, I've never seen an actual snake in person before. Meeting a fifteen-foot talking snake would scare anybody. Maybe the creepy Temple and that stupid skull door helped put me on edge. That might have prejudiced my reaction. Jonah is fond of him and if he likes him, then I'll try to like him, too.

"What was that thing you said to him when you first came in? That 'jee hek say koy tep' or something?"

"*Jwi héxé en koitep*," Jonah says. "It is the greeting of the Order of the Temple. You can use it too. It means 'Satisfaction in harmony be upon you.' When a Knight greets you, you respond, *Nan lapè în sül avètk*, 'Enjoyment in peace among you.'"

That sounds romantic. I'll try to remember it. Maybe try it on Dathid and see if he knows it.

Jonah gets quiet again. We often have long periods of silence, but this is more like he's distracted.

"Is something the matter?"

"Hmm," he says as if I caught him doing something wrong. "No. No, everything's fine. We need to talk. I want to know how you feel about all of this."

"Well, it's a lot for a first day. I hope every day isn't going to be this hard. I like Kyrbast. I saw my mother!" I shout, then become self-conscious and lower my voice. "I saw her. She looks like me. Or I look like her. It was so amazing. Well, more than amazing, but I don't know how to describe it. She was right there! Right in front of me. Oh, Jonah, I wish you could've seen her. She's very pretty."

I get quiet remembering my mother. The sadness is creeping up on me. I push it down. I will not be sad, because it's a happy thing. I saw my mother for the first time and that makes me joyful. I change the subject and tell him about Albína, and Lenox, and the many other interesting things that have happened to me on my first day at Cromsmead.

Jonah listens with interest to everything I'm saying, but I'm talking so fast he can only nod his head.

As we near my room, I wrap it up. "Oh, and then his tail uncurled! I thought I would hit the roof or maybe the floor. I'm still not used to people not looking like people. Although you don't look anything like a person and I like the way you look. I was never afraid of you. Not even when you jumped through my window in the middle of the night."

I sit on the sofa next to him when we get to my room. "I've missed you," I say.

He gives me a sad, sympathetic look. "I've missed you too." I lean on his warm shoulder. "So do you feel comfortable with Master Sarpedon?"

I don't want to lie to Jonah or insult his friend. "I'm relatively confident he won't eat me."

"Master Sarpedon is a vegetarian. Most Knights are."

"Do I have to be a vegetarian? That sounds awful."

"Well, the human Templars were allowed meat three times a week, but you had to eat in silence. You also had to take a vow of poverty, and they had a firm belief that if you were not working or training, you were praying."

"Well, I can't get any poorer. Meat three times a week would be more than I got in Queens. Good luck with the silence, though. And working and praying seem to be the only things to do here anyway."

"Sometimes you really impress me. Those were old rules, written in a different time. You're the only human Templar left, so you can probably bend the rules a little. And for your information, you're far from poor."

241

I'm reveling in the fact that I impressed him when his last statement makes me pause. "What do you mean?"

"You're the sole heir to the Rhomstead estate. You are, in fact, Lord Rhomstead. And I assure you, everyone has done their best to keep the estate functioning properly in case you returned."

"So I'm rich?"

Jonah makes a face. "Well, I can't speak in human terms. Curra don't have the monetary system humans have, but yes, you could return to Earth and be considered wealthy."

"How could I do that?"

"First off, you would rule a house that's smaller than this one but with more ground. And if you haven't noticed, Ashra is where many of Earth's rare precious stones and metals come from."

I nod. I've seen all kinds of jewels and odd metals decorating just about every inch of this place. "It's like I won the lottery. I feel guilty for not being ecstatic. But money never meant much to me. I was fine being broke, as long as I had enough to eat."

"One of the ironies of being a Knight. You're good at accumulating wealth, but you have no need for it," he says as he stands. "Well anyway, it's there if you need it."

"It's time to get ready for dinner," he continues, turning his back to me. "The elves keep it formal, so you'll have to dress. I'll escort you down in a bit. Did Albína show you how to summon her?"

I shake my head and Jonah walks over to three ribbons hanging on the wall. I remember Kyrbast having the same thing in his lab.

"These summon different people. Since the only one you know is Albína, this one is hers." He pulls the yellow ribbon. The door between Albína's room and mine opens and Albína steps out.

"I'll be back shortly." He kisses my head and leaves.

CHAPTER 34

I close the door and turn around to find Albína by my closet with a wide smile spread across her face.

"I have something for you," she says in a singsong voice that emphasizes her excitement. Her smile grows surprisingly larger when she unfolds the black dress in her arms. "I had them rush this so you'd have something appropriate to wear tonight. I hope you like it."

A smile spreads across my face. Elves don't wear black, which means this dress was custom-made. Albína abhors black, especially on women. The fact that she rushed this unfrilly dark dress just for me touches my soul in a way I can't explain. It causes my stomach to do a little flip and my chest to hurt. Someone went out of their way to do something nice for me because they thought it would make me happy. I didn't know people actually did that.

"Thank you," is all I can think to say.

I put the dress on. I'm trying to remember the last time I had a dress, but nothing comes to mind. Maybe I've never worn one. I wish Auntie would've taken pictures of me when I was younger. It's hard to believe that I never wore a dress, but it's possible.

I like the high neckline and long sleeves that are relatively simple compared to what the elves wear. The tailored bodice fits my body, and when I give Albína a spin, the skirt flares out around me. It's so fun feeling the dress float around my knees that I twirl a few more times until I get dizzy.

I step in front of the mirror to see if I'm as attractive as I feel. My heart sinks when it's still plain old Agatha. The dress is pretty, though. I just wish the elves had resisted the urge to add the gold embroidery. Starting at my shoulder is a gold dragon-snake creature that weaves its way down to my waist then circles around my back to end in the front, just above my knee.

"You never know. You may start a trend," Albína coos as she adjusts the dress. She's all smiles until she stands back to have a look at me. She frowns, and I want to rip the dress from my body. I'm just not a dress-wearing kind of girl.

"Maybe I'm getting used to your fashion sense, but the goanna seems a bit much." She touches my shoulder and says, "*Tovab coim.*"

The embroidered goanna slithers across my body. I throw my arms out and freeze. I don't even breathe. What the heck is around me? I thought it was thread, but it can move. It tickles as it slithers across my belly, but I'm so frightened I don't make a sound. It only takes a few seconds for the goanna to wrap itself around my waist twice and tie itself in a knot over my hip.

"That's much better," she says while she adds a clip to my hair. Once she's satisfied, she asks, "Are you alright?"

I'm as still as a statue with my arms stretched out at my sides because I don't want to touch the embroidery. It might bite me or squeeze me or something. I wish she would've ordered it to the curtains. I force a smile to my face and lower my arms because I don't want her to know that I'm afraid of my pretty dress.

When the goanna doesn't move, I smile for real and I give her another spin. Only this time I do it to see if the goanna will move again. It doesn't.

I take a deep breath and then stare awkwardly at her. We're both waiting for Jonah to fetch me, but in the meantime we're alone with nothing to do. We stand in uncomfortable stillness for a few moments until I can't take it anymore.

"So," I say, but run out of words. *Ask a question*, my brain demands but refuses to produce the actual question. I hope she can't see my panic as I frantically search my empty mind for anything else to say. Too much time has passed from my opening, *So*, amplifying my self-consciousness. This situation is rapidly leaving awkward and barreling straight into painful. I need to say something.

"I don't know anything about you, Albína." When in doubt, state the obvious. I forget which teacher said that, but I could kiss her right now. I do a quick exhale and catch myself. I was so nervous, I forgot to breathe. I take a few short breaths, trying to be sly, but she's onto me. With the added oxygen, my brain forms a question. "Are you married?"

By the time I leave my room, I know that Albína is widowed and her husband died in battle a long time ago. She has five grown children, all of whom are married, and one who works for the embassy, which makes her proud. She's been in the Queen's service for most of her life, loves her job and the royal family. She had her own apartment here at the castle, but she likes the one attached to my chambers better because it has a bigger closet. I heard many other facts but can't keep them in my head because they came at me so fast.

When Jonah and I arrive at dinner, we seem to be the last ones to arrive again. "Are we late?"

"No, you're the guest of honor. You have to arrive last," he explains. Elves have rules for everything.

This time instead of placing me next to the King, Jonah puts me next to a still-miserable Dathid, who is sitting next to the Princess.

Dathid stands, giving me a clear view of his wife. "Hello," she says with a big smile.

I'm not sure if I'm supposed to bow or something, so I opt for a small smile and a brief "Hi" with an equally small wave.

Dathid pulls out my chair and I quickly sit. When he's seated next to me, he thankfully blocks me from any more conversation. He takes a drink and I catch him subtly laughing at my dress. I don't take offense. He's laughing at the elves' sense of style, not at me.

There's no chair on my other side, so Jonah takes a seat between Princess Elaeria and the Queen. I'm alone in this big room with all of these weird elves staring at me and nobody to make conversation with except Dathid. This is going to be a long night.

Dathid leans in to whisper with a chuckle, "Nice goanna."

It pleases me to elicit a smile from him, but I like the elves. I'm still deeply touched that they tried so hard to make me happy. Dathid has a right to not like them, but I don't want to disparage my nice dress, so I lie. "I like it."

"Well, in that case, I won't tell you what to say to make it go away."

"You can do that?" I whisper back.

He chuckles at my quick change of attitude. "Yep," he says into his cup as he takes a drink. "We can put it over there on that awful unicorn tapestry. The elves would probably love it. Give it some more color."

The tapestry is pretty, but it's also extremely colorful, just like everything else the elves touch. The shiny gold goanna planted in the middle of the busy needlework would give the tapestry the one color it doesn't have.

"That's not nice," I say with a giggle.

Food is served and our conversation ends. This time, when the waiter pours the bright yellow liquid into my goblet, Dathid doesn't pull it away. I'm curious about how it tastes, so before he changes his mind, I grab it and take a quick sip. It's sickeningly sweet, like cough syrup with extra sugar.

I make a face and he laughs. "I didn't think you'd like it."

"Ugh. That's awful," I whisper while covertly wiping my tongue on my napkin.

Dathid laughs again, which draws the attention of Princess Elaeria. She glances at him and then at me. Her gaze isn't critical, more like astounded. She seems curious to know what could possibly make him laugh. However, I'm not sure she's pleased with his jovial mood.

Our lack of conversation gives me the opportunity to reflect on my day and my hosts, which inevitably causes me to compare the elves to the faeries. The elves are so foreign, old-fashioned and otherworldly, but the faeries seem almost human. Granted, they're more beautiful than any people I've ever seen, but with their wings folded they appear human and they act more human too.

"Dathid, how come faeries have more in common with humans than the elves do? I mean, I don't know. I was led to believe that elves were magical and stuff, but they were more humanesque. Faeries were more mystical, something like a butterfly, I guess—still magic, of course, but elusive. Or is that offensive?"

He's thoughtful for a moment. I probably should've asked Jonah this question because asking people about their race and ethnicity and stuff is rude. They should give me a book or something. Dathid and I are finally on good terms, so I don't want my stupid mouth and even stupider brain to mess that up.

He swallows his bite of food, wipes his mouth, then looks to his wife, who's deep in conversation with Jonah. He scans the crowd, then turns to me while resting his head on his hands. He's trying to block our conversation from the others at the table.

"Well," he says quietly, "the humans and the elves have much in common. I'm surprised you don't see the resemblance. I think that because the elves lived on Earth for millennia, you share many similarities. Although humans and elves didn't have much interaction until close to *Peme Nav Wusht*."

I guess he read my confused expression because he translates. "*Peme Nav Wusht* is what we call the sealing of the portals."

He takes another drink and continues. "The timing worked out well for the elves. They lived in areas that had temperate weather. As the humans invaded those territories, they were slowly pushed back to Ashra. Some were trapped on the other side when the portals closed, but they've all since died out."

Dathid scans the room and takes a deep breath. He chooses his words carefully when he whispers, "Elves don't really like humans. As I said, the humans took their lands. They warred with the humans for centuries until they gave up and left. It's odd that you don't see the similarities, though. Elves shaped much of the human culture."

He waves his arms to point out the grand room and all its luxuries. "They were living like this when humans had very small numbers and were living in mud huts. Not only did humans adopt their feudalistic politics, but much of what humans know about agriculture and husbandry they learned from the elves."

"The elves don't like me?" I ask. "They seem so nice."

Dathid lifts his head from his hands. "Of course they like you. I'm speaking in a broader sense. None of these elves were alive in the time before *Peme Nav Wusht*. They've never had their lands stolen, and other than the occasional Wizard, they haven't seen a human for generations."

I'm relieved. I like the elves. Well, one elf—Albína. We're becoming friends, and I'd hate to think that she doesn't like me because I'm human.

"The differences you're seeing are mainly in their appearance. They are awfully pointy. Other than my wings, I could pass for human."

"You're way too pretty to be human," I blurt out, then pray for death.

He laughs. "I've heard that before," he says to ease my embarrassment. "Did you know that faeries have never lived on Earth?"

"What? How?" I stutter. "Then how do we know about you?"

"It's possible fairies were spotted while hunting on Earth, but not likely. It wasn't a common practice because we're temperature-sensitive. Your change of day could be fatal. I think most of the human stories are mainly from humans who have come over here. Before the Knights were posted at the portals, humans would often stumble through one. If it survived, it was usually escorted back by a faerie. We don't eat humans."

After a moment I say, "You know, that's the most amount of words you've ever said to me."

Dathid gives me a crooked smile. "I've had a lot to drink."

That makes me laugh. He can be charming when he wants to be. "So if faeries have had little contact with humans, how come we seem to have so much in common?"

"Well, as I said, we look a lot alike. I can only speak for my clan when I say we're fond of your culture. When our clan first settled here, that portal was rarely used. There was nothing on the other side. Occasionally, we would see a human, one of your..." He pauses, trying to remember the name.

"Oh, I forgot the English word," he says, as he puts his hand to his mouth and struggles to remember. "What do you call the humans who were there first? The ones who were there before America?"

"Native Americans?"

"Yes, Native Americans. Should've guessed that one. Well, sometimes a Native American would wander in, or if we were hunting over there, one would see us. It wasn't until we started seeing the towers that we took an interest in your culture."

"Interest? How?"

"We read a lot of your books, magazines, and newspapers. Our library is probably five times the size of the largest library on Earth. However, there are other faerie clans, in other parts of Ashra that have little in common with the humans."

I'm so engrossed with what Dathid is saying that I jump when the music starts. I hope he doesn't have to dance again, or worse, that I'll have to dance. Thankfully, an elf with an intensely sparkly hat parades to the dance floor with a woman who is covered in so many feathers she looks like she's dusting the floor, not dancing on it.

Dathid leans in. "I don't suggest you hang about for the dancing. You've an early day tomorrow."

I'm relieved that I don't have to stay. Last night was fun, but I'm more of a solitary person. Once is enough for me.

"Give me a moment and I'll escort you back," he says dismissively as he turns to speak to his wife.

He's talking to her in Naga-Nuru. That's three languages he's spoken so far. How many more does he know? Jonah chimes in with something in the same language and then Dathid stands and pulls my chair out. He holds out his arm and I grab it. I want to know if it's an elf thing, the holding of the arm, or if the faeries normally do it, too. But I won't ask because it's probably rude.

It's much quieter when we leave the hall. Every elf we pass suspiciously eyes Dathid. They don't do much to hide their disdain, and it's making me uneasy. I can't imagine how he feels.

"Do you feel safe here?"

"Yeah," he says, none too convincingly. "For the most part I do, but not very comfortable."

"It must be hard to be married to your enemy." No wonder he was so unhappy about the journey here. I shouldn't have judged him so harshly.

"That's probably the hardest part."

I thought he'd say more, but he doesn't. Our comfortable silence slips into awkward.

"Well," I say in order to change the subject, "the nice thing about your lack of friends is that it's made me your ally. You're a lot nicer when everybody's afraid of you."

"I've always been your ally," Dathid says, genuinely hurt by my little joke. "I've sworn my life to you. I'm truly sorry if I gave you the impression that we aren't allies."

"No, I'm sorry. It was just a stupid joke. You've made a lot of sacrifices bringing me here and I appreciate it. I do. Thank you."

He doesn't acknowledge my apology or appreciation, but I let the matter drop when we arrive at my room. He makes me wait outside while he checks to confirm that it's safe inside. It's unnecessary, but I don't say anything. It makes him happy, so why fight it? He opens the door for me when he's done. He looks uncomfortable.

Before I can invite him to have a seat on the sofa he blurts out, "I'm leaving tomorrow."

"What?" is the question that leaps from my lips while my brain hopes that maybe I misheard him. One of my only two friends in the world—sorry, *two* worlds—is abandoning me tomorrow.

"I'm sorry," he says lamely.

I didn't realize how close I had grown to Dathid. The thought of him leaving makes my chest hurt. Betrayal and abandonment swirl around my brain.

"Why? You've only been here a day."

He takes a deep breath. "Well, as you can see, I'm not welcome here."

"But your wife is here!" I shout. That may not be the best argument, but it's all I've got.

"I'm sorry," he says again. "I was to escort you here and I have done so. I have responsibilities in Manahata that I dropped when you needed me. I must get back to them."

It's wrong of me to want him to stay, but I don't want him to go. "You'll be exceptionally busy. You probably won't even notice I'm gone."

I can't say anything. I've never been good at making friends, and I'm even worse at keeping them.

"I'll come back," he says. "When you're ready to go in search of the key, I'll be there with you."

253

A weight lifts off my shoulders. "Do you promise?"

"Yes, of course, I promise."

"Pinky swear?" I quietly joke.

"You want me to give you a pinky!"

"No," I laugh, holding up my pinky.

Dathid wraps his finger around mine and stares into my eyes. "I bind myself to you in the most sacred covenant of the pinky swear. I will return to you and always be at your side whenever I am needed."

I hug him, which surprises both of us. He's momentarily stunned but recovers quickly and hugs me back. "I vow to you, Agatha, that I will be here when you need me," he whispers to the top of my head.

We break our embrace and I escort him to the door. "You won't leave without saying goodbye?"

"I swear."

CHAPTER 35

After Dathid leaves, I numbly change into my nightclothes and hop into bed. Today has been a long day. I'm exhausted, but my stupid brain won't shut off. It's still busily processing the overabundance of information I've received. I can't believe that I've only been in Cromsmead one full day. It feels like a week. I hope every day won't be as tough as this one.

Albína comes in and I try to convince her that she doesn't need to babysit me, but she insists. Just like last night, she knits while I stare at the clouds on the ceiling.

"Is there anything to read? Dathid said the faeries had a large selection of books from Earth. Is there anything here?"

"I don't know. I could check for you."

"No, that's okay. I'm just awake. My brain is at capacity anyway, so a book might really damage it."

I lie awake, staring at various parts of my new room for a long time. I'm not in the least bit tired. When there's a knock on my door, I leap from the bed, but Albína is already answering it.

"Good. You're still awake," Jonah says as I run over to greet him.

Albína hands me a bathrobe and wishes me a good night before she leaves. Jonah and I sit together on the sofa.

"Did Dathid talk to you?" His tone is making me nervous.

I nod.

He grunts. I have no idea what that means. Maybe he'll miss Dathid, too.

After a long pause, he blurts out, "I'm leaving, also."

"What! You can't leave! You can't leave me here. You can't!" My heart seizes, forcing my blood to race to my fingers and toes. I wobble like he hit me. I want to strike back. "You bring me to this strange place and then you abandon me. How could you do that? I don't want to be here without you!" My sobs make my words unintelligible. I can't look at his pitying face, so I stalk to the other end of the room.

I pace until I'm out of breath and sweating, or maybe that's the fear. I stare out the window at the bright, sunny night and let my tears fall silently down my cheeks. I feel every bit of the strangeness of this land. I can't believe I put myself in this situation. I'm profoundly stupid. I want to hate Jonah for bringing me here and deserting me, but it's my fault. I never asked the right questions. I just trusted him and now here I am, lost and alone.

I sense him walking up behind me. He hands me a hankie. I don't want anything from him, but I need that stupid hankie. I grab it, but refuse to look at him. He tries to put his hand on my shoulder, but I shrug it off. He gives up and walks away. It's like he's walking out of my life. But that's what people do, right? Walk out. I shouldn't be surprised and I shouldn't be so mad.

I stay by the window thinking nothing and everything. I imagine this place without the comfort of my friends and I don't like it. I don't like this place. I don't like the strange creatures or their strange customs. I don't want to be here.

When my composure returns, I turn to talk to Jonah but he's gone. He didn't even say goodbye. The room tilts and my head swims. I'm alone, really alone. It's just me. I'm all I've got, and I am not enough.

"Jonah," I whisper. I want to yell it as loud as I can, but my voice is gone. I'm about to run after him and beg him to not leave me when his shadowy form ascends from under the sofa.

My panic is so quickly replaced with relief that it makes me giddy. I giggle for no reason and say, "That's still creepy." I blow my nose and we huddle on the sofa. "I can't do this without you." The tears start again.

"That's why I have to go."

"I don't understand. Why are you making me do this by myself? I don't know anybody. I want to go home."

He gently turns me to face him. "I've been in numerous meetings with an untold number of people. You're our only hope. Everyone wants what's best for you, but we all have different ideas as to what that is."

"So they're getting rid of you so they can do whatever they want with me," I say, my anger mounting.

"No," he says firmly. "Plans for your training have been laid out. Master Sarpedon has complete say in your training and safety. Your schedules have been made and everything is put into motion. I'd be…an interference."

"How could you be an interference?"

"Well, first of all, before I answer that, you need to understand that I have some people back in Brooklyn who miss me. I need to explain to them what happened. Also, I need to be trained."

I've seen Jonah fight twice, once against a whole squad of red soldiers and another against a huge monster. Jonah does not need training. "What are you talking about?"

257

"Well, I've only loosely followed a Knight's path. I protect the curra in New York City, but that's more of a *grab-them-and-run* situation. There aren't many swordfights. I was trained to use a sword many, many years ago, but it has been a long time since I held one. There was never a need. To put it plainly, I'm terribly out of shape," he says with a self-conscious smile that makes me feel guilty for forcing that confession out of him.

He sobers and continues. "I also don't know how to be an escort for a young human female. I was the one who brought you here because I was the one who found you. And you trusted me. It's the judgment of the council that I receive some training in that area too."

"So you're coming back." I push the hope down. I don't want to get too excited in case I'm wrong.

"Yes. Dathid didn't tell you we were coming back?"

"Yeah, he said *he* was coming back. He didn't say anything about you!" I'm shouting with both relief and anger. He could've saved me a lot of pain if he'd told me that first.

"I'm sorry. I will be back in a few…" He pauses, trying to think of a good time frame I'll understand. "Months. It will feel like a few months."

"Months?" I whine.

"The time will fly by. I'll be back before you know it." He pulls me to him and gives me a sideways hug. I never knew there were so many different types of hugs.

I lean against his shoulder and ask, "What's the second thing?"

He tenses. "Huh?"

"What's the second thing? You said 'first of all', that means there's at least a 'second of all.'"

"You are clever," he says and then tenses up. "There is a second. The council thinks that my being here will hamper your growth."

I'm not one for extreme emotions, but this news makes me so enraged I might hit something. For now, I jump up and pace the room. "That's stupid! Who is this council and why am I not on it!"

He pauses and then nods his head. "You're right. You should have a seat on the council. It is your life, after all."

"Well, I need to make a few changes." I'm strengthened by my rage. I turn to Jonah and hold up a finger. "First of all," I say with a pause so he can appreciate the drama of using his words, "I want a seat. Secondly, I want Dathid to have a seat. Thirdly, I want you to be in charge! If they want me to do this, they'll have to give me a say!"

Jonah salutes me with a smile. "Yes Sir, Lord Rhomstead. Acting like a Knight already and you've only been in training for one day. You're going to be a handful once you know what you're doing."

I sit back down. The anger briefly covered my fear, but now that it has expelled itself, the sadness is creeping back up. Jonah is leaving. What'll I do without him? I'm here, all alone, with awful people who push me around without ever getting to know me.

"I'm going to miss you," he says.

"Yeah, me too." I lean against him. He puts his arm around my shoulder and we stay that way until I fall asleep.

CHAPTER 36

The birds are singing so loudly I can't think. Albína shouts the command that shuts them up, and everything goes quiet. I take a couple of deep breaths to get my thinking straight. That's an awful way to wake up. I look for Jonah, but he's gone. He must have carried me to bed after I fell asleep.

"Is there a volume control on those things?" I ask Albína.

"They do seem a bit loud. I'll read the instruction manual this afternoon and see what I can do. Sir Jonah is taking you to breakfast, so you need to get dressed," she says in the singsong voice that means she has a surprise for me. She pops into the closet and returns with a pair of black pants and a long black sweater almost identical to the one I wore here.

My heart leaps almost as far as I do when I jump out of bed and nearly land on her. "It's perfect! Thank you, Albína."

I hug her without thinking and then feel the fabric of the lightweight leggings. They're made out of the same soft fabric as most everything here. The sweater is a heavier knit, but it's also velvety soft.

I race to the bathroom and grab the jars of colored powder. "Please show me how to do this so I don't have to be waited on," I ask, pulling a scoop of the green powder

260

out of the jar. I love baths, but I don't like having to ask permission before taking one.

"That's too much." She grabs my hand and shakes out the appropriate amount. "Now, sprinkle that in, and another. Be careful with the yellow. It has a tendency to spill and is difficult to clean up."

I throw the powders in the tub and applaud when it fills with water. I want to know how they do that. And how do they get it to the right temperature?

"A quick bath. We haven't much time if you want to see your demon before we go," she says before closing the door behind her.

I do as I'm told, but I don't have time to dry my hair. Albína is appalled that I'd let others see me this way, but I want enough time to visit with Lenox.

We wind our way around the castle. It's only my second day, but I'm already learning my way through the maze of corridors. When we reach the rooftop, Lenox has his head happily buried in a large bird. He reluctantly looks up and sends Albína scurrying back and slamming the door behind her.

He walks over to me, but I stop him because his mouth is covered in bird goo and feathers. "Now this is just gross," I explain while wiping off his mouth with a rag I found in the supply box. Lenox stands still for his grooming until I'm satisfied with my work. "There. Now you're back to your old handsome self."

As soon as the words leave my mouth, Lenox does his inspection. He doesn't like my wet hair. He smells it for a long time and then tries to eat it.

"I just washed that. Don't be getting bird guts in it."

He stares back at his meal.

"All right. I only wanted to make sure you were okay. Are you okay?"

I wish he could talk, because although he can understand me, I haven't a clue what he's thinking.

"Go eat your breakfast. I'll be back to check on you later."

He wastes no time returning to his meal and I retrieve Albína, who's hiding inside the doorway.

"I thought you were starting to like him."

"I'm trying, Miss," she answers while fixing my hair.

Jonah meets me at the entry to the castle and escorts me to a pub in the village whose name translates to 'The Brewer's Daft.' Dathid is already waiting out front, and when we walk in, it's quiet and practically empty. The elves keep a strict schedule, and breakfast is over.

The place is rather simple by elfin standards, with the exception of an inordinate number of spiral staircases scattered about. Some of the staircases are functional, but most lead to nowhere, ending in open space or at a beam or the ceiling.

I follow Jonah and Dathid as they wordlessly pick up a table and move it to the corner. Then they gather three chairs and invite me to sit.

"So you just grab a table and put it wherever you want?"

"Yes. How else would you do it?" Dathid asks.

"In America, most of the furniture in public places is stationary. You can only move something with permission of the management," Jonah explains.

"Sounds uncomfortable. What if you don't like where you're sitting?"

"Well, you either deal with it or you may be able to get another table," Jonah answers.

Dathid looks dumbfounded. After a moment of contemplation he asks, "So you leave the table you're at to go sit at another one?"

"If another is available."

"Huh," Dathid says with skepticism about the stationary furniture. "Sometimes I wish I could see the other side. It all sounds strange and magical."

"Magical?" Why would he choose that word?

"Yes. We read a lot of your literature and we see the lights of your towers. Television sounds fascinating. And the sun...one minute it's there and the next it's gone? Sounds terrifying. And you have so many rules for everything."

"*We* have a lot of rules?" I ask. "No one has more rules than elves. In New York, I'm allowed to eat when I want and wear what I want and no one cares. Here there's a rule for everything."

"Yes, humans love rules. That table rule is a good example," Dathid says defensively. We continue our debate until the food arrives.

I don't want them to leave me here alone. I have so much I want to say but I've already said it, so I don't have anything else to add.

After a few minutes Jonah says to Dathid, "You should have a seat on the council."

He answers with a mouth full of food. "They'll never allow two faeries on the council. My father has more experience anyway."

"You have a lot to offer, too."

"Thanks. I wasn't fishing for compliments. I just meant that my father should be there, and if not him, then my sister. She's the heir. They're much better at the politics than I am."

"Agatha doesn't need a politician. She needs people she can trust. And you're underselling your value. You have a wealth of knowledge she'll find useful."

Dathid turns to me with a crooked smile. "Well, if the elves ever give you a problem, I'll show you the best way to gut 'em."

Jonah shakes his head. "You have traveled over a good portion of Ashra, and you have encountered and fought many of the enemies she'll be facing. No one else on the council can say that."

Dathid folds his arms across his chest and leans back in his chair. "I hate politicians."

"Good," Jonah says. "I'm going to order the fruit cup. Would you like dessert?"

"Yes, do they have that cake we had last night?" I ask, and Dathid cringes.

"They have something like it," Jonah says, but I'm not paying attention because Dathid looks like he's going to be ill.

"Why are you looking at me like that?" he asks.

"You look like you're going to be sick."

"I can handle the smell of most elfin foods. Bread's tough, but dessert is disgusting."

"Okay, no dessert," I say.

"Go ahead and get it." It would've been a kind gesture if his face had cooperated, but he looks as if he smells something rotten.

Jonah deftly changes the subject, and we laugh and joke well past the end of the meal.

When the conversation dies down I ask, "So, when are you leaving?"

"When we're done here," Jonah answers.

I push my plate away and rest my chin against my hand. "I don't want you to go."

"We don't want to leave," Jonah says.

I'm knocked slightly off balance when Dathid bangs his elbow against mine and whispers, "*I* want to leave."

I smile at him. It's surprising how close we've become over the past couple of days. I trust him. I guess I always did. It took me a while to adjust to his demeanor, but it's just the way he is. This might be what it's like to have a brother.

We follow Jonah out of the pub and back to the castle. "Well, it's nice being outside," I say, trying to be chipper.

"Let's see if your feelings change once the physical training begins," Dathid says.

My heart drops to my stomach when Jonah turns down the path to the stables. "You're leaving now?"

He puts his arm around my shoulders as he nods to one of the grooms. How can he comfort me while planning his departure? The groom runs into the barn and returns with two unicorns already saddled and packed.

"Right now?" I shout. This is too fast. I thought I'd have more time. They're abandoning me. I want to grab Jonah and fall into a fit of temper until he promises to never leave me.

Instead, he hugs me and kisses my head. "We're coming back." He gently puts a finger under my chin and lifts my head so he can look into my eyes. "We're coming back," he repeats.

I wipe the tears that are forming. "I'll miss you."

"My thoughts will always be with you. Train hard and listen to Master Sarpedon. He knows best," Jonah says, then mounts his unicorn. I let him go without expressing all the words of protest that are racing through my mind.

I turn to Dathid, who looks so uncomfortable it would make me giggle if I weren't so sad. "I have a present for you," he says as his groom hands me an elaborately quilted bag.

"Why?"

He smiles. "Because I think you need it."

I open the bag to find an array of paint containers and brushes. I'm speechless. I've never had my own paints before. Or any paints, really. I used to scrounge for anything with color, and mixed and matched until I created something usable. "I don't know what to say," I whisper to the inside of the bag. "There are so many colors."

"Well, your walls looked rather dull. Those are Manahata paints, not the cheap elf stuff."

My head snaps up. "I couldn't. The Queen would kill me. She already doesn't like me. I couldn't ruin her room."

"It's your room. She can't kill you until you do what she needs. And if anyone tells you to stop, tell them you're under orders from the Crown Prince."

"Thank you," I say. "I wish I had more words for such a thoughtful gift."

"Jonah says I should be more like him." He grabs me and gives me an awkward hug before quickly releasing me.

"Oh," he adds as if he remembered something. He clutches my head about the ears and roughly drags me toward him so he can kiss the top of my head.

That makes me laugh.

He laughs too. "Okay, maybe I need to work on it a bit." He can be so charming when he tries.

Dathid mounts his unicorn before I can say any real goodbye to him. Then he salutes me and says, "*Jwi héxé en koitep.*"

"Enjoyment in peace among you," I whisper, and half-heartedly salute back.

They both give me a wave. Then the two of them trot off, and I watch until they disappear around the corner.

I look down and kick at the stones under my boots. I'm all alone in a strange world with no friends and nowhere else to go. I lift my head and force my feet to take me back to my room. What am I supposed to do now?

Candy Atkins is a full-time writer who lives with her husband and two kids in Orlando, Florida. She's an avid reader and lover of all things fantasy and sci-fi. Her debut novel, *The Lost Knight*, is volume one of the six-part *Lost Knight Series*.

Her life's journey has taken her from dining with the President to being on food stamps to running her own company. And since all author bios end by naming and quantifying pets…she also enjoys spending time with her boxer, Butler, and Wynona the cat.

To learn more about Candy Atkins and her books, visit www.CandyAtkins.com, follow at @Candy_Atkins on Twitter, like her at Candy Atkins Author on Facebook, and find her at Candy_Atkins on Instagram.

Acknowledgements

Alone we can do so little, together we can do so much.

-- Helen Keller

To everyone who reads my words, thank you. Thank you for your time, your commitment, and your support.

To my hubby, my soul mate, my best friend, and my biggest cheerleader. Thank you for believing I could do this. And thank you for counseling me when I believed I couldn't.

To my editor, Harry Althoff. Much like Goldilocks, it was difficult finding an editor who wasn't too mean or one who wasn't too nice. It was such a privilege to work with someone who was "just right" and cared about my characters as much as I did.

Thanks to my bestie Deborah Harnden. Your support in my darkest hours will always be a highlight in my life.

Flora Smith, the sister I never had and the bravest person I know. Thank you for propping me up and sending me "back out there" when I absolutely didn't want to go. You never didn't believe.

Thank you to my first readers, Savannah Nash and Katie Glading and the entire Ryder family: Chris, Hilerie, Austin and Aeryn. Thank you for taking a risk and spending your time on an untested novel. Your feedback and support was invaluable and much needed. You guys are the best.

Thank you to everyone who worked so tirelessly to make my dreams come true. Autumn Rain Glading for being the woman with a plan. Tameka Mullins, the wordsmith, who both inspires and excites. Bonnie Douglas, the one who was with me from the beginning. Jaye Rochon, the creative visionary. And the women of Bearly Marketing for your tireless effort in making it all happen.

And thank you to Agatha Stone for saving my life and helping me wade through the most difficult of journeys.

The Lost Knight Extras

Pronunciation/prə͵nansē'āSH(ə)n/

Just in case you're not fluent in Naga-Nuru or Gàidhlig or any of the many Ashra languages...here's a guide to help you discuss your favorite places and characters.

20 Questions with Candy Atkins

A sit down interview with the author, discussing how Ashra and Agatha came into being; and a frank discussion of what it's like dealing with a learning disability

A Sneak peek at the mind-blowing sequel The Lost Girl

Be the first to get of glimpse of what lies in wait for Agatha.

Pronunciation

PEOPLE

Dathid: Dath-id

Albína: Al-bee-na

Queen Ekecheiria: Queen Ek-a-share-ee-a

Princess Elaeria: Prin-cess E-lay-er-i-a

Kyrbast: Keer-bast

Master Sarpedon: Mas-ter Sar-pa-don

Gurador: Gore-a-door

Grucht Leisck: Groot Leash-k

Stratagor Ziras: Strat-a-gor Zeer-as

Matban Tadin: Mat-ban Tad-in

Oberon Thunderclaws: O-ber-ron Thun-der-claw-s

PLACES

Manahata: Man-na-hat-ta

Cromsmead: Croms-mead

Gwa Twouroch: Gwa Tor-oosch

Usuóko Ocean: Ew-soak-ko Ocean

/prə͵nənsēˈāSH(ə)n/

FUN THINGS TO SAY

Curramonstrusos: (Kur-ra-mon-stoos-os) Sentient beings of Ashra

Jwi héxé en koitep: (J-wee hex-ay en koy-tep) Templar greeting meaning 'Satisfaction in harmony be upon you.'

Nan lapè în sül avètk: (Naan la-pay en-sol-a-fect) Templar response meaning 'Enjoyment in peace among you'

Nüwa: Nee-wa

Gàidhlig: (Gaa-lik) Not to be confused with Scottish Gaelic

Jörmungandr: (Your-muhn-gun-dar) Sea serpent

Rosicrucian: Rose-ee-kroo-shen

Latuus birds: Lay-too-s birds

Sonti: (Saan-tee) Jump

Kaddamoll: Kad-a-mol

MAGIC WORDS

Vido cluana: (Vee-do Cla-na) Shut up

Talush ba dio: (Tal-ush baa-dee-oh) No idea what it means. Kyrbast picked up a chair with this spell.

Tovab coim: (To-vab koy-m) Makes embroidery move

20

QUESTIONS WITH THE AUTHOR

1. How did you come up with the idea for Agatha?

So, back at the turn of the century, I was sitting in a meeting for the finalization of my bankruptcy. It was a time in my life where I was fighting too many wars on too many fronts—this was just another battle. I was sitting in the conference room surrounded by ten lawyers who were all gathered around the table fighting over who got what. I wasn't allowed to sit at the table. I had to sit in a chair off to the side and observe. On the table was the plan that dissolved what was left of my life.

There was nothing left. I had this image of a bare carcass thrown on the table and vultures pecking each other's eyes out over a few pieces of tendon still holding at the spine.

I sat there silently watching them and thought, "When are these men going to remember that I'm a person? That I'm a single mother, all alone, with two children under the age of six? That what they're battling over is the remains of a lot of hard work and sacrifice? And this is a devastating moment for me."

The answer was never. But it got me thinking about what it would be like to physically leave the human race. How would I respond to being thrown into a world where no one is like me? Forced into a situation where I'd have to fight, but be totally unqualified, overwhelmed and desperate?

2. Where did the inspiration come from to sit down and write?

I wanted a voice. I'd been silenced for years, not by any one thing, but by everything. I was scared and alone and silent. I remember praying to God to give me a voice and let someone, anyone, hear it. "Praying" is too nice a word; it was one of my many God rants.

At the same time, I was reading a study Bible—I can't remember the passage but the study guide said, *'God likes it when we use our gifts.'* I thought, "Great! My gift is being organized. How can I make career out of that?"

What I didn't realize was that storytelling—conveying difficult concepts into easy-to-understand language—was my gift. I had been telling stories my entire life. It's why I was drawn to operations management. It was why I wrote popular manuals. And why my friends and family were always quoting me.

Around that same time, I got an idea for a shadow monster that wouldn't leave me alone. I wrote fifty pages before I ran out of words. His story wasn't very interesting, but the girl he met was. I remember staring at Jonah's story, hitting the new document icon and thinking, *Agatha sounds like she might have an interesting future.*

3. Why does Agatha start her adventure on her thirteenth birthday?

At first I wanted to highlight just how unprepared she would be for her mission. But then my daughter, Liv, turned thirteen and I realized how important it was for there to be some literature based on girls this age. There is so little available. Girls disappear from most media when they turn twelve and don't reappear until they're almost fifteen. If they're on a long-running television show, their characters become shells. In recent years there have been a few girls with a developed character arc at thirteen, but not many.

4. How did you build your world?

I don't build worlds; I build people and watch them react to their environment.

5. Why fantasy?

I love fantasy because there is only one rule – *Don't break your own rules* (unless you're Dr. Who or a starship captain. Then you can do whatever you want).

In real life, just having a conversation has a multitude of rules we must follow. But in world building, the author must establish everything. Can I talk over you? Are you allowed to ask me anything? Do we have to sit in these chairs, or do you have to do a lap around the room before I can answer? To me, answering those questions and establishing the rules is what builds the world.

6. Why did you build a world without time?

I didn't realize how important and how meaningless time was until it was taken away from me. At the time I wrote *The Lost Knight,* I was gambling with years of my life, my family's lives, and my children's childhood. Time rules us all. I needed to take that power away. I also had no idea how hard it would be eliminating time from a novel. I don't recommend it.

7. Your main character dyes her hair purple, and another character is purple. The skies over Manahata are purple. What's your favorite color?

Yellow. That's funny. It wasn't until we started working on the cover art for the second book in the series, *The Lost Girl* that I realized how much purple I put in my world. We call Lenox the two-eyed, no-horned, flying purple people eater. It's a song. Google it.

8. Would you dye your hair purple?

I have. Well, my bangs. I'm not sure that counts. But when I did it I had to use clothing dye because hair dye wasn't available in those colors. It was a brutal process. First I had to strip all the color from my hair, which turned it a terrifying yellow, and then dip it into almost boiling dye. But yeah, my bangs have been yellow, pink, purple, and red at various times in my life.

9. In your books you're pretty rough on teachers.

Yeah, that was not my intent. My children have had some great teachers. However, the school stories in *The Lost*

Knight Series are true; all of that happened to me. I changed the names. I would like to say that the only teacher whose name is real is Mr. Hallman. He was my favorite. And I'm sure he called on me when I didn't know the answer, because I never knew the answer. He was my fifth grade teacher, and the only thing I can recall was that he was nice to me and taught us about the explorers.

10. What were you like at thirteen?

Painfully quiet. I still didn't have a complete grip on my dyslexia. It affects my reading and math skills, but it had a devastating effect on my communication. I'm not a shy person, but it takes my brain some time to formulate words and push them out of my mouth. It's gotten better over the years with practice, but at thirteen I rarely spoke.

11. You've been very open about dealing with dyslexia. How do you think it has held you back?

I don't think it has. I mean, I have trouble speaking sometimes. I will insert the wrong word here and there when I speak, which most people find funny. I find it funny, too. Me and numbers are never going to see eye-to-eye, and I will always write *form* instead of *from*. I can live with that, because having this brain made a lot of wonderful things happen for me.

Dyslexia is like having legs that can run a thousand miles, but not learning how to walk until you're thirty. It's a superpower. A very hard-to-control superpower.

I was locked in my head for most of my young childhood. I had to learn my own way to communicate, so by the time my brain caught up to everyone else's, I had superior communication skills and numerous outlets for self-expression. I think that's why so many successful creative people are dyslexic. My only regret is that I can't read my own words out loud to people. But if my brain worked liked everyone else's, I wouldn't have had the words in the first place. I wouldn't trade it for anything and I feel blessed for having it.

12. What did you want to be when you grew up?

An Olympic gold medalist in the Three Day Event—that's horsey stuff. And a marine biologist. I love horses. Lenox was my girl. She was a warmblood breed called a Trakehner. She was a big girl. I loved her. She was truly the greatest horse. She died a few years back. I put her in the book so she would live forever.

13. How did you find writing as a career?

I didn't. It found me. I was an operations manager for most of my adult life. It required a lot of writing. I've written over fifty manuals, from JCAHO accreditation to how to build a house to code in Florida. I wrote for fun, too. Mostly stories for my children. That's how my board book *Monsters and Jam* came into the world.

14. You talk about *Life Changing Books*. What are your life-changing books?

The first has to be *Through the Looking Glass*. I read that for fun in high school. I read *Alice in Wonderland* and loved it. I thought *Through the Looking Glass* was Part II—it's not. That book changed the way I looked at reading. I never knew words could be put together like that. It had such a profound effect on me that I kept the book. I still have it.

Tale of Two Cities has to be next. I read that in my early twenties. I hated every word of it until I got about three quarters of the way through. I could only read four pages at a time because it put me to sleep. I was so happy when I finally got to the end. The last page blew my mind and changed everything I thought about what I had previously read. It is by far my favorite novel, and I have read most of Dickens' works because of that book.

The Hobbit took four attempts before I finally read the entire thing. It's my grandmother's favorite book. Every time we would walk down a long hallway she would say, "It's like we're in a hobbit hole." She gave me the book in the fourth grade. She even read parts of it to me, but I couldn't follow it. I bought it on impulse in a bookstore when I was an adult. And I agree with my grandmother: everyone needs to read this book.

Animal Farm. I know I'm supposed to say *1984.* I read *1984* in 1984 and agree with everyone who loved it, but I read *Animal Farm* first. It had a horse character and I will read anything about a horse. I was pretty far through the book when I realized I wasn't actually reading about a farm.

Pride and Prejudice. What can I say? Mr. Darcy is my ideal man.

15. Okay, movies. What are some of your favorites?

I feel the need to explain what makes a favorite movie for me. I can type away at my computer for hours, and I can read a book from cover to cover without a break, but I struggle to sit through an entire movie in one shot—even a fantastic one. A movie has to be really great for me to see it again. The list of movies I have seen more than once are as follows:

Star Wars, episodes 4–7.
Fight Club
This is Spinal Tap
The Lord of the Rings

16. Favorite TV Shows?

Anything reality! I'm a people watcher so…"Big Brother," "The Bachelor," "MythBusters," all of them.

I've seen every episode of every "Star Trek" and all of the movies.

My favorite Captains in order are:

1. Sisko – He dealt with a lot and had the most personal growth.
2. Janeway – We share a birthday! She should have been first on my list, but no Starfleet captain would put innocent lives on a distant planet above the lives of her crew.
3. Picard – I know either he or Kirk have to be first, but you asked so I'm answering.
4. Pike – I think the show would've gone in a better direction had they stuck with him.

5. Archer – It kills me to put him here. I loved *Quantum Leap*. Netflix needs to remake that.
6. And of course, Kirk.

I've also seen every available episode of Dr. Who. 9, 10, 2, 3, 4, 11, 1, 12, 5, 6, 7, 8, and 8.5.

17. Speaking of remaking shows, if you could, what show would you like to see remade?

I know as a certifiable nerd, I'm supposed to say *Firefly*, which I would love to see remade. But if I could only choose one, I would pick *Stargate Universe*. I know it's controversial, but they left those characters in stasis for a thousand years. Not cool. And portals.

18. Agatha enjoys painting. Do you paint?

No, but my mother does. She's an amazing painter. I wish I had her talent. I can draw. I thought I would be an architect at one point, but the closest I got was Operations Manager of a design firm.

19. What's in store for Agatha?

Nothing good. I think readers can tell that her transition into elf-life is not going to be a smooth one. Plus, she's training to be a Knight. New friends and new enemies.

20. Will we see Dathid and Jonah again?

Of course. They're a team.

Agatha's story has only just begun...

Find out what lies in wait for Agatha
in this mind-blowing sequel.

Coming July 20, 2016

If Stratagor Ziras doesn't kill me, my training regimen will!

Every day I wake up and go through the motions, but they've figured out that I'm not a Knight. I can't ride, I can't fight, I can't do magic, and worst of all, I can't see whatever it is I'm supposed to see in this stupid Orb.

Nothing is what it seems here. Everyone says they want what's best for me, but who can I trust? The wheedling minister? The crocodilian creature that's trying to lock me away? The Queen who wants me dead? Or the devil himself?

I don't know what I'm more afraid of: the enemies that have made several attempts on my life, or my allies now that they know they've made huge a mistake.

THE LOST GIRL

CHAPTER 7

The royal audience made me late for my second day of physical training; *always tardy* is going to be added to my permanent record. I don't know what I'm doing wrong. I mean, I know I'm not doing anything right, but I don't know how to fix it. I don't have anyone to talk to about it, either. If Dathid were here he would support my dislike of Queen Ekecheiria. I could really use some of his snarky remarks and funny stories right now. But then again, he doesn't think I'm good at anything, either.

Jonah has faith in my abilities and believes I have what it takes to be a Knight, but he would defend the Queen. Not her insulting me, of course. He would just explain away all her evilness by only seeing the good side of her.

It doesn't matter; I agree with Ekecheiria. I'm not a Knight. I'm just not good at any of this. I'm not strong enough, smart enough, or brave enough to do what they need. I want to throw myself at her feet and tell her she's right about everything.

I wish I wasn't so alone. I wish someone could help me, not with learning magic or riding a unicorn, but help me figure out what I'm supposed to do. This is so important and I'm failing. The task is too big, too overwhelming, too everything. I am Agatha Stone, foster kid of two crazy hoarders who ignored and imprisoned me. I'm no hero.

I pull a muffin out of my pocket and eat my simple breakfast while I search for my riding instructor. I don't find her, but I remember that I'm supposed to get my own unicorn ready so I retrieve Stryder from his stall. He nickers when he sees me, and that makes a smile crack my sadness. I pet the wide white stripe traveling down his face, but he lifts his head so I can scratch his furry black neck. When my fingernails reach his shoulders, he nods his head and smacks his lips.

"You're so silly," I say with a laugh I desperately need.

Stryder would let me scratch him all day, but we're already behind schedule, so I put a halter on him and lead him to the crossties. We're alone for only a short time when Levise finds us in a grooming stall and apologizes for being late.

"I had to give the stable master, Mr. Galnoy, assurances that it's fine having a pegasus live indoors," she says with a face that suggests she wasn't entirely truthful with him. We share a giggle about that while she helps me finish grooming. I ride the same three unicorns I rode yesterday and it goes about as well.

Levise still has to pick me up to get me in the saddle. It's so humiliating because we're the same size and she throws me up there like it's nothing. Then I spend all morning trying to get the unicorns to move, only to have them go the wrong way. *Walks in circles* needs to be added to my list of failings. I know it's just walking and stuff, but by the time I'm done and get the last one cleaned, fed, and in her stall, I'm whipped.

I'm supposed to meet Kyrbast for a magic lesson, but I get lost again on my way back to the castle. I need a map of the grounds because these paths don't make sense. Add *Gets lost all the time* to the list. I'm close to the outer—I mean, the curtain wall. Albína insists I use the correct words. This wall surrounds the entire castle and is the opposite way I should be heading. Maybe I should turn around and retrace my steps, but I think up ahead is a path leading to the Temple.

A set of thick arms wrap so forcefully around my chest that air leaves my lungs in an audible whoosh. I can't see who grabbed me, but another man picks up my feet. There's a flash of orange skin before my head is violently turned to the side and all I see is the wall as they carry me off.

My heart is thumping so fast the beats are indistinguishable. No one knows I'm out here! My lungs are so constricted that I can only get a short gasp of air before I use it all to let out a pathetic scream.

A sweaty hand clamps over my face, and my body tenses solid. His fingers are so long they wrap around to the back of my head and seal his palm over my nose and mouth. Two male voices have a brief discussion in an indistinguishable language, but it's hard to hear over my heartbeat pounding in my ears and my lungs screaming for air. I try to inhale, but no oxygen enters, just the taste of dirt and sweat from the hand over my face.

The man covering my mouth turns my head to force me to look at his broad orange face. He's human...I think: one head, two burly arms wrapped around me, and two feet beating against the ground as he runs.

He slowly moves his hand away from my mouth, but his large black eyes stare into my frightened ones as he softly grumbles at me as if to communicate that if I scream again, the hand comes back.

I'm afraid to take a deep breath so I slowly pull in a small shaky inhale. I want him to be certain I won't scream again. He smiles at me. I don't know if I'm more revolted by his crooked pointy teeth or my pathetic submission. I don't have time to consider it because he roughly tosses me over his red-armored shoulder, and pain sears through my guts as they take off in a run.

The jostling makes it hard to breathe and the pain makes it impossible to think. I should fight back. I should do something. I'm being kidnapped. But I can't fight this man or his friends, and if I scream again he'll suffocate me.

They stop at a ladder that's leaning against the curtain wall. As the large man easily carries me up, I see there are four soldiers, all of them thick as fireplugs and just as orange. I want to ask where they're taking me and why, but I want to cooperate and not make noise so they won't hurt me.

Once we reach the top of the wall, three soldiers lift the ladder and carry it to the other side. When my guy turns to supervise the work, I spot a large black winged demon flying toward us.

I don't know who the good guy is. These men are human. The monster flying at us definitely is not. I can barely make out the large curved horns and red skin before my guy spins around and drops me...

Don't miss any of the Lost Knight Series

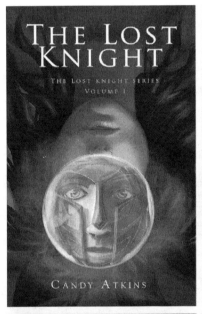

Made in the USA
Middletown, DE
18 December 2016